I0831283

Killing with Kindness

Killing with Kindness

Laura S. Devendorf

Different Drummer Publishing
2016

Killing with Kindness

First Edition 2014
Second Edition 2016

25 24 23 22 21 20 19 18 17 16 1 2 3 4 5

ISBN 978-0-9776623-3-3 (cloth)

Different Drummer Publishing
5836 Islands Hwy.
Sunbury, GA 31320

Cover Art

Polly's Chicken, oil on canvas by Phoebe Healey.
This provocative work was a gift to me from my deeply talented painter friend, the late Phoebe Healey. The suggestive, almost featureless blur of the child's face seems a portrait of innocence and promise. It is girlhood's edge of dawning—imprecise and awaiting time to define her.

She looks like—in fact, she could have been—me.

Laura Devendorf

Dedication

For Meredith, my inspiring editor, my daughter, my supporter, and my trusted friend.

Contents

Acknowledgements

A first book is like writing in a closet immersed in the deep, delirious aura of your own private thoughts and written words. You have no clue how your work will be received by real people in the real world—a place your closet is not. So, my thanks to all of the following who read parts of my work and offered comments. They include authors, a Broadway playwright, actors, a banker, an artist, teachers, a network TV comedy writer, a director, and a Hollywood movie producer—all of them thoughtful and discerning readers.

Meredith Devendorf
Don Devendorf
Charles Seabrook
Ron Onorato
Greg Jaynes
Stratton Leopold
Don Elda Boutwell
John Cariani
Bruce Taylor
Pam Melton
Cheryl Buck
Stuart Beringer
Madeline Jaynes
Louise Hoffman
Sandy Hudson

Foreword

I have avidly read Laura Devendorf's beautiful short stories that fill this book. The theme running through them: Someone sets out to do a favor, only to have the intended good deed backfire and trigger a slew of unforeseen miseries. Thus, the book's apt title: "Killing With Kindness." The lesson might be this: Doing good may come with a high price.

Many of us, no doubt, have been squarely in the middle of these kinds of predicaments, either as the well-intentioned do-gooder or the unfortunate recipient of a kindness gone awry. As such, we can identify with many of Devendorf's characters, like the couple who moved back to Georgia and, with a touch of compassion, kindly employed a down-and-out relative as a handyman, who then repaid their kindness with orneriness, deception and a work-shirking attitude.

But no matter what take-home wisdom you may glean from these stories, the most important thing is that they are wonderful and fun to read.

One other thing: The short story, a fine and often underrated art, is enjoying a revival, which was affirmed by the awarding of the 2013 Nobel Prize in Literature to Alice Munro, one of the world's consummate short story writers. Short stories can have profound effect on helping us understand the consequences of our actions, big or small. As Munro herself has said: "There are no such things as big and little subjects. The major things, the evils, that exist in the world have a direct relationship to the evil that exists around a dining room table when people are doing things to each other."

Perhaps the same could be said about kindness.

October 2013
Charles Seabrook
Decatur, Ga.

Introduction

These stories are both fiction and non-fiction, inspired by real people and events, but modified by both the clarity gained through time and the creative needs of the stories. Names and locations have been changed, and characters should not be presumed to be people you know, even though your private experiences make them seem so.

As a writer, I am drawn to situations that are provocative and that make me think. The stories in *Killing with Kindness* try to do just that. Even at the tenth reading shared with my editor Meredith, stories such as *Tracks* or *When the Wind Blows* or *Many Mansions* never end when the story concludes. Rather, they continue to spark animated discussion.

Much like being on a train where you can't get off, these are fate-driven stories that readers say compelled them to read straight through to the end.

I hope you enjoy the journey.

Laura Devendorf

TRACKS

The train is the great nullifier—the impotent space between life as lived and its continuation.

On this June afternoon, my thoughts ride with it on a graphite slide from where I live to my genetic home, Virginia. We glide through sun and shade-splotched rolls of hills and big-leafed forests, tangled with honeysuckle and memories. None to do with me now. But so familiar. Physically recalled. I summon the honeyed smell of it in green summer air. Mornings damp on my skin. And heat-soaked noons. And crickets cluttering the night.

I recall brown winter.

And the rain. Always the rain. And the mud—and the people, pressing like the heat and cutting me like the cold—all part of it. And I know that only pride and this mesmerizing summer beauty inspire a twinge of missing it and of wishing.

Long ago, Virginia was the gauntlet. And now I am on this train—late to my appointment with my past and the rusty idea of heritage and the old family—the crutch I never touch yet somehow hold, even while it defies my possibilities.

Darkness crowds the glory of late-day color and light.

"This is your dining car steward." The message comes loudly over the intercom competing with the clack of rails and the creak and groan of shifting cars. "This is your last call. If you wish dinner, please make your way to the dining car."

Yes.

The tables seat four. I'll have to sit with others.

But yes, anyway.

It takes a spectacular effort to ricochet down eight car-lengths and ram open sixteen air-locked doors. Everyone who arrives at the diner has that Olympian look about them. Breathless. A little disheveled. Certainly less than graceful as they are hurled by some sudden lurch into their seats.

At my table, I'm the first, and the steward seats me by the window.

Next comes a couple. Early thirties, I'd guess. Dark hair and eyes. Normal looking. Neat. Rather pretty, both of them, and each carrying a gift-wrapped package. She wears an odd mix of J.C. Penney clothes and expensive jewelry.

They are awkward, of course, getting seated. So I grin at them encouragingly. Her package falls to the floor, and while she bends down to retrieve it, he leans across the table and stage-whispers to be heard above the train, "It's our anniversary and I thought it would be romantic to celebrate it on a train."

Once seated, they smile, and he gives their names.

"Karen and Tony Shields."

I give mine. We smile again and turn to the menu.

"Steak, baked chicken, and veggie lasagna," he reads aloud. "Not much to decide."

And I add, "They can't really do much to destroy chicken."

"Right. So chicken it is," Tony says, and we all begin penciling in our order forms. The waiter takes them and staggers away.

"Are you going far?" I ask.

Tony grins, and Karen blurts out, "I really don't know. It's our tenth wedding anniversary. And I don't even know where we're going." She sounds more anxious than thrilled. She is carefully unwrapping the silverware—setting it meticulously in place.

"You don't?"

"No, she doesn't," Tony says. "It's a surprise. All of it. Where we're going, for how long, what we're doing..."

"I didn't even know what to pack."

Karen sounds a shade tense, and, as a woman, I am projecting. My sense of well-being as a woman is rooted in how I perceive myself, starting with how I look.

Yes. Looks. How must I appear to them, to Karen and Tony? Well-dressed in my understated suit—dignified—successful without airs—

confident? Yes, I think I put it all together to get that reaction. They'd never guess how many hours I spent shopping for just the right suit and this lovely lapel pin, packing and unpacking, making sure that I'll make the right impression when I get there. Get home. After all these years, I am going home, where they'll judge me even more harshly than most do. No, I definitely couldn't handle not knowing where I was going, and I wonder what kind of man this is who would put his wife in such an unsettling, even threatening, position. He reads my expression.

"I know it sounds strange," he says, "but it's an exercise in trust."

"Oh?"

Karen has begun rearranging the flatware. Concentrating on it.

"In the ten years we've been married, she has never been able to let go…to let me handle things the way the man of the family should or to...."

"Do you really have to say this?" Karen interrupts, knocking over the salt. She quickly begins dusting it into her hand and depositing it in her napkin.

"Karen, you know it's okay." He turns to me, talking over her. "Karen is one of the most caring people in the world, a really good person. Decent. Honest to a fault." Then he looks at her again, "You know you have nothing to be ashamed of."

"I know," she says, still looking down. "But can't we just…." She is picking up each stray salty grain missed by her sweeping.

In the awkward moment, I focus on the blur of town lights slipping by in the dusk outside the window. But he isn't finished.

"It's all right, Karen. Certainly *this* lady isn't going to think less of you."

Whatever the reference, would she really want *this* woman, a stranger, to share her privacy? I'm used to people who want to seem inclusive, being overly-familiar, thinking it will make me feel more comfortable, but this is too personal. I would really like to be somewhere else right now.

I wonder if my half-smile, fixed as it is, looks appropriately benign. But Karen isn't looking at me. Her agitation has ceased and she is looking at him directly.

"Please, Tony..." she pleads quietly.

"Karen, I said it's all right."

Now Karen turns to me, her dark eyes dull, her hands still, her voice a monotone. "I'm obsessive—clinically obsessive-compulsive, paranoid and neurotic," she states, deciding to say it herself since it seems inevitable. "My insecurities make me jealous and suspicious, and I have to control everything, every situation, and everyone." It's a recitation. "As Tony says,

'I'm a textbook example of what happens to you when you grow up in a family of alcoholics.'"

My face is still fixed. My feelings are in turmoil.

"You see," Tony elaborates, "I've been trying to get her over it; to put her problem right up front so she can accept it and learn to trust. So I've planned this trip from start to finish, and I haven't told her anything." And he adds, smiling at me. "It's all right. Really, it is. I'm a counselor."

All right!?! I'm projecting again, knowing that I'd kill any man who offered me an anniversary gift of clinical reconstruction. This whole trip business. What's it got to do with love and caring? It seems more like pushing her out of the airplane to cure her fear of flying.

On impulse, I ask, "Karen, doesn't it bother you not knowing where you're going? Doesn't *that* make you nervous?"

Tony answers, "She's really doing great. She hasn't asked once." He smiles approvingly at her. "She is really relaxed." I'm watching her pick at her cuticle. "She's just trusting me to take her wherever we're going."

And Karen adds, not looking up, "In whatever I happen to be wearing."

I say nothing.

Karen sighs.

"So where are you headed?" Tony asks me.

"Home. A family reunion."

"How nice. Did you have to take much time off work to do it?"

"No, actually. My time's my own."

"Really?" He seems genuinely surprised. "What do you do?"

"I'm a writer."

"Oh," Karen brightens. "I love to read. What do you write?"

"Novels, stories, travel articles, the latter being necessary sometimes." I smile at her. "You know. To adjust the revenue stream in my favor."

Karen actually laughs, "What do you write about?"

"Irony." She gives me an uncertain look, tempted but a little afraid to go there.

Tony fills in, "That covers a lot."

I agree. "...and it's usually uncomfortable. But we're all caught in it, aren't we?"

"In what ways?" he asks.

"So very many. But I just write about the part where we try to do the right thing for the right reasons, and it ends up accomplishing the opposite, in fact, something terrible. I suppose my kind of irony suggests the warning, 'look out for those dynamic unintended consequences.'" Seeing their sudden discomfort, I add, "Sometimes, that way of looking at life comes out a joke. Do you know O'Henry's *The Ransom of Red Chief*?"

Tony says, "I don't think I know that one."

Karen smiles. "That's the wonderful story where two disreputable con artists decide to make a lot of money by kidnapping a boy who likes to pretend that he's the Indian, Red Chief. Then, once they have him, this charming child proves to be such an accomplished monster that the kidnappers end up paying the parents to take him back."

We all laugh, when suddenly the train lurches and our fourth table partner is delivered. He collapses into the seat next to me. His is the look and attitude of studied anarchy. His worn, hip-slung jeans sag to the brink of putting his buttocks in full view. His running shoes, once white, are mottled hues of age-yellow, grass green, and other colors whose origins I prefer not to explore. He is bone thin, and his head is shrouded in about two pounds of knotted, shoulder-length hair.

I almost laugh out loud as, suddenly, I'm struck by the image of a huge Old English sheepdog who once terrorized our neighborhood. With all that hair, you couldn't see his expression to tell whether he meant to lick or bite. His weapon was surprise, and I wonder if our fourth guest's fur will be as purposeful.

We stare at him with some curiosity while Tony makes introductions. "I'm Tony, and I'm a Health Department counselor, and this is Angela, a writer, and," he says proudly, "…my lovely wife, Karen, mother of our two great kids."

We look expectantly at guest Number Four who just mumbles and pushes two long hunks of tangled hair behind his ears so he can read the menu. He puts the card back down so he can wipe the smears off his wire-rimmed glasses with the most starkly clean and graceful hands I've ever seen.

"Anything worth eating on this thing?" he asks without looking up.

"We've all decided to try the chicken."

The waiter arrives.

"What kind of beer you got?"

"Bud...maybe some Miller Lite."

"That crap? Guess I'll take the Bud."

We shift in our seats—look out the window which now is black with country night.

With those long sculpted fingers, Number Four fills in his order and then begins playing with his fork, digging it into the tablecloth.

"So, where are you headed?" Tony asks.

"North."

"Vacation?" though that seems unlikely somehow.

"Nope." Long pause.

"Are you still in school?"

"No." He appears to enjoy sabotaging Tony's amiable, polite search for conversation.

Tony doesn't give up, "Have you graduated?"

"Yeah."

"Where'd you go?"

"Brown."

This doesn't register with Tony. "What was your major?"

"Philosophy."

Tony's voice shows that he is wearing down. The struggle is distancing them, but Tony tries again. "So. What do you do now?"

"Music. I do music."

"Really," Tony's energy level is suddenly restored. "So do I," he grins. "I play professional guitar."

Four rejects the attempted personal connection with a disinterested, "Yeah?"

Glad to refocus on Tony, I ask, "But I thought you were a counselor?"

"Oh yes, I am. But I put myself through college playing jazz guitar." Tony is so…so ordinary with his neat clothes and trim haircut that it's hard to imagine him blown out in some dingy bistro. "In fact," he goes on, "when we got married, I didn't have a degree or a job or any work experience except for playing. So I supported my family on my music."

"Then you must be good," I say.

"He is," Karen affirms, not looking at any of us.

"Well, I've never had a weekend off in fifteen years."

Number Four mutters something unintelligible.

"Then why did you go into counseling?"

"I loved guitar. But I didn't love the life."

Number Four yawns.

Tony looks directly at him, "I saw so many troubled wannabes and druggies wasting their lives when they were never going to make it."

"How would *you* know," Four snaps.

"Easy. They had no discipline. No self-control…just depending on another pop to free them up to play a little better and too stoned to know that, usually, they sounded worse."

Four shakes his mane and smiles patronizingly. He's heard this uncool line before.

Karen is changing the golden rings around on her fingers.

"Of course," Tony continues, "They always thought it was someone else's fault they hadn't been 'discovered.' Sometimes I thought I was the only person in the business who saw it for what it was—at least it seemed that way since everyone kept coming to me to straighten out their lives."

Four expresses his disdain by pointedly staring at passengers lunging up and down the aisle.

"I just seemed to have a knack for it. When I saw that I was actually helping people, it started feeling really good. That's when I realized that counseling was my calling."

"Calling?" We haven't lost Number Four after all. "Oh, please! You're just stupid, man. Why'd you get some nine-to-fiver boring shit."

Karen and I are taken aback, but Tony, who has heard it all, never misses a stride.

"That's easy. It made sense. It had a point to it. You know yourself, about the uncertainty."

"So?"

"I had a family. In music there's just too much risk. And there was no guarantee I was ever going to make it."

"It takes time, man. You have to hang in there."

"That's what they all want to think, but that's too intangible. My dependents are real."

Four chooses to ignore that, "Your music was makin' the nut. At least, you let us think so."

"Yes. Barely. But there's more to it. I grew up dirt poor and I couldn't watch them…."

"Not that tired line."

"I take it you don't have a family."

"Are you kidding?"

"So you can't know how hard it is to disappoint the ones you love. To keep explaining why we can't afford to go anywhere or have that new bike at Christmas. It seemed too selfish and unfair."

"Ah, they played the old guilt trick on you, did they? Obviously, man, you have the wrong family."

Karen fixes Number Four with hatred, "To make your point, you don't have to be rude."

"I'm not rude. Just a realist. What do you really want from life? Be honest. If you don't get it, it's because you didn't want it badly enough." He points a finger at Tony. "He's all about justification. His life's an excuse."

Karen has listened long enough. Her voice has risen noticeably. "It has nothing to do with guilt or justification. It has to do with maturity and choice. Have you ever been responsible to anyone other than yourself?"

Four looks at her. She's absorbing the whole of him. She looks away, her voice cool. "I guess not."

"Look," Tony reasons, "My family doesn't expect or demand anything. It isn't that. It's how I feel when I watch my wife and kids happy because of things I'm able to give them, like a new bike, or jewelry that they *don't* expect."

"Yeah, I noticed all the gold."

"Well, I know it sounds like a bromide, but giving to others really *is* the gift you give yourself."

"Gifts. Things. You keep talking about things. Is your relationship reduced to that? Bikes will rust. Jewelry breaks or gets lost. What then?"

"You don't understand. Seeing them happy is everything. It's the greatest high of all." Tony's voice softens, "It's what I live for."

"Live," Four mutters. "You mean you have less guilt. Shhhhiiiii..." he hisses. "You've got no life."

"You're wrong," Tony tells him very seriously. "I have two wonderful children and a beautiful wife who is deeply good and caring."

"I think you recited that litany before."

Tony ignores him. "I'm the lucky one. I have what everyone wants…a tight family unit where we love and share and respect one another. They are my life, and I owe them everything."

Four looks at him mockingly as if he just popped out of a Cracker Jack box. "Are you born again or something?"

Tony is wilting. "It's hard to explain...." he trails away. Then tries again, "I guess...I guess they call it 'old-time values', my friend…home, the comfort of family, honest hard work, caring about others." He sees Four's smirk and adds, "As they say, 'don't knock it 'til you've tried it.'"

Four tilts back in his chair and locks his hands behind his head. It increases his size alarmingly. "I don't buy all that noble crap. You know, most people won't admit it, but they're all dying of frustration or collective boredom and they're scared shitless to do anything about it. So, they explain away their failures and bury their regrets with platitudes. Just the way you do. If they looked at their lives realistically, they'd explode. Me...I'd just go for it."

"I'm sorry for you," Tony says. "You haven't experienced the contentment of putting others first."

"All right then, let's do it your way. If, as you claim, you really want to give your 'dependents' something that matters, then you'll go for the big one. Be big time. Be a star. That's when you'll make everyone around you happy. Yeah. Then we'll talk about real respect—people proud to be connected to you. Give up the excuses, man, and go for it. Be somebody important, that's what banks. Not just being some wimpy nothing everybody uses or dumps on."

In the abrupt silence, Number Four turns to me. He looks long and hard, and then he says, "You, of all people…you should know what I'm saying."

Karen cuts him off, "Leave her out of it. Go for what? We love and respect him just the way he is. A man of honor and substance."

"Substance? That's just a euphemism for 'ordinary.'"

"Don't say that!" Her hands are fists. "There is nothing ordinary about him. Besides, how would you know about our kind of admiration and appreciation? What have you done with your life that compares with the accomplishments we see in his?"

"So he's your hero because he sacrifices everything for you and the kids. So you can have those rings you keep playing with."

"Now wait," Tony protests.

Karen rushes in, "How can you say those things? Of course we want him to realize his potential."

"She does," Tony says. But he can't say more because Karen is propelled by rage.

"But there are other considerations, and you're saying he should leave his family and just chase the dream."

Four grins at her. "You don't get it, do you? Nobody admires a failure. All he's got to give is what he's made of himself, what he's accomplished. How recognizable his name is and how many people applaud it. A star. Get it? The top of the heap. It's what everyone wants to be connected with."

She could cry. But she doesn't. Instead, she stares him down and begins coldly, "So, according to your criteria, Tony should just leave us to fend for ourselves while he's out anointing his ego…or not…if it turns out he isn't good enough. And how long will that take?"

"Maybe you already think he's worthless."

"I never said that."

She waits for a reply, but none comes. Number Four just leans back in his chair to enjoy watching her take the bait.

As she plunges in again, her voice thickens with sarcasm. "So we should just lead our lonely, separate lives content with the privilege of belonging to him." She sees a glint of response she can't read and continues, "I'd miss him, of course. Why wouldn't I miss him? It would have nothing to do with him personally, it's just that life would be barren without his shimmering celebrity surrounding me. But, according to you, I'd be getting the best part. Just think how fulfilled I'd be walking down the street by myself and overhearing, 'That's her! That's Tony Shields's wife. Isn't she the lucky one?' That should fill my hours nicely."

Number Four's interest is obviously aroused. His eyes crinkle with humor as she goes on. "Or imagine the blessed day when he actually visits and I walk down that street again *with him*, seeing heads swing in recognition and smiles radiate toward us—when, for that moment, I am allowed to share his aura. Why, I could live happily for a year on that."

"Well," Number Four laughs aloud, "I see I've awakened the 'gone undercover' brain I suspected was there and ready to explode. Do go on."

She can't stop herself now. She looks at him with all the simmering, unsaid frustrations of her own existence. "And, of course, you'd never have me worry about his endless, lonely nights away from me on the road, nights filled with worshipful, needy, irresponsible girls with long blonde hair and perfect skin and firm bodies that they roll seductively in invitation...or maybe just the comfort of a few too many drinks that grow into an abiding habit…or…."

Number Four stops her. "Whoa, whoa! So what really scares the crap out of you is that he'll shack up with some gorgeous piece of ass, while you're stuck in your pedestrian little life with two kids, getting dumpy and dull, and that you'll lose by comparison. The fact is you're saying the same thing. Nobody wants to be connected to a loser. For a minute, don't think about yourself. Think when he's dead. What will his kids remember about him? How many bikes he gave them? Get serious. He could have been a son-of-a-bitch and gotten drunk every night and bedded every slut out there. They'll never mention it. We all have selective memory, and what they're gonna remember is the stuff they can brag about...what their daddy accomplished...how important he was. Be pragmatic about it, and you'll admit, if he has a big name it will give them a leg up in life, and isn't that what you should want for them?"

"Oh, please."

Number Four focuses on her eyes making their contact dark and personal. He asks quietly, "When someone you don't know asks what your husband does, what do you say about him? Do you say that he sits in some crummy little office all week long listening to people whine about who's to blame for their inadequacies and that he does what he's meant to do one stinking night a week in some smoky little nowhere just to earn a few bicycle bucks and get his private soul fix for a pitiful three hours?"

He pauses, looking at her while Tony and I wrestle with the silence.

"I bet not. Admit it," he says with venom. "You summon up the very best credits he can claim, probably going way back to high school, and you embellish the hell out of them to make them as strong as you dare." He pauses again, before nailing his accusation into her. "You know damn well you do because it makes *you* important, and all the drudgery that is your limited little life won't seem as boring and meaningless as it really is."

"Wait." I protest. "Please stop. This has gone far enough."

Number Four turns his stare on me. "You understand the power that comes with being important. To get real respect you have to have real accomplishments, recognizable things that *force* others to accept you. You…of *all* people should have a fix on that. For Christ's sake, woman. You're black."

Now that he has exempted no one, Number Four returns his focus to Karen.

"Like everybody else, once the gush has gone from the relationship, what you want most from him are bragging rights. No. Don't deny it. When you begin the recitation of his merits, it's only his success you tell about. The niceties stay buried someplace inside you that's reserved for thanks and forgiveness and simple things you privately appreciate but that you can't explain to anyone so it doesn't sound like a quote from *The Bridges of Madison County*. It's only his success that counts. And if you really give a damn about him, you'd make the sacrifice because you know that success is also his ticket to being wanted and, most of all, respected. A man needs that. You can cage the shadow of him if that makes you feel safe rather than risk the big reward of having him whole and wanting you, just you, because he is free to choose. But ballsy women," he pauses to smile at her, "never understand that until it's too late."

Karen's hands are trembling visibly.

Tony reaches to hold them. "Easy, Karen. It's all right. He just sees it a little differently than we do."

Four displays amused contempt, a demeanor transferred to his dinner which has finally arrived. He picks at it. We work through our own meals, the air between seasoned with staggered bits of silence and struggling conversation. Four is a volcano parked in the middle of it which we dare not provoke and cannot surmount.

Finally, as he puts money on the table and rises to leave, he looks at us and says, "Happy thoughts?"

Once he's gone, it takes a minute; then there is a visible relaxing of shoulders and raising of heads.

At length, Karen takes a deep breath and says, "What was *that*? Speaking of someone who needs to get a life!"

Everyone has stopped eating. Grateful for a chance to begin again, Tony picks up the long slender box festooned with curly golden ribbon. "It's time," he says, smiling, "for important things."

Karen, retrieving her own gift, asks, "Who goes first?"

"You do," Tony says.

Hesitantly, she takes his gift. "This ribbon is just gorgeous. This package is beautifully wrapped. It's almost too pretty to open," she chatters, picking slowly, very slowly at the ribbon knot.

"Go ahead, open it," Tony urges, his voice full. "I think you'll like it," but his eager face betrays that he knows, with certainty, that she will.

She stretches the ribbon, tugs it off, and methodically unfolds the paper which falls to the table, revealing a gold jewelry store box. For a long moment, she just holds it, as if the revelation of its contents will begin something she doesn't want to unleash, but then, carefully, she lifts off the top and just as slowly, removes the long strip of soft white cotton covering the contents.

The bracelet beneath glows with golden leaves set afire with the flowers of a dozen diamonds. Quarter-carat size. It is exquisite and tasteful and, obviously, unspeakably expensive.

Tony is beaming deeply with expected joy.

Slowly, very slowly, she lifts the gleaming treasure from its snowy bed, almost as if she is fearful of holding it.

Tony cannot slow his own enthusiasm. "Put it on. Put it on." And she places it over her wrist and attempts to fasten it. His hands move in to help, fumbling to catch the clasp and encircle her slender wrist with his devotion.

She has said nothing.

He hasn't seemed to notice. But the void is deeply awkward. So I say, "That's the most beautiful piece I've ever seen. It is stunning."

Still, she says nothing, and on what silent history I am treading I cannot know. So I say no more.

Tony moves closer to see the tiny metal end, his fingers troubling with the delicacy of the clasp. It will not close.

Karen is staring at it now. "I think it's defective," she says. "I think there's something wrong with the clasp. It should fasten and lock right away."

Tony has removed it from her arm and is examining it, anxiously. His face is still, the moment of anticipated pleasure draining away.

Karen extends her other arm. "See, this bracelet you gave me for my birthday has a much sturdier catch and a double safety." She moves it closer to Tony's face, but he is engrossed with the balky catch.

"Good jewelry," she continues, "always has a strong double safety catch. Like this one."

Tony doesn't comment. His fingernails are pushing and pulling the bracelet ends trying to unstick or loosen them while Karen talks critically, authoritatively, analytical, on and on. "I can't understand why they didn't put the proper safety catch on this new one...." His fingers grow more frenetic. "...since it's obviously a much better bracelet. You can see how much heavier it is. It's obviously so much more expensive." She stops for breath.

He doesn't comment. But in the pause, there is a tiny clipped sound. A piece of gold gleams on the tabletop. He has broken it.

His fingers curl into fists as she states the obvious, "Oh no, it's broken." His knuckles whiten.

Seeing his hurt, she says hurriedly, "It's all right. They'll fix it." His silence is cold and empty. Dark. "It's not your fault. You just need to take it back. It has a warranty and they'll fix it. I don't know why they put such a light clasp on it. But they'll repair it. Just take it back to the store." And she stops and looks at him. "You got the warranty when you bought it, didn't you?"

"I just picked up the bracelet yesterday."

"Well, didn't they give you the warranty?

"I...I guess they'll mail it."

"Did they tell you they would?" And when he doesn't answer. "Who sold it to you?" Nothing. "Do you know the salesperson who sold it to you?"

"I know who she is."

"Who? Is she the one who usually helps us?"

"I know who she is. Don't worry about it."

She sees the signs, struggles to stop herself to derail the relentless noticing and ordering, to stop the comments that she doesn't want to say which suggest displeasure that she doesn't feel—the unabated saying them and then tempering them with solace, but saying them all the same.

She takes the broken gift from his hand where it still dangles and examines it.

She gropes for reclamation of the ruined moment. "The diamonds are so large, Tony. And marquis!"

He smiles a little sadly, "Yes, I knew you wanted marquis. That's why I got it."

"They are lovely. Just lovely," she searches their glittering surfaces with pleasure. Then she hesitates. "Oh....oh...." She drops her head and brings the bracelet closer. "Look, Tony. Look at this." She proffers the band for him to see. "They're NOT marquis!" His head jerks toward her. "It's two little round ones placed close together to *look* like marquis."

He grabs the shimmering, tasteful, life-bought, too-expensive treasure and probes it with his eyes. "You're right," he says. "They aren't marquis."

"They look just like it," Karen says. "I really thought they were."

"So did I." There is an emptiness in his voice. "That's why I bought it."

"But they're beautiful anyway, Tony. And you can still get the bracelet fixed. It's a good store, and they'll do the right thing. They'll make it right."

"I really did think they were marquis," he says. But he isn't really talking to her anymore.

Interloper, voyeur, whatever role I'm assuming, I'm still here. I don't want to be but I am all the same. So I search through the moment's unclaimed fragments and I say, "Karen, what about your package for Tony?"

"Oh...oh yes." And she picks it up from the table and offers it to him uncertainly.

He takes it without enthusiasm.

"Do…open it," she prompts, propping up the moment with affected cheer.

Mechanically, he pulls off the ribbon, and the paper, and reveals a framed document. He looks at it. Puts it down on the table. Nothing more.

"Don't you know what that is?" She asks, picking it up again, holding it for him to read. "See? These are quotes from our high school yearbook," and she points below them, "and this column is my update. A summary. Ten years of us."

He nods. But says nothing. So she turns the plaque to me. "See...."

Across the top it reads: GRADUATION—JUNE 3, 2003

Under it, in the left-hand column, are the yearbook quotes: "ANTHONY SHIELDS, Band, concert orchestra, jazz band, football, swimming. Voted: Best personality. Best friend.

Class Prophecy: Will have 20 gold records and six Grammys by age 40 when he's too old to care."

In the update column under it labeled "JUNE 3, 2013," Karen has written: "Professional counselor and musician, best father, best husband, best friend."

On Karen's side, the yearbook says: "KAREN PEABODY, Valedictorian, Senior Class Treasurer, Honor Council, Glee Club, Debate Team, Yearbook Staff. Voted: Girl Most Likely to Succeed.

Class prophecy: Will graduate from Harvard Law in 2008 and become the first woman Chief Justice of the United States Supreme Court."

Under today's date she has put: "KAREN SHIELDS, occasional legal secretary, still dark-haired, five pounds heavier, wife, mother, baby-sitter, cleaning lady, cook, nurse, chauffeur, laundress, seamstress, always there...ever hopeful."

The entire document is scrolled in gold and meticulously hand-lettered. It is a gift of self and a summing up, as a woman does when considering to whom and for what she has given ten years of her being. Who is he? And who am I alongside him? What were we supposed to be? And who are we now, together?

I find it honest, without guile, an unsettling, telling summary.

Tony doesn't even comment. I can't be sure he even read it. He offers her no clue. Nothing.

She waits, a thin cloud of lonely resolve darkening her eyes. The silence is too hard. She begins to rise, a move made more awkward by the swaying train.

We are almost strangers again as she looks at me and says, "Well, I guess we've kept you long enough. Have a wonderful trip. Where'd you say you were going?"

"Charlottesville."

Then, kindly, "Everyone will be glad to see you again, I know."

Then she asks, as if I had never said, "And what is the occasion?"

"Our family reunion."

"Yes...." she pauses and looks beyond the window at the lights dimpling the night. "Family. That's the best reason for doing anything. Isn't it?"

I smile at her. Tony and I shake hands.

And they leave so she can spend the rest of the night trying to erase her words, to bring him back. Knowing it's too late. And so he can search for yet new ways to quietly reassure her that he understands—while forgetting about the magic.

And—wherever it was I thought that I was going—will be different.

AT THE END OF THE ROAD

The plan was bold and risky.

Imaginative, too, I thought—and mine—and I was determined to see it through to the end regardless of the consequences. I needed to add only one more small detail to complete it.

I needed Julia.

Julia was wiry and strong and full of purpose. She was perfect for the job, a fact I knew she'd recognize immediately, once I'd explained it all to her. So, I sought her out.

"You're crazy!" she stated flatly, looking at me from under her short brown bob. Then she went on to say precisely why she had no intention of getting involved in my scheme— "not now, not tomorrow, not in a hundred million years"—a scheme, she concluded, that would "probably get us all killed."

So much for Julia.

But there was always her sister, Libby. Libby—well, Libby was always willing.

For the past two summers, Julia, Libby and I had vacationed with our families on my parents' isolated, coastal Georgia farm. As city dwellers the rest of the year, we were thoroughly intrigued by its rural uniqueness. It never mattered to us that, back then in 1939, there was no air conditioning, no telephone, and, in fact, no electricity. We immersed ourselves in the rituals of farm life. We swam and fished and shrimped the rivers and prowled the marshes, observing the birds, raccoons, mink and opossums which took their sustenance there.

We watched moons scatter silver over the rippling nighttime tides. We saw dawn's gathered mists soon burned away by hot and breathless mornings. And in all the months we spent there, we never grew complacent about the country's gifts nor lost our love for its magic and surprise.

Being isolated also meant we had to rely on each other for company, and from the beginning, Julia and I had been best friends. We shared everything—secrets, fun, and, in particular, the tormenting of her little sister. Without us, Libby had no one, and she yearned to be included. Which is why little Libby, of the auburn hair and big dark eyes, became such easy prey.

We never included her in anything. It was tacit policy. Unless, of course, we needed someone to perform some awful job assigned to us by our parents. Or, better yet, we could use her as "*the enemy*" in games where we ambushed her from trees or pelted her with chinaberries from the hayloft.

So, when I offered to include her in my plan—to involve her in a *secret mission* that didn't even include Julia—Libby never thought to hesitate. Julia warned her against it, but I'd gotten to her first and had made sure her judgment was in full retreat. That was the easy part. Libby was, after all, only five.

Julia was eight.

And I was almost seven.

At that age, my compassion was selective. While it didn't include many humans, it did embrace all our parents, my Aunt Ruth, the men who worked the farm, and most of the animal kingdom.

It did not include snakes. Nor my Uncle Floyd.

Floyd was my uncle by marriage. He and my sweet-faced, kind Aunt Ruth lived next door, and their weathered white frame house was the center of our little river-front community that included the small guest cottage where Julia and Libby were summering on one side and the one my family used for vacations on the other.

My father detested his brother-in-law, whom he considered lazy and resentful. But, as we spent most of the year in Savannah, some forty miles away, he needed someone to manage the place. Whatever else he might be, Floyd was available.

So my uncle, with his thin-blue, angry eyes resting in his bone-mean face, orchestrated people and things pretty much the way he wanted with little supervision or resistance from my father.

Technically, Uncle Floyd was the farm's overseer, a title he took quite literally. In his bib overalls and faded shirt, he looked weathered and tough, just like the rest of the farm hands—except that he was white. So, to set the hierarchy straight, he'd tell the men, "If I was as know-nothin' as you boys, I'd be out there where you are all day long with my face in the business end of some mule. But since I'm the overseer here, I'll tell you what needs doin', and I'll see to it that you do it."

"Yessuh, Mista Floyd. Yessuh," was heard repeatedly every morning while he gave out the day's instructions. Then he puttered around the barn until the creak and jangle of harness and the thump of wooden wagon wheels and the final "gee" and "haw" were muffled by the woods that flanked the road to the cornfields.

Having thus "overseen" the day, Uncle Floyd would amble on back home and into his kitchen where he could be found most of the morning, tilted back in a wooden chair, with his white-socked feet propped up on the enamel-topped kitchen table, chewing on a length of broom sedge and talking to Aunt Ruth while she worked away.

Which is where I found him that particular morning.

Grinning, he watched me as I climbed the steps, crossed the porch and padded onto the kitchen's faded linoleum.

He greeted me as he always did. "Mornin', Br'er Fats."

"Good mornin'," I answered politely, looking at my feet where my bare toes twitched and thumped uncomfortably.

As usual, he had made me miserably aware of my childish shape. In his gaze, my trace of baby fat seemed elephantine. And there was no way to hide it in the flowered sunsuit which was much too spare to camouflage the rounded arms and legs that stuck out gracelessly from inside it. My stick-straight, short brown hair was also much too brief to hide the blush rising in cheeks which, in his opinion, resembled "an advanced case of the mumps."

He let me wait there. Looking at me. Until finally, he said, "So, Br'er Fats...an' what kin we do for you today?"

"I came to see if Aunt Ruth wanted me to hunt for eggs," I answered without looking at him.

It was my favorite pastime, one worth even braving an encounter with Uncle Floyd. I liked doing it early, before Julia and Libby showed up and I'd have to share the adventure.

I knew where every one of the thirty hens had their nests. The old red sat under the porch, and the white lay in the milk cow's manger. The funny-looking speckled hens went deep under the house where the chimneys met the dark, cool earth. I knew them all, and I'd run excitedly to tell Aunt Ruth if a hen had laid two eggs or to give her the somber report if a nest were empty.

A hen whose nest had been bare for days was an aging white called Snow. And it was about her that Uncle Floyd now spoke.

"You know, old Snow ain't layin' much. I think she just might be ailin'. You wanna help me find her and see if we kin take care of it?"

"Sure!" I said eagerly, finally brave enough to look at him. Snow never stayed still for me, and I loved it when someone held her for me and I could touch her.

"Get some corn and we'll go lookin'."

The chair bumped on the floor as he untilted, while I ran to the corner of the dilapidated porch, to the familiar croaker sack and dug out two fistfuls of shelled grain.

He stood up slowly, yawning and stretching, his feet searching for his shoes. Then we headed out together calling to the distant chickens where they scratched the ground for bugs.

"Heah, chick, chick...heah, chick," he cooed as a few feathery heads appeared. "Now throw 'em a little bit. You gotta make it worth their while."

Stopping by the wood pile, he rested his foot by the big axe on the chopping block and waited.

Obediently, I tossed a few golden kernels into the black dirt.

They came scurrying now. They ran across the grassless yard, past the rusty hand pump poking up stoically from the open ground and past the barren roosting tree below which the dirt was peppered with murky green and white droppings until, finally, they were clucking and flapping at our feet.

Uncle Floyd worked his way toward Snow until he could reach down and gently close his hand to still her wings. With the other, he scooped her up, her yellow legs dangling through his fingers. He stroked her quietly as he began to look her over. I reached out happily to touch her.

"Can't see nothin' wrong," he said, as he searched her carefully.

Snow "Gwaaaked," and fixed him with her tiny blinking eyes, but she didn't struggle.

"Ya think she's just old?" he suggested, turning her now from side to side.

"Might just be," I answered.

He nodded, studying her a while. Then he turned. Slowly he placed her on her side on the block, putting his foot down firmly on her to keep her there. Terrified, the old hen squawked and struggled while a cacophony rose from the other birds as they raised their wings and fled.

He held Snow there as he reached for the axe.

"No, please." I begged. "No....NO, DON'T!!!"

But he raised and aimed it carefully—then brought it down with a splintering force that broke the wood beneath as it split away her head from the rest of her twitching body.

Snow's head, her eyes still staring up in terror, lay severed on the stump.

When Uncle Floyd released his foot, her body flapped violently and fell to the ground. Then it raised itself and went staggering around the yard, wings instinctively extended in a dance that searched for life and balance—dipping and dragging from side to side, blood spurting everywhere from the empty neck.

Hot tears flooded from my eyes. I rubbed at them with the back of my grubby hand, allowing the last few golden grains to fall onto the red-stained dirt.

"Oh, Uncle Floyd, why?" I sobbed. "Why did you make her die?"

His pale blue eyes fixed on me. "That's dinner, young'n. Everything out here has t' be good for sumpin'."

Then he turned to the hen once more and waited until her useless fluttering stopped, and with a final, falling spasm, she lay still. He went over to her, picked her up and began yanking out her bloody feathers.

"Bye, Br'er Fats," he called after me as I ran from the yard. "Come see us real soon, y' hear?"

Isaac had just brought in a load of wood for the iron stove on which our meals were cooked, even in the one hundred degree noon heat of summer. I nearly bowled him over as I flung myself up the brick steps and into the kitchen.

"Whoooooah, there young'n," he said as he caught my arm. "What's de matter?" He studied the grime of yard dirt and tears on my miserable face, and his soft, dark eyes expressed his concern.

Isaac was my truest friend on the farm. His tall, lean, brown-skinned frame seemed as strong and permanent as a tree. I trusted him. I confided in him. I loved him. And I would do anything he said.

"Awright, chile," he said, "tell me all about it."

Squatting down, he listened patiently while I burbled out my story of what had just happened. When I'd finished, I sniffled and looked at him for sympathy.

"I know it don't sound good t' say so," he began while searching for a way to take the sting away, "but your Uncle Floyd is right."

"Nooo!" I protested.

"Yes, he is." Isaac said. "That's the way things is on the farm. Folks gotta eat. An' that's what them animals is here for."

"But..."

"Now ah knows you don't wants t' hear that," he interrupted, "and it's true enough, your uncle—he did'n' need t' do it just that way. But them chickens you likes t' feed, well, they gets t' eat 'cause we needs 'em fat so's we can have 'em for our own dinner. We needs 'em so's *we* can stay alive. It's just the way things is, chile, an' you gotta learn t' accept it."

He regarded me steadily until he knew his words were a part of me—when my understanding, although grudging, was complete. Then he smiled and said, "You chirren wanna go down t' de pig lot with me this evenin' when ah takes watermelon down t' feed them hogs?"

"Oh, yes!" I responded, grinning. Who in his right mind wouldn't?

Then Isaac knew he could release me into the kitchen, where, if I begged convincingly enough, there'd be a cookie or two, and, he was certain, there would also be forgetting.

It took four cookies, by actual count, to soak up the remainder of my grief, at which point I'd been put out of the kitchen like one of the cats who insisted on sneaking in when the door was ajar, ever hopeful that they'd get a handout. Their attempts were usually met with immediate ejection, but it didn't seem to matter. The game was played for its own reward. They never stopped trying. Nor did I.

Victorious, for once, and sated with sugar, I sought out Julia and Libby.

We built the City of Oz out of dirt and oyster shells and twigs for our captive population of fiddler crabs.

We swam.

And lunched.

And napped.

Napping was that terrible period when we were made to lie down somewhere to rest—without talking, or giggling, or anything. It was necessary, our parents said, because the midday heat would sap our energy. Which was a ploy, of course. We never ran out of energy; our parents did. We sulkily submitted to the ruse, but we never forgave them for it.

We met Isaac at the barn at five o'clock. He had Millie, the best mule, hitched and waiting, and we piled on the loaded wagon for the two-mile trip to the pig lot. Isaac shook the reins, and Millie moved off, pitching us from side to side as she pulled her cargo down the lane laced with roots and dented with potholes.

Once out on the road, we would jump down occasionally to rescue a sherd of Indian pottery or a bit of broken china from the dust. Then we'd have to run to catch up to the moving wagon. Grabbing hold and jumping back on was made even harder by four other little hands all energetically trying to prevent it. If you started laughing, you were done for, since the game was to tickle the ascender until, convulsed with laughter, she fell down on the sandy ruts and had to walk back home.

That day, Libby was the one who found herself face down on the road.

"Libby can't catch us," we taunted her as the wagon pulled away. "She's too little, and her legs are too short!" A little mean talk always seemed to ratchet the victory up a notch.

She howled at Isaac to stop and, taking pity on her, as he always did, he *whoa'd* Millie to a halt and waited.

"Not fair!" Libby pouted as she regained her place. "NOT FAIR!" she shrieked. After that, she petulantly refused to talk to us as we lurched the rest of the way to the pig-lot.

The hogs, meanwhile, had heard the distant drum roll of approaching watermelons and had gathered in a pushing, shoving, snorting mob to await their arrival. They squealed approval as we lumbered into view, and it was mayhem by the time we hove-to at the side of the pig lot fence and got ready for the fun.

The watermelons were enormous. And it always took two of us—or two-and-a-half if you counted Libby—to hoist one off the wagon floor and inch it up the side.

"Push, Libby, PUSH!" we'd shout. "Higher! You've gotta get it higher!" until with one final, magnificent assist, we'd set it spinning over the edge to crash into the chaos below where it squashed like a fleshy water balloon, its red, mushy insides and slimy seeds splattering all over the scuffling contestants.

We loved every raucous, messy minute of it.

The hogs loved it, too, and Isaac indulged us all.

When the cache was spent—when the laughter had died down—when the sticky snouts had stopped tilting up to us expectantly—only then did we collapse in a heap to watch the sun set hotly behind palmetto scrub and blackened silhouettes of pine—lying on our backs on the wagon floor, watching for the evening star, singing silly songs and talking, while Millie and Isaac—wearily, ploddingly, dutifully—delivered their happy child-cargo back home.

We had been over at Aunt Ruth's house feeding the chickens when she appeared and signaled us over to her porch. Wading through the flurry of hens, we assembled at the bottom of the steps while she addressed us.

"Now, girls," she began seriously, which always merited our attention, "tonight we're havin' special guests, and I'd like very much for the three of you to join us for the evenin'."

"Who's comin'?" we chorused excitedly. No one ever visited.

"Our preacher and his wife," she answered with a proud smile. "They're comin' here for a special prayer meetin'."

Julia and Libby smiled at her sweetly, and Julia said, "How nice."

"Oh," I mumbled, disappointment showing.

Aunt Ruth gave me a hard look, "Now shoo, go 'long and ask your parents. They're comin' about seven. You won't have to dress up."

During the school year, Julia and Libby were every-Sunday churchgoers, and their parents thought this prayer meeting would be a healthy fill-in for a summer of blatant religious neglect. My parents, on the other hand, disdained all formal religious functions. They never went to church nor sent me there.

"Do you want to go?" my mother asked.

"I don't know," I demurred.

"Well, you're old enough to make your own decision. You don't *have* to go, but you can if you like."

Well, truthfully I wouldn't "like." But this prayer meeting was next door. I could hardly ignore it nor the more pertinent fact that my cohorts would be there, privy to all manner of unknown happenings that would take place and about which I would know nothing. They were sure to lord it over me. So, after supper I took a bath, put on a clean sunsuit, and, head down, I kicked sand and chased a stray fiddler and otherwise prolonged my reluctant journey to Aunt Ruth's and the mysterious meeting that was to take place in the front parlor.

No one that I knew of had ever used the front parlor for anything. It was easy to see why they had avoided it. It was bleakly formal with whitewashed bead-pine paneling, scrubbed bare floors and furniture that was dark and stiff and forbidding.

Julia and Libby were already in place on the settee, a torturous affair with straight oak slats for a back and a thin, black horsehair pad covering a hard-board bottom. The remaining places to sit consisted of rigid chairs with deer hide stretched for seats. The fur was still intact, and the hide felt sleek and satiny, much like a living animal, if you stroked it the right way. Rubbed backward, it was as bristly as a porcupine.

I was assigned to one of these. My feet didn't touch the floor. The seat was too wide for me to brace against the back, and if I moved at all, my bare legs would be perforated by those hairy needles. It was going to be a long evening.

There was a clock to tell me just how long. It was the one fussy thing in the Spartan room, its face held high by a windswept bronze-draped lady with baskets of grapes at her feet.

According to the grape lady, at precisely seven, the preacher and his matching wife arrived.

He was all in black, his features sharply chiseled—sort of like the furniture. Smiling at us somberly, he patted each child on the head as we were introduced. He was delighted to find his flock now swollen by three, and he promised to make a special effort—meaning long—on our burgeoned behalf.

We started out with hymns, except that there were no hymnals for the children. We couldn't read the big words anyway. But amazingly, Julia and Libby seemed to know the songs by heart, each one of which had at least ten verses. We, or rather they, sang them all while Aunt Ruth sat starchily before an ancient upright piano pounding out tinny melodies that were mostly intact but devoid of superfluous nuance.

At the end of the singing there were prayers. *LOTS* of prayers. While we bowed our heads, the preacher started talking to God about death and stoicism and pestilence and floods and retribution and penance and the weather, the last of which was always of major interest on a farm. I peeked every once in a while to see if all heads were still down. They were. And it wasn't until I heard the mumble of "Amens" followed by the rustle of bodies straightening and books being closed that I was sure we were at the end.

It was 8:30. Our usual bedtime. I rose to go.

Frigid looks shot from the preacher's wife and Aunt Ruth, and the sneer sent my way by Uncle Floyd sent me climbing back onto my prickly perch. I looked to Julia for reassurance and she returned my look with one of smug amusement. And Libby—Libby chose to ignore my gaffe completely by daintily smoothing out a turned-back ruffle on her sunsuit.

The preacher remained silent.

Waiting.

Looking at the ceiling.

Once I was resettled, he took a deep breath, sighed, and turned languidly to focus on this rank new prospect so sorely in need of instruction. Still silent, he stared at me steadily, carving every detail of what he saw into his deepening purpose.

Finally, he began. At the Beginning. With Adam and Eve, who, I was startled to learn, were wearing only fig leaves. He described the beautiful Garden of Eden where there was a huge tree loaded with crunchy apples. It seemed stupid, but God had told Eve she wasn't supposed to eat any of them. Then, down out of the tree to talk to her about it came this huge, HUGE SNAKE!

I winced.

Contact!

The preacher smiled. Now he could get on with the real pith of the matter, a dissertation on Original Sin. He broadened that to include omnipresent evil wherein all of us were unrepentant sinners, capable of unimaginably heinous acts of violence, aggression, seduction, illicit fornication (whatever that was), thievery, murder, and the like.

Even though I hadn't the foggiest idea what he was talking about, I felt uncomfortable—even personally responsible. By now he was spreading the hopelessness of our condition among everyone in the room, and their attention was absolute. So he proceeded with what we should do about it.

"We have to grow, brothers and sisters—grow as God's children—grow as Christians—grow as people—to MATURITY!"

I understood that word. I was back within receiving range. He detected it immediately and moved over to my chair. He leaned down to me, his face just inches from my own, and said, "...but we can never hope to escape the prison of our own selfishness and self-love if we do not *mature* as God-fearin' people—if we do not learn *patience*!"

I squirmed.

"And," he continued, looking at me balefully, "and...if we cannot be *still*, how can we hear the words of Jesus Christ, our Savior?"

As if to set my stillness in a vise, he reached out and imprisoned my pudgy face tightly between his hands. "If we are not *still*, we cannot understand the words, and if we cannot understand the words, how can we hope…to be *SAVED!*"

"Saved?" I stammered. It just came out. In my experience, being saved meant something imperative—like being saved from drowning—or from being eaten by pumas—or bitten by rattlesnakes—or—or something!

"Yes," he hissed into my face, "SAVED!"

I didn't know how or from what, but, for a moment, I was utterly convinced that "saved" was what I needed to be.

Releasing me, he turned now to the others, raising his arms heavenward. "For without being saved we are condemned, brothers and sisters." He shook his fists, *"Eternally condemned!"* he shouted, "TO HELL ON EARTH!"

Deer hide punctuated the point as I backed into the recesses of my chair. He swung back to me again. The beady burning pupils of his eyes bore into mine which were now huge with awe. "Condemned eternally to hell on earth and to the fires of damnation...FOREVER!"

There was a mumble of "amens." I sat transfixed, his black eyes possessing me—piercing me—penetrating through me, into the deepening dusk.

At nine o'clock they lit the kerosene lamp, and the darkness of furnishings, people and night windows all shimmered and wobbled against the acrid white of the walls. It hurt my eyes. I couldn't see things clearly any more. The smoky stench of burning kerosene hung in the summer night. My stomach growled while Julia and Libby sat primly, assuming angelic looks as they concentrated on the wavering image of the preacher. They were trying not to giggle.

By 9:30, hundreds of insects were flying suicide missions into the hell-fires of the flaming lamp. I watched them find their frantic way down the glass chimney, doubtlessly into "Eternal Damnation" where they were crisped to nothingness…FOREVER!

"Amen...amen...amen, brother."

My eyelids were supporting anvils. "Amen," I mumbled trying to hide a yawn.

Everyone looked at me. I must have said it in the wrong place.

At 10:30 there was the switch and play of flashlights somewhere out in the dark. There was muffled talk and laughter—magnifying—nearing. Parents were coming. It was two hours past our bedtime.

It took another fifteen minutes to disengage us during which I sagged against my father's leg. But finally, we could stumble down the steps and into the succulent night.

In bed at last—just before my body had no substance and my thoughts fell fuzzily away in sleep—I divined that religion must be designed as a test of human endurance. It had left me with half my childhood spent. And, if given a choice, I'd never partake of it again.

It was *always* pancakes on Sunday morning—thick, deep-fried, crunchy fritters dripping in fresh butter and syrup and always served with homemade sausage, smoked bacon and wet, sweet melons from the garden.

What wasn't usual was that today I was wearing a dress.

"If church isn't until eleven," I complained, "Why do I have to be at Aunt Ruth's house at nine?"

"You haven't seen Floyd drive," my father said with a deep, imagining-it laugh.

So, I finished my breakfast and trudged across the yard with even less enthusiasm than I'd had the night before, wondering how—knowing what I now knew about religion—I ever could have let myself get talked into going to church and enduring it all over again.

I wasn't sure.

The previous night when my parents had finally rescued me, I had been too near sleep to listen to their conversation with Aunt Ruth. It seems that she had been ecstatic over what she perceived would be my imminent religious conversion. She felt appointed, perhaps missionized, to push me over the edge. As a result, she had begged my family to send me to church with her the next day.

"Please, George. Please, Louise. I'm sure she'll really love it." More convincingly she added, "Besides, how can she know if she likes it or not if she's never been. Julia and Libby are going with us, and she'll be with her friends."

"We'll talk to her about it in the morning," was all they promised. "But if she's willing, what time do you want her over here?"

"At nine o'clock," she answered.

"But isn't the service at eleven?" my mother asked, knowing that the old country church they attended was only four miles away.

"Floyd drivin'?" came from my father. Aunt Ruth just lowered her head and gave a little titter.

Early that Sunday morning I had sat cross-legged on the bed while my mother brushed my hair. It was our ritual, our time to be mother and daughter—warm and close. It was my favorite moment of the day with her before friends and duties and problems and play separated us from our shared privacy.

"You really like Aunt Ruth, don't you?" she asked.

"Oh, yes."

She stroked a stray lock into place. "Would you like to do her a favor?"

"Sure," I replied. I'd do anything for Aunt Ruth.

"She wants very much to have you go to church with her today."

"Ooohhhhhh!!!!" I wailed, springing to the floor and facing her. "Do I have to?"

She smiled at me indulgently, "No, of course not." And she patted the bed in an invitation to sit back down on it. With some suspicion, I did. She stroked my hair some more.

"It would really mean a lot to her if you went. She is certain you'll enjoy it, and, as she says, you've never been."

"But I went last night."

"That was really quite different," Mother said, adding for inducement, "It really is a wonderful old country church." She crossed to the closet and turned to smile at me again. "You might try it for her...just this once." Then she brought out my white sailor dress, and I slipped into it without a murmur.

The big robin's-egg-blue Ford had already been backed out of the shed onto the grass alongside the house so we wouldn't track in sand and chicken droppings from the yard. Away from home, Uncle Floyd always took trouble with appearances, and before venturing out he always washed the car. Today, it was sparkling.

As were most 1929 models, the Ford sedan was also very tall. So he helped Libby climb in first, then Julia, then me.

"Awright. Watch your feet, Br'er Fats," he warned. "Don't get 'em on the seat." Then he and Aunt Ruth got in the front, and we were ready to go.

Floyd cranked the engine while the rest of us rolled down the windows for air. It was already in the low-90s, and the sun was beating hard on the metal roof. With the engine purring, we just sat there for a good ten minutes—baking in our big blue shiny oven. Sweat drizzled down my legs which were now sticking to the seat. It even oozed into my dampening sandals. I fanned my skirt at my face, but it didn't help much. Julia and Libby, while soaking, too, remained unrumpled and sedate.

Finally, we began to move forward, blazing out of the yard at a heroic five miles per hour.

"You chillun just don't understand about takin' care of things," Uncle Floyd explained, unasked. "Like this here engine. You gotta treat it kindly. Let it get used to goin' before you ask it to do anything big."

Out on the dirt road now, he pushed the Ford up to possibly ten full miles per hour, still not enough to generate any breeze. My neatly brushed hair was now plastered to my head with sweat.

"Take speed," he went on. "That'll sour an engine just like lightnin'. That's why you'll never catch me doin' more than thirty, even on the paved road."

I could almost hear my father laughing.

"...an' the bumps...like on this here corduroy road. Why, if I wasn't careful, I'd bust ever' spring in this automobile before the year was out. An' I intend for this here vee-hicle to last. That's why I'm not likely to...."

But I had stopped listening. Instead, I turned to stare out the window at the fans of wet green ferns edging the road as it cut through gatherings of cypress, their grey knees bulging up for air above the tannin-stained swamp water.

With a sudden burst of light, we broke free of the forest edge, and I saw the open fields, now blue where morning glories clustered and dotted with grazing cows. Then came the houses, shacks really, grey from weathering, their shutters propped open from glassless windows to catch the breathless air. They were set high up on cedar stumps. Scrawny dogs of questionable parentage sprawled under them in the shade while chickens scratched around in their sunny, broom-swept yards.

Flanking nearly all the wooden front-porch steps were mounds of color—phlox and daisies and petunias stuffing the centers and spilling over the sides of discarded, white-washed rubber tires. Nearby, there were tumbling disarrays of poles and rusted tin that served as barns and holding pens for the farm animals.

By now I was almost grateful for our lack of speed as I watched hogs wallowing into cooling inky bogs inside their pens. And I laughed as indecisive biddies scattered from their mother hens at the sight of our monstrous blue enormity glistening down upon them.

And—for the first time—I saw the horse.

As we drew close, he lifted his head slowly to look at us. It was then that I saw his eyes, so tired from age and hunger. I saw the stains where biting flies had sucked their fill from his frail neck, and I saw the bones of his ribs and hips and shoulders stabbing at the taut, unfatted skin.

The old brown horse kept looking at us, following us with his eyes until the blue Ford's tires drew our track out of sight around the bend.

"What did you see that's so interesting?" Aunt Ruth asked.

"That old brown horse," I replied.

"He is sad, isn't he," she answered, in a way that seemed to mirror my own concern.

Then Uncle Floyd intruded. "Don't know why they don't jus' shoot the old nag! Ain't worth nothin'. He's half starved to death, and those people never give him any feed. Don't know why they just don't kill him and let the buzzards have what little's left."

"Good gracious, Floyd," Aunt Ruth exclaimed. "Do you really think he's that far gone?"

"Without nothin' to eat," he growled, "that old horse won't make it past the first hard freeze. They oughtn't to keep him like that. They oughta just put a gun to his head, blow his brains out, and put him outta his misery."

"I suppose you're right," she said thoughtfully. "It might be a kindness."

"That's not a kindness!" I blurted. How could Aunt Ruth say such a thing? I searched for an explanation of my own. "Maybe...maybe he's their friend."

This only made Floyd laugh. "You young'ns don't know nothin'," he sneered. "You think you kin fix anything by bein' sweet and carin'."

"I DO care," I protested. "I DO!!!"

He just laughed harder, relishing my stupidity for the next half-mile which took at least ten minutes to complete, while I sat, angry and impotent in the back seat, silently repeating "*I* care—*I* care—*I* care—*I* care" to the distant horse, still seeing and feeling his sad eyes following us while I fought the tears in my own.

"Church" in the white wood building was indeed different from the night before. Inside, enormous windows made the interior bright with sunlight. The thirty-foot-high ceilings created an echo chamber which lent ethereal richness to the music, especially to "Swing Low, Sweet Chariot," my favorite Negro spiritual that even the white folks sang. As the preacher rolled into his *"hell-awaits-all-disbelievers"* sermon, the reverberation was thunderous. Even I was impressed, and it didn't seem so long at all until I could satisfy my real desire—to drive back by that shabby farm and see the old brown horse again.

This time, the horse stood dozing in a pool of deep shade, reprieved for a while from the stinging torment of insects settling on his meager coat. But as we neared, he met my eyes once more and followed us until the vision of our bouncing, glimmering blue chariot swung low and was blotted out by the darkness of the moody swamp.

We roared into the chicken yard at our accustomed pace that didn't even unseat the flies that had settled comfortably on the hood at church and had ridden with us, undisturbed, all the way back home.

We all got out, pulling at our dresses to unstick them from our clammy legs. Julia and Libby said, "Thank you, ma'am," and skipped off down the road toward their house.

Before I could do the same, Aunt Ruth placed her hand on my shoulder to stop me.

"Won't you stay for dinner?" she asked.

"I think Mother's expectin' me."

She tried to entice me, "But we're havin' your favorite—fried chicken."

I thanked her but said "no" and trudged on off toward home.

I wondered if dinner was going to be Snow.

I never missed a Sunday at church after that. I endured all manner of heated attempts to rescue my dysfunctional soul, but I never heard most of them. I usually concentrated on a dirt dauber's progress with the nest it was building on the window frame outside. Over the Sundays, the grey mud blob had swelled to impressive proportions because the dauber had placed it too high to be whacked down with a broom handle, or to be threatened at all without the aid of an enormous ladder.

For variety, I also counted the congregation of flies that gathered weekly in a pine-stained patch of sunlight on the wooden floor. Sometimes I watched white summer clouds move dark grey shade across the windows and hoped that it didn't spell rain which would spoil our afternoon in the river.

I did learn all the verses of all the songs. And, as did the rest of our congregation, I futilely whipped the dense, wet air with paddle-shaped cardboard fans that were placed in the hymn book rack behind each pew, compliments of the Gum Branch Funeral Home, *"The Loveliest, Most Caring Place In Liberty County To Make Final Preparations For The Journey To Eternal Rest."* Still, I always found myself just waiting until we rose and mingled toward the mossy steps, shook the preacher's hand, and filed away into the real world of dirt and trees and car—the big blue Ford that Uncle Floyd parked carefully to catch the shade. Once inside it, we could set out for home, and to the place in the road where I could glimpse the old brown horse again.

On the way to church each Sunday morning, just before we came to the spot where I could see him, I'd pray. I prayed with all my might that he had changed. I imagined that flesh had suddenly softened his bony frame—that his head would rise alertly, ears pricked forward—and that he would look at me today with eyes that shone with welcoming recognition. But each time the gleaming car burst from the swamp and I'd see him, at last, the eyes I met were deeper set, the taut skin more defining of encroaching death, and his drooping head hung lower in acceptance—and in waiting.

When, finally, I understood that his life was ebbing, the journeys home were filled with sadness. I still would search for him each time, just to connect, just to look at him and keep my pledge alive.

"I care...I care...."

But Uncle Floyd was right. It hadn't changed anything. My hopes became as hollow as the emptying eyes the brown horse fixed on me each time the shiny-domed blue Ford pulled us through the glistening heat to and from the House-of-Saving.

During this time, my unflagging faithfulness to the weekly trip had convinced Aunt Ruth that her mission to "save" me was approaching fruition. She often put her arm around me when she spoke and gave me a close, warm hug.

Uncle Floyd showed his own approval by sharing news about the farm. My father's farm was Floyd's fiefdom, his seat of power, and he protected all information concerning it with a dark ferocity. Now, though, during these Sunday drives, he made me privy to all sorts of inside information, by far the most intriguing of which were the reports he leaked about *the hay baler*.

His descriptions of it approached the supernatural.

I had never seen a hay "bale." The men always brought the sweet cut grass in trucks and wagons and pitched it up loose to the loft where it was stored for winter.

The hayloft was our favorite place. Hours were spent there chasing mice out of holes between the rafters, or playing *King of the Mountain*, or just lying deep in the fragrant, pillowy grass while summer rains beat a blunt tattoo on the corrugated metal roof.

From what Uncle Floyd said, I suspected hay "bales" would end all that. But fascination with a machine that could reduce veritable mountains of grass into tiny rectangles quickly overrode my reservations. I could hardly wait.

"Patience," Uncle Floyd had cautioned. "It's comin' soon."

A few weeks later he announced, "It's comin' Saturday."

Before anyone knew it, Saturday became tomorrow.

Then, "the very first hay baling in Liberty County" was about to take place on our farm—today! It was epic. It was historic. Even my father made plans to come.

On that magic morning, Julia, Libby, and I assembled at the barn to watch, seating ourselves in a line high up on the wagon bench to assure ourselves of the best possible view.

"You young'ns look like a bunch of crows on a wire," Uncle Floyd laughed, exposing his good humor. He relished being center stage for such a moment. With the baler set up behind him, he stood before our group and authoritatively explained how he planned to make the contraption run.

A mule would walk around in a circle while attached to a ten-foot pole that was connected by chains to a gear box. When the mule moved forward, the gears would engage, sending the loose grass down the conveyor and into a hopper. There, it would be fed into a compactor, then be bound with twine and finally dumped onto the ground.

Millie, our favorite, was the chosen mule, and, to make her go, Uncle Floyd had hired Jesse, a small, ten year-old black child, for twenty cents a day, to ride her.

We all expected the performance to be seamless. But to Uncle Floyd's embarrassment, the equipment was far from the 20th century farming marvel he had advertised when he talked my father into buying it. Again and again, the mule was made to *whoa* while rebellious hanks of straw were unclogged from the uncooperative system. And the more restless his audience became with the endless stage waits, the more agitated Uncle Floyd became.

"Whoa, Millie, you stupid mule!" he roared and then looked menacingly at Jesse. "And you, boy."

The child looked down at him and smiled, "Yessuh!"

"Why you actin' like you're as stupid as a mule yourself. Can't you see we need to fix this thing? You're supposed to make that mule stand *still* while we do that. Why you so dumb, boy?"

With this, Jesse squinched lower on the mule's razor back and murmured, "Yessuh," the smile gone in the strike of words.

Eventually, to Uncle Floyd's chagrin, my father left.

It never took much to amuse us girls, however. We remained fascinated by the slow, heavy birthing of each grassy cube. We clapped each time—every five minutes or so—when one inched its way out of the machine and hit the ground with a final thud.

Now, once again, the mule had been *whoa'd* to a standstill, while the men unplugged the machine, and again Uncle Floyd was up to his elbows in the gear box. The sun had cleared the trees and filled the scene with yellow light which also brought the flies. They buzzed and hummed around the mule. They settled in to bite, and the blood they leeched attracted even more. Jesse dutifully swished at the ones which fought for space on Millie's neck and rump, but he couldn't reach the mule's back legs and belly, to which the knowing flies now flocked.

Millie swished her tail and stomped her legs in a vain attempt to dislodge them.

Floyd bellowed at the boy. "Jesse! You worthless nigger, you hold that old mule STILL!"

"Ah's tryin', Mista Floyd," Jesse replied. "These here flies is turrible. They be eatin' Millie up."

Millie pounded her belly with her hind leg and angrily kicked at the dirt behind her.

"I told you NOT to let that mule move FORWARD!" Floyd shouted.

Millie stomped and kicked in frustration, her hind end beginning to pitch and sway. "Whoa, mule. WHOA!" the frightened child pleaded as he hauled on the reins with all his strength to stop her. "WHOA!"

This time the agitated mule obeyed him after all. She stopped leaning forward on the harness; instead, the steps she took were backward.

Just a few of them. Just enough.

And with an almost imperceptible grind of metal against metal, the gears engaged and caught Floyd by the hand.

His hideous scream assaulted us and terrified the mule. With a slap of chains and leather, Millie bolted, dumping Jesse on the ground. Still tethered to the pole, the mule frantically ran around the circle while Floyd, his right hand trapped in the meshing gears, shrieked in anguish.

Before the men could move, Uncle Floyd fell backward to the ground, suddenly free to clutch his injured hand, moaning and crying, blood pouring from between his fingers and trickling down his arm.

Isaac and the other men rushed to him. "Mista Floyd! Mista Floyd!" Isaac pleaded. "Lemme see. Take ya han' away now and let Isaac help you." Floyd rolled and pitched, still moaning horribly. "Please...Mista Floyd, please. Ya gotta let go so's ah kin hep ya. Ah needs to see."

When finally Uncle Floyd released his hand for Isaac, we saw it too. One finger dangled from a thin, skin sinew, and another one was missing. Blood spurted out of the short remaining stumps.

None of us moved.

Not Julia. Not Libby. Not I.

Not one of us said a word.

Uncle Floyd grabbed at his hand again, writhing and moaning, "Son-of-a-bitch! Son-of-a-bitch! Jesus! Goddamn it's gone. My finger's gone. Son-of-a-bitch!"

"Jes a minute, Mista Floyd, an' ah'll find it for you," Isaac said, his voice quivering with concern.

He got down on his hands and knees and poked around under the baler and came up proudly with the curled remains of Floyd's finger, two end joints complete with fingernail, caked with dirt and blood, but still together.

Floyd cried out again.

Isaac tried to calm him. "I bet if'n you hurry, them doctors kin put it back on for you." He turned to the other men. "Somebody go get Miz Ruth an' tell her t' bring Mista Floyd's car. Hurry now!"

One of the younger men sprinted off and soon distant bright blue flashes announced the Ford's approach as it shot through shade and sunlight with Aunt Ruth behind the wheel. Not once did she even try to avoid a fallen branch or hole. She sent bits of wood and black mud flying as she sped into the yard and slammed to a stop by her husband's writhing body.

All the men gathered to lift Floyd off the ground and put him in the car where he slumped against the seat. Someone took out a soiled handkerchief and gently wrapped the finger in it and placed it on Floyd's lap. Isaac carefully closed the door.

The dirty, spattered car pulled off at once. When it cleared the barn, it must have been going forty miles an hour.

The next day, Julia and I finally managed to ditch Libby so we could talk about what had happened. We had been forbidden to discuss the incident, and if Libby heard, we knew she'd tell on us.

"Did you know they didn't find Jesse 'til this mornin'?" Julia whispered as we sat hidden in the branches of our favorite tree. Even with no one else around, it was scary to speak out loud about it. Clearly, we were risking serious trouble.

"Noooo. What happened to him?" I whispered back.

"I heard he got an awful whippin'." she reported. "They used a chinquapin switch on him. An' I heard Mama say that he kept beggin' 'em and tellin' 'em he didn't mean to do it."

"I know," I said. Anger made my voice rise. "It wasn't *his* fault."

"Shhhhh." she warned. "They blame him, though."

"Uncle Floyd's always gotta blame somebody," I muttered, "...especially somebody who can't fight back."

We both went quiet—pensive. Then I said, "That cut-off finger..." I was almost talking to myself. "Just like..."

"What?"

"His finger...the cut-off end of it. It was spurtin' just like a chicken's neck."

After the baling incident, Uncle Floyd kept pretty much to himself. When he came back from the hospital, there was a big bandage covering his hand, and we couldn't tell if the fingers were back on it or not. The word was "they got one of 'em sewed back on." We'd just have to leave it at that, until he took the wrapping off and we could see for ourselves.

With the bandage on his hand he couldn't do much either, including washing the car. So he stopped going to church, and Aunt Ruth, ever dutiful, stayed home to keep him company.

So, for several weeks I didn't see the brown horse. I thought about him, though, and one day I asked Isaac about him.

"Isaac, do you ever see that old horse up the road?"

"Oh, I sees 'im ever so often," he replied.

"Does he have a name?"

"I 'spose he does, but ah don't know what it might be."

"Is he still starvin'? Does anybody feed him?"

Isaac stopped what he was doing and looked me in the face. "Now why you wants t' know 'bout no old hoss, chile? What you gots on your mind t' do?"

"Oh, nothing, Isaac, I just wondered. That's all." But I figured I'd better not ask again.

Within a day of the baling, Julia, Libby and I had already slipped back into our summer ways. We swam daily in the warm salty river where the swift current both threatened and toned our strengthening bodies. We picked juicy scuppernongs from the grape arbor whenever we were hungry. And every evening we went to the barn to help the men throw yellow ears of dried field corn into the mangers, where the mules tore into them with a ferocity born of ten-hour-days spent plowing through a drag of earth so black that it was endlessly thick with weeds in spite of ripping at them day after day, from early dawn till sunset.

Julia and I also had returned to our persecution of Libby.

It was inevitable.

Most important, it was fun!

Compared to us, we decided, Libby was a mental midget. After all, she couldn't even read.

Letters of any kind could always be used to manipulate her.

"Y–C–I–Y–D–I," Julia said to her one day while we were out climbing the cedar tree in front of my house.

"What?" both Libby and I replied.

Julia shot me a swift, conspiratorial look. Then, turning back to Libby, she repeated the letters in her most derisive sing-song. "Y–C–I–Y–D–I!...Y–C–I–Y–D–I!"

"What's that mean?" Libby's tone held a certain apprehension.

"I don't know if I should tell you," Julia said mysteriously. "It's a secret password." Turning to me, "You think we oughta tell her?"

"I don't know," I replied, knowing how the ritual always played out. Then I climbed over to Julia and the two of us went into a huddle.

"OK, what *does* it mean?" I whispered. She told me while we worked out the plan.

"It's the password to a secret club, Lib, and you can't join unless you do what we tell you for the initiation."

"What's *in-ini-shay-shun*?" she asked suspiciously. It was a very long word and she'd never heard it before.

"Oh, nothin' much," I put in. "It's just a little somethin' you have to do to prove you're *big* enough." 'Big' was always the key word. "And..." I added, "there's no way you can join if you *don't* do it."

"Oh." Libby was in a tight spot. "I don't know."

So, Julia gave her the final push, "And you're out of *everything* if you don't."

With that, Julia climbed down from the tree, and I followed, acting as if we were going to leave. From the ground, we looked up at Libby and waited.

It didn't take long.

"Okay," came the resigned reply. "What do I have to do?"

"It's easy," Julia told her. We were struggling to suppress our giggles, but Libby was too concerned and too far away to notice. "You see that limb up there?"

"Which one?" Libby asked.

"That one up there," I instructed, "The one above you."

Libby looked upward cautiously. She was a little afraid of climbing trees—which, of course, we knew.

"That one?" She pointed to the branch just above her head.

"Noooo," Julia cooed. "The one above it! Just climb up there."

"But I can't." Libby protested. "I'm not supposed to go that high."

"Y–C–I–Y–D–I," I called out to her mockingly.

Again we waited. We were always patient when the result was going to be soooooo delicious.

Libby thought about it. Then, finally, she said, "Oh, awright...." and she began to climb to the limb some twelve feet above the ground.

From where we stood, it did look pretty high, now that little Libby was way up there. But there was no going back.

From where Libby clung, the potential drop was obviously terrifying. She wobbled and clutched at a branch. For a minute, we thought she was going to fall. Then she got her balance and sat still as stone.

"What do I do now?" she asked, a whimper of fear registering in her voice.

"YOU JUMP!"

"NO...NO, I CAN'T. I CAN'T!!!" she cried.

"Sure, you can." Julia shouted back. "It's easy! It's all soft and grassy down here."

I shouted our final encouragement, "Y–C–I–Y–D–I! Y–C–I–Y–D–I !!!!"

Libby looked down at us for a long indecisive moment. Then she took a deep breath—pushed off into air—and plummeted to the ground.

She landed in a heap and didn't move. We just stared at her first in disbelief. Then in panic!

We ran over to her. "Lib!...Lib! Are you OK?"

Her eyes were closed. In a moment, she moved a little, moaned, and slowly reached for her ankle. Julia and I looked at each other. We really hadn't meant to hurt her. What to do? We didn't want to go get our parents.

Julia knelt on the grass beside her, "Libby, are you awright?"

"I don't know," she sighed, her eyes fluttering. "My ankle hurts a lot." Then Libby opened her eyes wide, looked straight up at us, and asked in a clear, cold voice, "What does *Y–C–I–Y–D–I* mean?"

Julia stood up and backed into me. We looked at Libby together. In silence.

"Tell!" she insisted petulantly still lying there where she had landed. "You promised, and you have to tell."

Since it was Julia's game to start with, I turned to her. "*You* tell," I said.

There was a lengthy pause while Libby and I waited. Finally my co-conspirator sighed and, with resignation, kept her promise.

"It means. . . . .*You're Crazy If You Do It.*"

There was a loud wail from the ground. Others heard it, too. Then they saw. Suddenly, all of our parents came running to the fallen-sparrow-vision of Libby lying listless on the grass.

The moment wasn't lost on Libby. She had that look of revelation—of vengeance spreading over her face that made us cringe.

Julia blurted fiercely, "Don't you tell. Libby, don't you *dare* tell."

"We mean it," I added quickly. Just in time. Just before the parents reached the tree and gathered anxiously around her.

They asked Libby lots of questions while Julia and I attempted to become invisible. Libby milked the melodrama like a pro, as they poked and prodded and flexed all of her limbs. At last they decided that, although nothing seemed broken, they had better take her to the hospital for examination. They lifted her gently and placed her in her parents' car, and, in a moment, they were off to Savannah, leaving the two of us standing in their dusty wake—wondering anxiously if Libby would spill it all.

Apparently not.

The confirmation came that afternoon with the arrival of her parents. They were cheerful.

"Libby is fine," her mother reported, smiling, as she relaxed into one of the wicker porch chairs. "She is simply being kept overnight for observation. She'll be released tomorrow afternoon, and I'd like to have you girls go with me when I pick her up. Oh, yes," she added, "Lib said to be sure to tell you that she just can't wait to see you."

In unison, we looked down at the floor.

There was no way out of the trip to town. We were trapped. Julia spent the night with me, and we brooded over it all night long.

⁂

The next day, as we whizzed up the highway to Savannah, I couldn't stop wishing that Uncle Floyd were driving. All too soon we pulled into the hospital parking lot, and all too quickly we were on our way up to Libby's room.

And to Libby.

The door had been pushed ajar in anticipation of our arrival. And inside, there she was, propped up in the crank-up bed wearing a beautiful *new* bedjacket, her auburn hair neatly brushed and pulled back with a pale blue ribbon. And that wasn't all. Scattered around her on the bed were a doll we'd never seen before, a new game and two huge, still-unopened packages wrapped in beautiful paper. She was flanked by baskets of summer flowers. And—she was sipping languidly on a chocolate milkshake.

"Where'd you get that milkshake?" Julia asked her, testily.

"Oh, this?" Libby purred. "This is the second one I've had already. The one I had yesterday was strawberry."

"How come?" I demanded.

"Because I'm hurt, and I can have anything I want to make me feel better."

"We're all delighted that you are better," her mother said. "And that means we get to take you home and have you back with all of us again."

Libby smirked at us. "That will be nice."

Julia and I stood there sullenly until her mother spoke, "Now let's hurry along, girls. Help me gather up all these things, and, when we get them loaded, we'll help Libby to the car."

It took half an hour to collect all the flowers and loot and Libby's belongings and to make the endless trips up and down the stairs. Libby, meanwhile, sat like a princess sipping her milkshake and watching us labor, a satisfied grin imbedded in her face. Then, while we watched, they lifted her gently into a wheelchair and she was ridden away, holding a spray of daisies in her lap, to the elevator in which we were not allowed to ride. At the car, an attendant placed her carefully in the front seat while we scrambled into the back searching for space among the collected treasure.

It was a long and quiet ride home.

It was followed by a long and miserable week of having to include Libby in everything. The entire incident was still too fresh to risk provoking her into telling anyone what really happened.

Almost imperceptibly, during this time we also became busier. The three of us were sent to pick grapes, and, in exchange, we were the ones allowed to stomp them barefoot in galvanized wash tubs—seeds and pulp spurting everywhere as we pressed out the juice for jam and jelly.

"It's very European," we were told, which added a certain glamour to the grossness of the process.

Vegetables were brought in to be put up in Mason jars and stacked on the rapidly filling pantry shelves for winter. Corn was harvested, the best of which was shelled and saved for grinding into grits and meal, while the rest was stored for the farm animals in a metal-lined room to keep it safe from invasion by determined rats and opossums. The smokehouse was cleaned and readied with stacked wood, and the men built sod-roofed, A-frame huts to store potatoes. Finally, the cattle were brought closer to home to facilitate winter feeding, and the hogs were brought from the pig lot to the barn.

During that time, Floyd's big blue Ford remained parked in its shed—dusty, strung to the walls with spider webs, ornamented with an occasional chicken, and splattered all over with droppings.

Uncle Floyd remained taciturn, even abrupt. If we invaded his area during the day, we were dismissed with a preemptory, "Go 'long young'uns and find some place else to play. We're busy here." He never even bothered looking up. He just knew we were there, and we knew we'd better scatter.

One particular afternoon he stopped what he was doing and came over to us as we started to play around the barn.

"You young'ns better go 'long," he began as usual. "I don't want you over here today. I don't want you comin' anywhere near this barn, ya understand?"

"Yes sir. Yes, sir," Julia and Libby replied.

"Why?" I asked instead.

"That's none of your business," he answered sharply. "What we're doin' has nothin' t' do with you, and if I catch you over here it'll be trouble." He stared hard until I looked down at my feet. Then he walked away.

Behind him we could see steam rising from a huge vat that, until this moment, no one had ever seemed to use for anything. A fire was burning in the oven-like brick chamber that supported it. It was mysterious and strange, and we lingered, looking at it until Uncle Floyd turned to us again and, this time, angrily waved us away.

We ran off past the barn to the connecting mule lot and climbed the fence. But we didn't go away. Instead, we sneaked alongside it and into a stall, climbed through the manger, into the barn, and through to the wagon shed on the other side near where the men were busy doing something. And we hid.

The vat was right next to us so we could hear the men working around it. But hiding also meant we couldn't see a thing.

"We's ready, Mista Floyd," we heard Isaac say. "The water's boilin' good now."

"Good," Uncle Floyd said. "Go get 'em boys."

There was a moment of quiet when we knew the men had gone away somewhere, followed soon by angry squeals as they seemed to be scuffling with a hog who had no intention of doing what they wanted.

We could hear the squish and suck of boots in the hog pen mud and a thump and scrape as the squealing intensified. Something heavy was being dragged across wood and men were calling to each other.

"Git 'im, Isaac."

"Hang on now, Ned."

"He's a comin' over t' ya."

Other men were now struggling with the angry hog, wrestling him closer and closer. They were just outside now. The heavy grunts of the men mingled with the high-pitched squeals of the hog.

"Git 'im now, Ned!" Isaac called out, his voice imperative as the scuffling grew more intense, as strong male bodies crashed into each other and slammed into the fixtures in the yard. "We can't hold onto 'im much longer."

It was Ned now, "Hold 'im fast. Ah can't git a fix on 'im less you keep 'im still."

"No!"

"NOW!"

"Ah'm a tryin'!"

"Don't let 'im...." The pounding and confusion was chaotic.

"QUICK!! KILL 'IM QUICK! HE BE GITTIN' AWAY!!!!"

With a mighty splash, the hog hit the water in the vat just outside our hiding place.

The scream was horrifying and so penetrating that clapping my hands over my ears did nothing to alleviate its poignancy. It sounded—*human*—as it cried out for mercy and reprieve. But even then, it was not like any I had heard before. It was the anguished, helpless scream of dying—boiling in a vat—while strong men yelled to one another, "Hold 'im down!" and "Hurry! Pick up dat axe"—until—with a final shriek of agony, metal shattered bone and split the cry with silence.

When the screaming stopped, I looked at Julia and Libby. Their little hands were also tightly clamped against their heads, their faces wet with tears—just like my own.

Libby whimpered, "I wanna go."

Julia put her finger to her lips to quiet her and sadly shook her head to tell her "no." We dared not be discovered. We couldn't go. Not now. Not all that long and wasting afternoon, when life was spent in a gruesome ritual of death.

We heard the screams of struggle again and again—stilled by the axe—followed by grunts and heavy breathing and water splashing as the men dragged corpse after corpse to and from the boiling pot, and, finally, with a thud, dumped them on the butchering table.

"The hair sho' come out easy from de hide when you boils 'em, don't it Mista Floyd?"

"Just tryin' t' make it easy for you lazy boys," Floyd would reply and laugh.

Endlessly, it seemed, there was the quiet squish and flop as the hog was shifted on the table to remove the bristled body hair. And then there was the steady whack of hatchets and knives, cutting up the remains into hams and bacon for the smokehouse.

Once, one of the men had said, "Look at dis one, Mista Floyd. What a fine ham that'll make come Chris'mas time." But worst of all was hearing Isaac say, "Miz Louise'll be mighty proud of havin' this 'n on the dinner table, that's a fact."

Through it all, Julia and Libby and I became one. An arm had slipped around me. When? I didn't know. Libby's head had fallen on my shoulder. I patted it gently. I reached out and held Julia's hand. Our little group sat huddled on the ground where we emptied our innocence into the lengthening afternoon.

It was long after the animals' feed-up time before we dared go home. We never looked at the vat, nor the tables, nor the hog pens. We went straight home murmuring "good-nights" but scarcely looking at one another, each one of us serving as a blunt reminder to the other two of our shared confusion and unhappiness.

We dared tell no one.

We could never ask, "Why?" We didn't even talk about it among ourselves. We had to find our private ways to reconcile it.

As August neared an end, I spent more time alone.

The marshes were still bright with summer green, but the storms were different now. Northeasters came with growing frequency, and there was talk of hurricanes. There would be no swimming on those days. So I would sit on the splintery dock for hours watching whitecaps frothing on the slate grey river and egrets battling against the wind, their whiteness shocking against the steely sky.

Soon, marsh hens squawked all day, and birds flew by in determined flocks vee-ing their way south, sometimes peeling off formation at near dusk to rest in marshy hammocks overnight.

Goldenrod began to trace the fields with yellow, and the leaves of sweetgums wore a rosy blush. Everyone knew that the mellow time was ending, that frost was coming. Soon, lonely colors would replace the summer lush. The marshes would become like fields of wheat, bronzed by dying winter suns. Then I'd be gone and not return until Christmas.

After the frost, winter would come bringing the death of more than just the growing things. When the last green stem was dead and dry tan stubble took its place, how would the old brown horse survive?

I went to Isaac.

"Don't you worry your head 'bout that hoss, chile," he said. "It don't belongs to us'n, and we got no part in other people's business."

"But Isaac," I insisted, "Uncle Floyd said he'd die when the hard freeze comes."

"Dat hoss is old, chile," he explained kindly. "He done see his time on dis here earth. He done his work an' he be tired now. So he be restin' and waitin' 'till it be time for he t' go."

"But if *you* fed him...."

"No, chile. You knows ah can't do that. The feed ain't mine t' give him if'n I wanted. 'Sides..." he added, "his teeth's bad now. Corn's for healthy hosses."

"Then...he will die, won't he?"

"He ain't got long," he answered truthfully. "Now, you go find them little friends and play and don't think 'bout that ole brown hoss no mo'. Just let 'im be. He ain't none of our business."

So I couldn't even count on Isaac.

By now I'd had enough of death and the calm way everyone accepted it. If the horse could just get some feed, I knew he would live. I did care and I had promised. So now it was up to me.

I went off to find Julia.

After the pig slaughtering, Julia had become distant, even cold.

"Are you crazy!" she said when I told her my plan. "You know what your uncle would do if he caught us."

"But you have to do it, Julia," I pleaded. "You're my best friend and you have to."

"No I don't," she stated flatly. "Why do you think you can save that old horse anyway? You know he's gonna die."

"No he isn't." I answered angrily. I could not allow her to be right. "And I don't know how you can say you won't help if maybe we could save him."

"You're crazy!" she snapped back with finality.

Neither of us understood that she simply could no longer deal with the possibility of death. Distance was her way of coping.

Mine was not to cope at all. I just refused to accept any of it. I would become a one-child Crusader, tilting against demise in any form. Crusaders mean to win.

So this time I sought out Libby.

While I had been keeping to myself, Julia had withdrawn from Libby, too. Once more, Libby's isolation made her an easy target. To Libby, the thought that the two of us would brave this thing together, as a team, was irresistible. I even embellished it by suggesting that, together, we could overcome Death itself, an idea which appealed to Libby's post-hog-slaughter anxieties as much as to my own.

We decided to act on Sunday. No one would be around the barn except at feeding time, and there was little risk of our being seen. We met there after breakfast, which gave us more than six hours before we had to be home again. We quickly filled the croaker sacks with what we needed, fifty perfect ears of weevil-free, dried corn that we had carefully sorted and put aside during the week, plus ten quarts of expensive oats we had hidden in a paper bag, enough, in all, to last a long, long time.

I was the one who tied the sack tops closed with baling twine. Libby still couldn't even tie her shoes.

We took the hidden path behind the barn that led through the woods to the swamp road and, finally, to the horse's pasture some two miles away.

Roots and stumps snagged at the loosely-woven burlap sacks which we had to drag because they were far too heavy to carry. By the time we reached the corduroy road through the swamp, our hands were red and stiff, and we needed to rest. We had covered only half a mile and, already, we were huffing and panting. There was a long, long way to go.

On foot, the swamp seemed different than it did from inside the safety of the towering Ford. Strange bird calls warned other creatures of our presence. A whoosh of water or the snap of a branch told us we were not alone, but we saw nothing other than occasional ripples arcing over the surface of the wine-stained water when stirred by some unseen slithering thing. It seemed a strangely sullen place permeated by a murky sense of silent watching eyes, and I refused Lib's pleas for time to make the pond frogs jump or to catch a dragonfly. Instead, I allowed us only a few minutes at various points to catch our breath and cool our palms in the stagnant pools. Then, we were on our way again dragging our load across the bumpy ground. The cypress gave us shade, but the humid air was dense and the morning heat was rising.

A mile into our pilgrimage, we cleared the swamp and the corduroy road. The hard-ridged footing gave way now to the soft, deep sugar-sand that formed the open, treeless stretch we'd have to walk until we reached our destination. Wearing shoes had never occurred to us. Our feet were tough from a summer of swimming off oyster shell banks and trekking over roots and cockspurs. But now the morning sun had cleared the eastern stand of cypress and it focused on the sandy road with a blistering intensity.

Libby began to complain. "Do we have to go any more? My feet are hot, and this old sack weighs too much. I wanna stop," she whined. "I wanna sit down and rest."

I couldn't finish the job alone. So we sat.

Rivulets of sweat trickled down our faces, legs and arms—itchy, greasy sweat, getting worse the longer we sat and baked in the road.

"It will just be worse if we stay here, Lib. We need to go."

Unhappy, she nevertheless obeyed.

The sand was deeper now, and it seeped into the open weave of the bags, adding several pounds of weight we could not see. Blisters were starting to form on my reddened hands—and on Libby's, too, I knew, although I didn't dare mention it.

With still half a mile to go, she sat down abruptly in the rut. "I won't go. I won't do it anymore. I'm tired, and I need a drink of water."

"But you know we're almost there," I pleaded. "Please, Lib, just a little bit farther."

"NO!" she said, jutting out her lower lip. "No, I won't!"

"We'll get a drink of water just as soon as we get there," I reasoned.

"I don't know why I ever came down here with you and I wanna go home NOW!" she said, ignoring me.

"But you can't, Lib." I was desperate. "You can't go back through all the snakes and 'gators in the swamp all by yourself."

"WHAT 'GATORS?! WHAT SNAKES?!" she screamed in terror.

"It's awright...it's awright." I tried to calm her. I could see a head or two pop out from neighboring houses, and I fully expected people to come rushing out to us at any moment.

"You MADE me come. You have to take me back!" She was getting hysterical. "Or. . .or I'll TELL!"

"I will. I will, Lib." I reassured her. "We'll go just as soon as we take this stuff down to the horse. It's just a little way now."

"You lied to me," she muttered. Her voice sounded like a stamping foot, and I was beginning to suspect that even if we didn't get caught, I might be in trouble anyway.

I had to convince her of the "rightness" of our mission. "No, I didn't lie to you Lib. I wouldn't do that. Remember, you felt really sorry for that poor old horse and you wanted to be the one to save his life. How can you just leave him to die? Not now—when we're so close."

She thought about it for a minute, "Well..." she said guiltily. "I guess I really don't want him to die." She paused. "Maybe I could go just a little bit more," she sighed.

"You won't be sorry," I promised. "Let's go. It's getting a little late." I shouldn't have said it.

"Late! Are we LATE?"

"NO...NO! We're fine. Really. Let's just go, Okay?"

I couldn't believe how hard it was to pull myself up out of the road. But having done so, I helped Libby up, and we slowly dragged the laden sacks through the burning, holding sand, our little bodies glistening in the searing mid-morning sun. Salty sweat burned our eyes and blurred our vision. But I knew exactly where I was going.

Libby complained half-heartedly, but she plowed ahead until we finally dragged ourselves, exhausted, to the fence where the old brown horse was waiting. We slumped onto the ground and closed our eyes and dizzily breathed the hot, still, thickening air.

We'd made it.

There was a soft nicker from the horse as he hung his head down over the fence to reach me. His hard and bristled muzzle nudged my hair. Slowly, I opened my eyes and looked up at him. He was the saddest, thinnest, mangiest horse I'd ever seen. But the eyes that looked at me were all that I had imagined. They were neither clear nor bright, but they were looking at me in welcoming recognition.

Softly—very softly—I cried.

Wearily Libby and I stood up again to unload the treasure from our sacks. We dropped it over the fence, and the horse tore into it, eagerly, first muzzling through the oats because they were easy for him to manage while we stood there watching him, slowly understanding what we'd achieved. We had saved him, given him life. He raised his head to nicker to us, and we began to laugh—then to hug each other, joyous both for him and for ourselves.

Watching him had rejuvenated us. While he ate, we looked for water and discovered an old claw-footed bathtub which furnished water for the cattle in the field. Gratefully, we drank from the pipe which trickled the clean, artesian water into it. We cooled our legs. We splashed our faces, and then, giggling with joy, we splashed each other.

Arms entwined, we went back to our friend and just stood a while there smiling. We had done it. We had started it and finished it. It had been hard—and miserable, and scary—but we'd done it anyway—all on our own—not for ourselves, but for someone else.

Even little Libby understood.

By now, the sun stood nearly in mid-sky. It really was late and we had to go.

It didn't matter that the journey home was no less long nor painful—nor that we were hot, and tired—nor that our hair was stringy and our clothes covered with stains. We spent the first part of the walk home hardly noticing. We held each other's hand and talked and felt just wonderful.

The last half-mile was anguished. With each misstep, the hard swamp road reminded us of our sore and blistered feet. Our hands hurt horribly. They had been rubbed raw by the abrasive burlap, and we stopped often to soothe them in the wet, cool swamp. But we didn't complain. Finally, we didn't even talk. We didn't need to. We were adrift somewhere golden—in sweet, private space where we were beautiful and incredibly complete.

There was just a week remaining of vacation now. For Libby and for me, everything glowed. The world was a special place, and we were special children in it. We never noticed the occasional concerned glance from Aunt Ruth or Isaac. We'd stopped reading into every look an ominous prelude to exposure. We felt safe in our haloes of fulfillment.

And we hadn't yet run into Uncle Floyd.

There seemed no need for apprehension when at last I did. I'd been gathering eggs for Aunt Ruth, and, when I came out from under the house, he was standing there by the wood pile.

"Mornin' Br'er Fats," he greeted me in the old familiar way he'd hadn't used since his retreat into himself following the hay baler accident. He was smiling at me broadly.

"Mornin', Uncle Floyd," I replied, returning his smile.

He walked across the yard to me. "Whatcha got there?" He already knew, but it seemed to me he was just trying to be nice.

Proudly, I held out my moss-lined, egg-filled basket for him to see. "I've got ten already."

"That's good. That's real good," he remarked, grinning.

He paused, looking at me calmly before he continued. "You really like these chickens, don't cha'?"

I smiled again.

"You're really big on animals, ain't cha'?"

I nodded.

"You used t' mention an old brown hoss up the road. Seems t' recollect you thought somebody oughta feed the poor old thing, you know, fatten it up t' see it through the winter."

He knew.

"Well...just thought you might like to know. Somebody took your advice." He waited, his eyes keen on my face while I prayed silently that he wouldn't go on.

"Yessir, somebody made that old hoss a present. Lots of corn and expensive oats. Like Christmas. Well, that old broke-down hoss sure did appreciate it. Ate up every scrap." His face turned as cold as his eyes before he said, "And I bet you know who gave it to him."

What did Uncle Floyd plan to do? His face was predatory and inscrutable as he waited, watching me. Then he asked, "Ever see a case of colic?"

I didn't answer, but he hadn't expected me to.

"Over-eatin' brings it on as often as not. Now a mule won't eat more than she needs. But a hoss, he'll eat anything you put in front of him. And he'll just keep on packin' it in 'til he gets the world's biggest belly ache."

Oh, please. Don't let him hurt, I prayed. Please let the brown horse be all right.

"Now a hoss can't stand much pain. And if he's hurtin' bad enough he goes down on the ground and starts rollin' around tryin' t' git away from it. And if he keeps up that rollin' long enough, well, he'll tie his guts all up in knots. There's no savin' him then, of course. He's done for. It's just a matter of how much pain he can take before it kills 'im. Unless, of course...." He let me briefly hope. "Unless, somebody's nice enough to put a gun between his eyes and pull the trigger."

"Oh, no...oh, no," I murmured, tears crowding the corners of my eyes. "They didn't."

"Oh don't you worry about that. They didn't shoot 'im."

Oh please, God, please my heart begged.

"They just let 'im suffer 'till he got so weak he couldn't even swish away those mean tormentin' flies that were crawlin' all over 'im at the end."

By now the tears were running freely down my face.

"Took two whole days for that old brown horse to die." Then he added, "Funny thing, I never thought he'd put up such a fight. You s'pose he had a reason?"

All the "whys" I'd ever wondered didn't matter. I was remembering my friend. I was hearing his gentle nicker and feeling his stubbly muzzle on my hair. I was touching his shabby, blood-stained coat and remembering how rough it felt beneath my fingers as I stroked him, offering kindness. And most of all, I was remembering his eyes, his soft, old, tired eyes, with their look of welcoming recognition.

"Maybe. . ." I started haltingly. But I couldn't finish. So Uncle Floyd concluded it his own way.

"Well, Br'er Fats, y' know what they say, don't cha'? *'The road to hell is paved with good intentions.'*"

I'd been to church.

I'd been down a lot of roads.

I knew.

HOT PRETZEL

She didn't care if every vile thing in New York had blown all over it. She never came to the city without buying a hot pretzel from one of the street vendors who set up shop out there on the dirty cluttered sidewalks. She blotted out all the horrific stories her friends loved to relate whenever the subject of street pretzels came up, that litany of disgusting things to which, they insisted, every pretzel in the city had been exposed. They were right, of course, but she didn't care. She bought them anyway, one per trip. When she was alone.

At last, there it was, a pretzel stand right across the street from her hotel at Madison Square Garden. The neighborhood was grim. It was night, and she was alone. But she could easily slip across the street and buy a big salty one, still finger-burning hot, to take up to her room, where she could enjoy it with her feet propped up while she watched the evening news.

She couldn't wait to take off the shoes she was wearing. What Machiavellian mind had invented pencil skirts and pointy-toed spike heels for walking all day on city pavement? She liked the "dressing up" part of working, the "being fashionable." She liked the confidence it gave her, knowing she looked successful in her expensive suit with her artful makeup and haircut. Admittedly, she felt best about that when she was freshly dressed in the morning, rather than now, late in the day when her leather pumps seemed two sizes too small. No, she didn't like that at all. She pressed the toe of her most painful foot against the back of her other calf. It didn't help.

And she was freezing.

The pretzel stand across the street was the usual wagon sort of thing with its big doughy twists kept hot inside a glass dome. It was manned by a short, mustachioed man who stood hunched near its warmth, the collar of his old black coat pulled up to its limits in order to overlap the knit cap he'd pulled down over his ears. Yes, it was very, very cold.

No one was stopping at his cart, and he looked tired and a little sad. It was near Christmas. Perhaps people carried too many packages to manage a pretzel.

She crossed the street.

Selling pretzels couldn't be much of a business, she thought as she watched him press his body closer to the warm stand. Not much. She felt good knowing that she could bring him a little money.

He turned as she approached.

"A hot pretzel, please," she said.

"Yes, miss," he smiled. As he did, his face wrinkled deeply around his dark eyes and it made him look very kind. He opened the dome door to a cloud of steam billowing into the night and reached in with a clean square of waxed paper to retrieve her pretzel without getting his hands on it. Then, he offered her the prize, a soft, hot, brown braid encrusted with sea salt. She smiled appreciatively.

His accent was heavy, but the words were clear and the tone polite, "That will be one dollar twenty-five cent, please."

Wearing fat woolen mittens and holding the pretzel made it almost impossible to locate her wallet and pull the money out. Her purse swung wildly as she fumbled through it. She was embarrassed by her clumsiness. So, when finally she retrieved the money, she thrust it quickly toward him. As she did, the old man's smile vanished. He grabbed her by the arm and yanked her hard toward him. "Come here," he growled. He had her shoulder tight in one hand while he pulled at her purse with the other.

"What...?" she stammered as she tried to pull away, but he held on, screaming now. Within seconds, three muscular teenagers in leather jackets and black pants were around her, banging into her, pushing at her, then moving quickly toward the old man.

"Go now," he said to her gruffly, "Go quick. They want your purse. Close it quick. And go."

She hesitated, then started backing away, clutching her bag to her chest.

They were already on him, all three of the young toughs. He was still waving her off and saying "Go! Go!" before he started yelling at them. "You leave her alone. You not gonna getta anything from her you feelthy hoods." They had him pinned against the cart. "GO! PLEASE!" he shouted to her, and she turned and ran across the street, horns blaring at her, to the hotel.

There was no doorman. No one on the street did more than glance the old man's way. No policeman to help. No one. She stood alone in the safety of the hotel doorway watching in dismay.

They were roughing him now, pushing and pelting him with fists and grabbing her money out of his hand.

"You getta outta here!" he bellowed above the traffic noise, trying to protect his head with his arms and drawing a little bit of notice now, the New York kind where they look, see trouble, and get out of there as fast as possible.

"Aw, you old fart. You ain't no fun," one boy shouted as he looked at the little bit of money. "You ain't worth nothin'. You ain't worth our time."

"GET OUTTA HERE," the frail old man screamed.

They shoved him hard again, bending him backward against the cart. The biggest one moved menacingly up close to him, into his face, mouthing words she could not hear. The city cabs honked, and tires screamed and buses bumped and hissed in the street. The teenager was telling him something. Something sinister. Something terrifying. She knew it.

For a long moment they bent over him; then, in jaunty unison, they sprang away—on down the street. Suddenly, the big one spun around into a boxer's crouch. The old man flinched as the young thug's arm moved toward him in a huge, menacing fist that opened slowly as he gave the old man the finger. Then, laughing, they were gone.

Upstairs, in her room she took off her shoes and sprawled into the chair with no sense of relief. She couldn't erase the old man's image. Or the fear. Tonight. Late. When the streets are empty and he starts for home. What then, she thought? Or, if not tonight, what about tomorrow night, or next week or…sometime. Just because he had helped her.

The pretzel lay in its little paper wrap on the table beside her. Cold now.

THE ROSE

She knew exactly what it was, the far-away screeching and thlunking that invaded the dawn. The cranes had started work in the distant train yard, swinging their heavy loads over the empty boxcars where their buckets yawned noisy waterfalls of coal and logs and stumps into the waiting metal bins. The sound came cleanly through air that was sweet with the damp, exciting smell of spring, yet still was crisp with winter's chill. Anna shivered. Her flannel nightgown wasn't enough to warm her through the wait which had been longer today than expected, but she dared not leave the window overlooking the lane behind the house for fear she would miss him.

The cranes were too noisy to hear his approach, to hear the familiar crunch of gravel and of bottles clinking against each other as the wagon jolted over the muddy holes. Suddenly, there he was, the dark bay, fine-boned horse slowing to a stop behind the alley gate as Ned jumped down with three cream-topped bottles for the family milk box. He read her mother's note inside and reached into the wagon for one more quart to finish the order.

The horse, meanwhile, had turned his head to watch, and just before Ned put his foot on the wagon step, the horse jingled his bridle and, without instruction, slowly moved away, straining against the weight of the wagon. Ned swung quickly into the back to busy himself setting up the next delivery. They were friends, these two, in sync in a shared routine. Anna was happy to be a secret part of it as she sat in her window perch each morning.

She had never spoken to Ned nor stroked the velvet muzzle of the little horse that dutifully made his rounds without command. Anna was only seven years old, and she was not allowed outside before breakfast.

Soon after the milk wagon called each morning, Evelyn, the middle-aged black cook, dressed as always in her starched gray uniform, would descend from the garage apartment behind the house, gather the bottles, cross the lawn, and enter the kitchen below Anna's room. Then, with a creak, the side gate would open, and Rufus, the black gardener, would pull his rusty bicycle into the yard and begin untying the old worn tools he used to make their garden a place of envy in the neighborhood. Rufus was spoke-thin, graying, and crowding eighty, but he worked a young man's day. And the start of it was Anna's cue to get dressed and begin her own. It was time for Anna to abandon her fantasies, a time to become lonely again. Evelyn, Rufus, Ned and the horse were real. But they were Anna's friends only in her imagination.

Anna didn't have any real friends.

She was not a pretty little girl. Her teeth stuck out, and in another year she would get braces. Even a special trip to her mother's hairdresser, intended to transform Anna's mousy straight hair into fashionable Shirley Temple ringlets, had horrifying results. After setting the rollers and seating Anna in a corner to wait for the perm to take, the beautician had forgotten her. By the time Anna was remembered, her hair had cooked to a tangled mat, and, for months, the only way to groom it had been with a wire dog brush. Anna's body verged on stumpy, and, instead of helping her image, her hideous hairdo made her chubby face seem puffy and her body frumpy. Even if she tried *not* to think of herself as the creature who greeted her in the mirror, there were always plenty of others to remind her. Especially, her mother.

Comparisons were easy to come by. "Doesn't Barbara have the most exquisite blue eyes?" her mother would say. "They certainly reflect the intelligence inside that handsome head of hers." Anna's eyes were gray-green and decidedly sad.

And there was Anna's ballet class attended by young girls who were destined to grow up into poised young matrons. Anna actually loved ballet. The music and the movement freed her to express herself, and she wasn't half bad when no one was looking. But the emerging swan she hoped to become remained a phantom to her elegant mother who, instead, commented ceaselessly on Anna's classmates. "Doesn't Sylvia move beautifully?" she would muse. "She is so accomplished, so lithe and graceful." Then she would look long and coldly at Anna with inferred comparisons. "Stand up straight, Anna," she would insist, and then turn away.

Her father expected nothing of her. He was tall and heavyset and older than her mother. Anna never dared to ask how old. He had the potent self-confidence of someone who has been important for a long time and who had neither time nor patience for the childish, fumbling uncertainty that described her. He treated her with the same cool, authoritative control he used with underlings who would never be his equal.

His basic requirements were that she always be neat, clean, polite, quiet, and on time, especially for her ride with him to school. "You must be in the car promptly at 8:15," he had told her the first day he had driven her there. For more than a year she had been punctual, until the morning she broke her shoelace.

"You must learn to do things for yourself, Anna," she had been told over and over. So while she awkwardly tried to tie the frayed ends back together, she heard the engine of his waiting car rev up in warning. The knot wouldn't hold. The engine roared again then shifted into gear. When she heard the tires move, she bolted out of the house, plunged down the steps, and raced down the drive after the car. But it didn't stop. Her father must not have seen her. She ran faster and caught up alongside his window as he reached the curb.

He rolled down the glass, "You're late," he said.

"I'm sorry, Daddy. I'm sorry." Panting, she ran around to the passenger side. But even as she touched the handle, he backed into the street and left her standing there. She watched, tears brimming, as the car shifted into forward and moved down the street.

"Wait, daddy, please wait," she called, impotent tears flooding her face. "I'm sorry," she began to sob. "I tried to fix it. It broke. Oh, please come back! Please let me tell you." She wanted so much to please him, to make him proud.

Her voice faded to a whimper by the time the car turned the corner and disappeared. Even at seven years of age, she knew it wasn't just about being late, or clean, or quiet, or neat, or polite. She knew she wasn't what he wanted his daughter to be. And there were no words to fix that.

The next morning, she was still putting new laces in her stubby brown oxfords when she heard the car engine racing in the drive. It was still early, she knew. But she panicked. Grabbing and dropping school books, she hurtled out the door and down the brick steps.

Her father had the window down. "Hurry up," he said predictably and then added, "Someone left something on the front seat for you."

What had she done wrong? She hurried to the car door, pulled it open and stared, disbelieving. On the seat lay a single perfect rose. Its straight green stem was wrapped in dampened moss surrounded by wax paper just the way her father always kept his prize camellias fresh before presenting them to their lady friends. The rose leaves were crisp, and the creamy flower glistened with spring dew.

Anna gasped.

"There's a note with it," her father said.

She reached for the folded piece of paper and undid it. The penciled script was perfect, like a rendered schoolbook lesson, and it read, "To Anna, a rose."

For a moment she flushed. Her family didn't grow roses. "Who…?" she stammered, looking at him to see if there was some mistake. "Is it really for me?" But, of course. It had her name.

Her father was amused at her confusion. "A secret admirer, perhaps."

Anna looked down, wordless. Thrilled. Afraid.

"Hurry!" her father said. "Give it to Evelyn to put in water. We'll be late."

She grabbed it and quickly took it to the kitchen.

Evelyn looked up anxiously from the dish-filled sink. "What you doin' in here?" she scolded. "You 'sposed to be in that car."

"Look what someone gave me!"

"Gave you?" Evelyn sounded doubtful. "Who?"

"I don't know. Do you?"

Ev just shook her head. "Sho is pretty," she acknowledged. "But you'd better run on, chile. I'll take care of it, and you can look at it some more this evenin' when you get home."

Anna thanked her and ran back to the car. Her father was already thinking about something important, and they drove off in silence. But Anna was thinking, too, and so she didn't mind.

She couldn't help looking at everyone in school differently that day. Might one of them have left it for her? The thought made her want to smile at them. But no. Children her age didn't get to leave the house alone. And no one else's parent would have done it. No busy teacher would have thought of it. Anyway, none of them ever focused any attention on Anna unless she had done something wrong, and that would never warrant giving her a rose. So, by the end of school she could hardly wait to get back home. The answer must be there.

"It's in water in that pickle jar over there," Evelyn greeted her before she had time to ask. "And, no, I don't got the slightest notion who left it for you."

Anna was disappointed, but when she caught sight of the flower that had opened just a bit more in the kitchen's warmth, the question no longer bothered her. All she knew was that it was really hers. Her very first. With a note and everything.

Her mother wasn't home, but Anna went right upstairs anyway to do her homework. She took the jar with her and set it on the little table where she worked two hours every day after school. Even when she finished, she didn't ask Evelyn to let her go outside or take thirty minutes to play a game of *Go Fish.* She just stayed at her desk, dreaming and occasionally leaning over to draw on the sweet rich fragrance that beckoned her.

At dinner, she smiled and ate all of her vegetables without having to be prompted.

"Any clues about your secret admirer?" her father teased, at which she blushed and shook her head. She was relaxed and so, it seemed, were her parents who invited her to join them in the living room after dinner while they listened to the news and then *Amos and Andy* on the big Motorola console radio. At her father's invitation, she sat at the foot of his chair, and he once patted her on the head. Then, voluntarily, she went upstairs to bathe and climb in bed with her stuffed teddy to whom she talked quietly about her incredible gift until the words held sleepy long pauses between them—and ended.

The next morning, after her routine alley-watch and breakfast she raced out to the car. And yes! There was! This time blush pink, a soft young shade that matched her cheeks. There was no note this time but she knew that it was hers. She ran inside to tell everyone, "Look, Mommy. Another. I got another!"

"So I see," her mother smiled. But her eyes spoke concern.

At ballet class, she danced with a lightness and purpose that belied her leotarded image. Even Miss Kerr, her teacher, noticed and told her mother, "Anna's improvement is remarkable. Today she seemed to float through all the routines. If she'd lose ten pounds and come to class an extra day a week, I think we could bring her along dramatically."

Focusing on the reality of her shapeless daughter planted solidly before her, earth-bound and awkward, she said, "We'll see."

Before Anna went to bed that night, no matter how much it hurt, she plowed the dog brush over and over through her matted hair. Tears crept from the corners of her eyes as she yanked and tugged, but she could feel some of the knots loosening up.

The next morning, she chose her clothes with care and polished her scruffy oxfords before she went to the window to wait. That morning, when Ned and the horse arrived, Ned looked up at her and waved.

Had he always known she watched them? She pulled back quickly behind the curtains.

Evelyn came, Rufus creaked open the gate, breakfast was served, and once again she was free to race to the waiting car to see if....And there was! Pure and white. A tiny rose that was fragrant and perfect in every way, a mirror of how she felt herself.

She was on her way back into the house when she met Rufus pushing the wheelbarrow down the driveway. He had his ancient rusty leaf rake with him, and she noticed that each of the long thin metal tines had been hand-wired onto the frame in order to squeeze out another year or two of use. She never noticed before. Now she was noticing everything.

"Mornin', Rufus," she said smiling, holding out the rose for him to see.

"Mornin', Miss Anna."

"Isn't this pretty?"

"Sho is, Miss Anna. Sho is," he answered, looking at the rose with a serious gardener's eye. "That's a sweetheart rose. Did you know?"

"No," she said smiling at the thought. "No, I didn't. How really nice."

She couldn't wait to tell the others. In fact, she had lots to talk about these days. It was as if a door were opening that allowed all her thoughts and feelings to run free. To her surprise, even her father seemed to listen. The morning trip to school was filled with exchange about simple things, the coolness of the morning, the certainty of spring, the happiness flowers bring, the traffic. Her father even smiled on occasion; he was actually paying attention.

The next morning, Ned paused as he filled the milk box and looked up at her directly, smiled and waved. Without hesitation, she waved back. The horse looked at him curiously because of the delay. She was part of their morning now.

At breakfast, her mother asked, "Are you sure you don't know who is giving you these flowers?"

"No, I really don't."

Her mother turned to her father. "Who in the world would want to give *Anna* flowers?"

Obviously, the gifts hadn't improved her mother's opinion of her appeal, but Anna remained serene. Her father, however, was aware of how much pleasure Anna took in them and he enjoyed the way they were affecting her, enough to say, "You look especially nice today, Anna."

"Thank you, Daddy," Anna smiled. "You know, I used to really want to know who gave me the roses. Now I'm not sure I even want to."

"Good girl," he said.

Today the car held a glowing yellow rose, and she met Rufus again on the way to put the rose in water.

"That's mighty pretty, Miss Anna," Rufus remarked. Anna noticed how old and shabby his clothes were, worn from dirt work and torn from making the world beautiful for other people. She felt hurt for him, but Rufus was saying, "That rose is the color of a bright, sunshiny day, don't you 'spose?"

She agreed.

"By the way," he added, "the mimosa is startin' to bloom. It smells so pretty."

"It is?" He knew it had always been one of Anna's favorite flowers. "I'll have to go look later," and she ran inside, leaving him to go about his chores.

When she came home from school, she visited the mimosa tree, and sure enough, there were soft, pink powder puff blossoms beginning to burst. She picked an open one and dusted her face. It offered the perfect touch and scent of spring.

The next morning, the car yielded the most beautiful rose of all. The outside of each petal was pale pink while within, it was deep yellow so that as the flower opened, each pastel petal seemed washed with gold. It was amazingly lovely. Even her mother commented on its beauty, but she looked gravely at Anna for a long moment.

That night, when she was supposed to be asleep, Anna heard her mother talking to her father in the hall.

"It's Rufus. I watched this morning, and I saw him do it."

Anna felt a stab of reality and her mind raced.

"Really," her father said without surprise.

"You know, it isn't right for a Negro man to be giving a young girl roses. It isn't normal. And she's all wrapped up in this."

"What do you want to do about it?"

Anna wanted to run out to them and blurt, "Oh, no!" but she felt paralyzed.

"I'll wait 'til you take her to school tomorrow," her mother replied, "and I'll talk to him."

So it wasn't anyone Anna ever imagined it could be or secretly hoped it would be. But she wasn't disappointed. Rufus was so kind—so gentle. He always seemed to understand what she needed, the small things that made her happy even when she herself had no idea what would. He made her feel worthy somehow. She wanted to tell him she knew, and she wanted to thank him. At the same time, she knew she would never be allowed to say it, most certainly not to him. Nor to anyone.

In the morning, with a deepening sense of sadness, she went out to the car. There on the seat was a blood red rose the color of what everyone, even Anna, associated with loving hearts. She wanted to cry, but she saw Rufus coming up the walk. When he reached where she stood, she placed the rose so flawlessly beautiful and soft against his weathered hands. She couldn't look him in the eyes. "Wasn't it nice," she said, "of someone to give it to me? I wish I could thank him." Rufus said he thought it was nice, too. Then she went into the house to look for water.

That night she heard her parents talking again. Her mother was saying, "So, after you took her to school, I had a talk with him and told him not to bring her any more. I had to be stern with him to make sure he understood. He seemed hurt by it. He said he meant no harm. The way he said it was, 'She just looked like she needed to feel nice, like she kinda needed to have a friend. I thought it made her happy, that's all.'"

Her father didn't comment.

"We just don't need to encourage that sort of thing. She's just too young to understand."

Anna cried herself to sleep. She didn't want to wake up or go to the car ever again. The next morning she felt too lost to watch the lane. She heard Ned come and go as she dressed, but she didn't look. She went downstairs to a silent breakfast. Then she gathered up her books, stepped outside and went down the brick steps to the car, knowing that when she got there, there would be nothing for her

THE CHRISTENING

I was five when my father bought Chip, an impressively expensive English Setter, to point up birds and retrieve them during dove-hunting season.

Even as a shy young farm boy, my father had dreamed of owning such an animal, a top-of-the-breed working dog that would awe his neighbors, a collection of country-hard men, made competitive and often mean by struggle and pervasive poverty. He, himself, had been taught to hunt to live, and by age ten he could outshoot most of them, an embarrassing fact that seemed to prompt their ill will. It made him their relentless target.

But with a dog like that—a top dog like that would earn neighborhood respect….

At age sixteen he left the farm to find work in Savannah, and by age forty-five, he had taken his early hunting prowess to more refined heights by winning *National Blue Ribbon Skeet Championships* in three shotgun categories. By then, he was already listed in *Who's Who In American Business*; but, even so, few realized the scope of his achievements. He deplored publicity. Instead, his imprint as a power figure was more immediate and personal. At a looming six-feet four inches, with ramrod posture, cut-to-the-chase directness and a laser stare, he was intimidating.

Certainly, he didn't need symbols or braggadocio to prove his merit. But unnecessary or not, he felt the old, enduring need to fulfill his long-held dream. He wanted, and now would own an expensive, prize-winning hunting dog—the undeniable emblem of success that could humble those country neighbors who had ridiculed him as a child.

It was startling to hear him brag expansively about a mere dog. Praise became hyperbole. And why not? In the past three years, the setter had been champion in every field trial he had entered, a record reflected by the price my father paid for him.

By the time the trainer's blue pickup pulled into the drive to deliver his prize, Chip had assumed the aura of *Wonder Dog.* The reception committee included everyone. My parents, the farm hands and I were all gathered there waiting as the truck door opened, revealing Chip sitting calmly in the passenger seat. He wasn't the enormous, ferocious, all-conquering creature I'd imagined. Rather, he was slender and sleek with gentle eyes. When the trainer invited him to join us, Chip exploded out of the truck, all exuberance and joyous wags. Yet, it required just one brief word from the man for Chip to sit quietly, panting and obedient, waiting for instruction.

Our congregation stood in awe.

It wasn't that we weren't used to "working" dogs. Our place, as did all the neighboring farms, housed a crowd of game-tracking critters the men had gleaned from the local feral pack. But they were a rowdy, unkempt mob whose only reliable talent was howling in unison to demand their evening pan of slops. Chip, by comparison, was *Class.* My father hadn't exaggerated. Just looking at this silky, elegant, well-mannered champion made it clear that we were in the presence of Dogdom's gentry.

"Would you like to see Chip put through his paces?" the trainer asked.

Assent from the assembly was eager, and we watched transfixed as the dog performed on command. When it was my father's turn to instruct him, Chip repeated his moves with like precision. Then, my father looked right at me.

"Young lady, would you like to try?"

"Me?" I stammered. Did he really mean he wanted *me* to work his prize hunting dog? With everyone watching?

Awkwardly, I repeated the commands. Chip looked uncertain.

"Go ahead. Just speak with authority."

My father was indisputably good at that, but I had to drag courage from my toes to do it. Miraculously, when I did, Chip responded perfectly. I blushed. I grinned. Time and again he did exactly what I asked without hesitation. In my five year-old experience, such power was intoxicating stuff, open to unimaginable possibilities and I knew, right then, that, with Chip as my student, he and I were going to have a remarkable summer.

As an only child spending summers alone in such a remote, isolated place, the coming of this intelligent creature provided the companionship I craved. Chip, in turn, was a "professional" dog who normally spent his mornings training and the rest of his day caged in a ten-by-ten foot pen. For the first time he could run free and while I had nothing to do with it, he gave me full credit.

We were inseparable. All summer, the two of us went about happily discovering things, digging up treasures, and splashing in puddles, but what I loved most was just sitting by him in the warm grass with my arms around his neck while he licked my dirty face in reciprocated friendship.

Although fall meant weekday separations for school, the weekends cocooned our growing bond. Soon, the harvested fields went fallow. Days were energized with cool air and most important, at first frost, the snakes went into hibernation, allowing us to expand our prowling into the woods and ditches and nearby fields. Chip could smell the season's change, feel it under his paws, and his expectation was immediate. He was eager, tuned, and ready for the hunt.

On the opening day of dove season, my father invited all the country neighbors to hunt with him. Or, more accurately, he invited them to admire Chip.

That morning, Chip matched my father's mood with his characteristically exuberant tail-wagging as they loaded the trucks and prepared to go to the fields. Of course, I was excluded. Children were always left behind when things promised to be really interesting, but I could imagine the scene well enough, Chip sniffing and pointing in the misty field, displaying his dazzling skills to the astonished admiration of all.

The fields that dawn were thick with frost, and the deep cold added to the men's eagerness to get started. Once everyone was in place, and with great drama, Chip was released into the tan broom sedge to point and flush the birds on my father's command. Chip did so promptly and repeatedly. But no birds flew.

Cat calls began to float through the chill as the waiting men hunched and stamped trying to generate a little warmth.

"That's some fancy bird dog!" came the first curt remark.

A mocking laugh responded.

"Yeah. My granddaddy's old coon dog could find a bird better'n that."

My father muttered in disbelief as the derision escalated.

"Who says you can't teach an old dog new tricks? That one of yours points *grass*!"

Guffaws rolled across the morning. It was like the old days when my father was ten—the men quickly warming to his humiliation by ratcheting it up a notch.

"Hey, John. What'd you say you paid for that critter?"

The money reference with its suggestion that he had been swindled was too much to endure. My father strode into the field to see why the birds Chip pointed hadn't taken flight. Chip remained frozen in point position, waiting. And there, just as Chip and I had spent all summer practicing, the dog stood nose to nose with a gigantic bull frog.

Great profanity arose from the spot and the other hunters went running to see; and then collapsed in laughter.

Which is why I was dispatched to my room the minute we got home. Not only had I corrupted my father's champion, but worse, I had mortified him in front of those judgmental country neighbors who were unlikely to let him forget that hideous day.

Ever.

The next morning Chip and I stood silently as the familiar blue truck drove into the yard. When the trainer stepped out, Chip bounced joyously to his side. On command, he leapt into the front seat while the man exchanged a few quiet words with my father. Then they drove away, Chip wiggling over to give his old friend a loving lick on the face while I watched, unnoticed, with tears drooling down my cheeks. Abandoned. Left alone to endure whatever role in purgatory my father would assign me.

It took a week, but I knew it had come the following Saturday when I was awakened at four a.m. and informed that from now on, I would be Chip's replacement. I wouldn't be working the birds. Instead, I would be relegated safely to the field's briar-tangled fringe where I would retrieve everything else. Thermoses of coffee. Lunches. Shotgun shells. Cigarettes, matches, gloves, anything needed from the trucks parked in the woods, and I would bring these things promptly, noiselessly, back to the field. In between errands, I must sit on the freezing ground, being painfully quiet, agonizingly still, and wait. Hungry. Cold. And uncomplaining.

No one took pity. By then, everyone knew that I was the dangerous dog-corrupter, and my censure was universal.

After a few Saturdays it seemed incredible to me that Chip ever had delighted in retrieving anything. Sourly, I thought, we had never had anything in common, and, with a sniff, I decided that our summer relationship was all a lie. In fact, Chip had deceived me.

Even worse, those Saturdays meant I had to roam the fields dressed in a way that marked me as a conspicuous interloper. Unlike real hunters who wore tan duck pants and jackets with a million secret pockets and elegant tall lace-up leather boots, I had to wear my old worn corduroy pants and brogans. In those days, children weren't spoiled with possessions, and our minimal wardrobes consisted of clothes essential for school, play and special events. We had brown lace-up oxfords for everyday and black patents for dress up. That was it. Even though I really needed waterproof boots and thorn-proof pants, those were for "later." In my case, with the Chip episode lurking, "never" seemed more likely.

Miserable as I was, there was a good side. Amazingly, at the mere age of five, I was allowed to go out with the adults, into their mysterious hunting world of frosted fields and wintry woods, places I now shared with them—albeit as an invisible non-person—in a season I soon learned to love even more than the languid barefoot days of summer.

Unfortunately, my new job didn't end after each hunt was finished. When we got back home and the men went laughing and talking into the house to warm themselves with a toddy in front of an inviting fire, I remained on the cold brick steps outside, picking cockspurs and beggar weed off my pants and socks, one sticky piece at a time, and then brushing off the caked dirt until I was judged clean enough to be allowed inside.

I told myself not to worry. Surely, in November when I turned six, my father would forgive me.

But he didn't.

Except for weekends, summers, and holidays, we actually lived in Savannah where my father worked, and I endured city life while having to go to school. Admittedly, spring was lovely in town, and that year, when the weather warmed enough to invite sitting on the porch, my father decided to teach me to play rummy. As in most games, he was an expert but he evened the competition by giving me a substantial handicap, an advantage so generous that my frequent victories seemed assured. My assumption was premature, unencumbered as it was, by one small fact. He always played to win.

"No one ever appreciates things that are made too easy," he'd say. "Winning at anything only matters when you've worked hard enough to earn it." So I'd focus determinedly, and whenever I did manage to best him, he'd smile approvingly and praise me. Briefly. Just long enough for me to enjoy the flush of triumph before announcing that he was reducing my handicap.

Once, during our afternoon game, as I was trying to deal the cards, he stopped me. Anxiously, I waited while he took the deck from my hand and turned my palm face down on the table. "Look how young," he said quietly. "Look at those dimples." He touched them gently. "And that soft, smooth skin."

I had never noticed.

Then he put his own hand next to mine. How new and small my hand looked next to his powerful worn one ridged with bones, its splotchy skin traced with a gathering of scars.

"When you get to be my age, I hope yours won't show that you've lived so hard." Then abruptly, he took the cards and finished dealing.

When school dismissed for summer, our family returned to the farm and my father commuted to the city to work. Those cool early mornings, before he had to leave, I'd hurry to walk with him. He never talked much except to point out something I hadn't noticed such as a bird's hidden nest or to give a name to one of the mysterious night creatures who left traces of their goings in the sand. It was knowledge shared from his country childhood and as we walked, he took me to his past, helping me absorb the earth-real wonder of it into my life as well.

On weekends the lessons escalated. "Now that you're six, it's high time you learned how to live off the land. There might come a time when land is all you'll have to keep you going."

When he issued such warnings, I didn't understand the urgency. We never seemed to want for anything. But imperative or not, such shared wisdom made me feel prepared for things and eager to learn everything that would protect me from vague whatevers, whenever they might surface.

Getting food was a basic way to start. First, he taught me how to rig a fishing rod, to bait the hooks and how to find the most promising drops. Then I learned to cast without a backlash. That difficult skill came with surprising speed because I loathed his mocking laughter that lasted as long as it took me to untangle the mess I'd made.

With casting mastered and ready to haul in a whale, I still needed to learn how to feel the nibble; then set the hook, and, when I had reeled in my fish, to grab that wriggling, slippery prize and, without drama or making faces, carefully remove the hook and add my catch to the others kept fresh in a galvanized pail of salt water.

By mid-summer, I had learned the proper way to handle boat lines, to catch the dock cleats with them and to make the boat secure.

In August, I graduated to mixing oil and gas for the outboard motor. He even allowed me to choke and start it too on mornings when we'd browse the river before the heat could rise.

Just for fun, on afternoons when the air was stagnant and sweat drooled down my face and legs, he'd take my mother and me for a ride in our fast little cruiser that he drove full speed, careening around river bends dipping side to side with me riding on the bow, shrieking in excitement as I hung on for my life.

I relished everything about that summer, our new companionship—the confidences, the learning, and the risks—that made my former relationship with Chip seem like a childish infatuation. Then one day out fishing, I dropped a large, fresh-caught bass overboard.

"Damnit!" my father snapped. "That's food you wasted. That could be somebody's meal for a whole day. Why don't you think what you're doing? What the hell is the matter with you?" I started to sob.

"Stop that!" he ordered. "Stop it right now! Don't you ever let me see you cry when there's nothing wrong with you." I sniffed to a halt as he shook his head in disgust. "Sometimes I forget you're just a girl."

That evening after supper, while he didn't make it an invitation, he let me watch him dismantle the outboard motor. And when he had finished, he gave me a ride back home up high on his shoulders so I could "see the world the way the squirrels do."

The summer's sharing softened my awe of him. And as school resumed and the fall hunting season approached, I knew things would be different. Just "how" came on the first dove-season day. At four a.m. without preamble, I was rousted out of bed, fed, suited up, loaded into the truck with all the rest of the gear and dispatched to the woods to resume my wild acres delivery service. Astonishingly, my father seemed all too comfortable with the arrangement. He never mentioned it or how pathetic I looked working week after week in the bitter cold, still inappropriately dressed in drafty corduroys and leaky oxfords. He wasn't the least bit sorry for me. Just oblivious. Halfway into this *second* dove season, I was still being treated like a dog.

Even my birthday in late November didn't bring expected change, and as December progressed with its continuing litany of frozen Saturdays, I lobbied, mutely, "Please. I'm seven now and much more mature. So maybe. For Christmas?"

On Christmas Eve it was twenty degrees when my father and I went into the woods on our annual pilgrimage to find our holiday tree. We sidetracked into the forest where he allowed me time to swing like Tarzan on the wild grapevines that dangled temptingly from live oak limbs. We roamed the damp fringes of the marsh and explored the upland, inspecting and rejecting dozens of cedars until, in an old, overgrown field, we found it, belled and thick and the perfect height for the tall ceilings in our old country house.

By then, I was shivering.

"Help me gather up some pine cones and straw and we'll have a fire going in a minute," he said. When the pile was tall enough, he lit it and we sat cross-legged on the ground, gathering its warmth until finally, my teeth stopped chattering. Then he began to talk.

"When I was a boy, I used to come out here to plow."

"That must have been a really long time ago. It's all grown up now."

He hadn't seemed to hear me. "And, just like today, we usually found our Christmas tree right here on the edge of this same field." He looked around as if waiting for something. "When I turned ten, my father sent me out here to get a wild turkey for Christmas dinner."

"All by yourself? And he let you shoot?" I was vastly impressed that any child should be awarded such responsibility and freedom.

"Of course. By then I was the best shot of the twelve of us at home, and he wasn't taking any chances. No bird, no dinner. Simple as that." He looked at me and grinned. "Shotgun shells were expensive and he gave me just two to get the job done."

"Oh, no!" I blurted. "Did he punish you when you missed?"

He laughed. "No need for that. I always got my bird." Then he beamed with mischievous pride, "The best part was holding it over my older brothers when I brought home the bird—*and* the unused shell as well."

Telling me was another lesson perhaps. No wasting?

Not even time. Not even today. He rose abruptly. "You should be warm now," he said, as he began smothering the flames with dirt, kicking the embers around and tossing on sand until no smoke was left. Then, in the gathering chill we went back to collect our tree and take it home to Mother.

By tradition, we all shared in the decorating. With much muttering and a few shocking "damns," my father strung the barbed cedar branches with bulbous, colored lights. Next, my mother adorned the tree with our old glass ornaments from the five-and-dime, and finally, I got to drape strands of crimped foil "icicles" which, according to my seven year-old skill, hung in clumps and tangles, intentionally unnoticed by my parents who vigorously praised my work.

The tree ceremony was followed by a light supper that I hardly touched. Then, carefully, I placed my little gifts for them that I had made in school, in a conspicuous spot under the tree. As the finale, we hung our red-topped gray woolen socks from the mantle and put out milk and cookies for Santa, before I was hustled upstairs for a quick bath and into bed in the cold fresh air of the sleeping porch. There, my mother read *The Night Before Christmas* before she tucked in my covers, gave me a kiss and went back downstairs to join my father in tantalizing chatter that, try as I might, I could only faintly hear.

It felt cold enough to snow. For a long time I lay there in the dark, the feather quilt pulled up to my nose. Thinking. Hoping.

I wasn't going to dream of sugarplums. What were those things anyway? I hated plums. No. I would dream that finally and at last, there would be a big box under the tree that was just the right size to hold my dream. I had waited and wished for two long years and, at seven, that was a lifetime.

I knew better than to ask for anything, or even hint, much less beg or whine. That behavior had been shamed into oblivion early on. Once, I had casually mentioned boots but it was predictably dismissed with, "Maybe when you've stopped growing." Sleepily, I remembered my father's lean Christmases and firmly told myself, "Boots are expensive…so it's Christmas, but that doesn't mean….don't think about it...you can't just have what you want just because you want it..."

"And, oh…" I remembered grimly, just before I drifted off, "There was…that Chip thing."

When I awoke, the sky outside was still black and alive with stars. They were dancing and playing—having star games again. Hundreds of them out there in the ending night trying to out-dazzle each other, some huge and bright, some twinkling and teasing, while the faint ones seemed to be running away to hide.

Stars were one of the rewards for being awake in the night, my favorite time to experience the wonder of things. Existing, as I did, in the silences of only-childhood, it was often darkness, not words, that evoked imaginings, that held the greatest mysteries, and that brought anticipation of magical things. Especially Santa Claus.

Suddenly, a purple light brushed the dark horizon where dawn would come. The stars soon faded and were gone. Then the light began heating with color. Rose. Rust. Crimson. Orange. Not long to wait now.

With the first golden flash of sun I was out of bed, pulling on my robe and slippers, and thundering down the stairs to "Merry Christmas" shouts from my parents who, somehow, had gotten there already. The firelogs were blazing, and our simple country living room glowed with the mix of golden firelight and the multi-colored lights from the tree. The mood of it shone with the irrepressible excitement of giving, of stockings now filled, and presents wrapped and waiting under the tree.

It was impossible not to spot the huge package waiting there. Could it...?

The stocking ritual came first. Mine bulged with promise and I gleefully pulled out a tiny harmonica, a little bell, a bar of soap impressed with a dog, and peppermints, and nuts, and oranges. I rushed even more than usual. I had to get to that enormous package under the tree. I had to or, quite possibly, die from anxiety.

The package waiting there was unnecessarily huge, a troubling detail that made my hands fumble nervously when, finally, I could touch it and begin to bare its contents. When the wrapping came off and the box was opened, there was yet another, smaller present inside. And inside that another smaller one. And yet another, each wrapped differently, in my mother's wonderful way of heightening the suspense, a goal achieved, in a flurry of paper and ribbon that seemed endless.

By comparison, the next box seemed too small and I choked back disappointment as I opened it.

Suddenly I screamed, "Thank you, thank you!!! Oh, thank you!" as the final lifted lid revealed two tall stems of dark brown leather with thirty brass ringed holes in each that were crisscrossed with leather laces from the boots' arches to their tops where they would land just below my knees.

Oh, that delicious aroma of new leather. The solid, tough feel of it. They were the most beautiful boots I had ever seen.

They were mine!

It was obvious that the feet were several sizes too large because I would have to wear them for at least two years. But an extra pair of thick socks would fix that. And there was more. In a second package next to them was a pair of real hunting pants made of strong tan duck in exactly my size.

My parents stopped opening their presents to watch, as giddy and happy and laughing out loud, I took a boot from the box and held it lovingly against my cheek, drawing in the scent. Then, my father added his own special gift.

"How would you like to christen those handsome boots today?"

"Could I?"

He grinned, "We'll go out to the dove field this afternoon, say about four o'clock. Just the two of us."

Forgiveness! Acceptance! It was truly Christmas! I was bursting with the restorative joy of it. My eyes brimmed. But I struggled hard and didn't cry.

At three o'clock I ran upstairs to change into my new duck pants and to find two pairs of bulky socks. Then, I raced back down and into the kitchen and sat on a little stool by the hearth to pull on my boots. The leather was unlined, and the rough surfaces resisted the socks defiantly. The struggle occasionally landed me on the floor but by four o'clock, tall leather shanks encased my legs with the professional style of a seasoned woodsman.

Walking in them was awkward. They were heavy and stiff. It was like lifting concrete. But, even though my father had to haul me into the truck by the seat of my pants, I didn't mind. I was ready for my first real participation in the country coda of survival. The hunt.

There is a loneliness cast by pale winter sunlight settling in the leafless woods that at that moment seemed as tantalizing as moonlight. Fallen branches littered the way and dead leaves crushed noisily underfoot, but every step and stumble that I took through the forest that chill afternoon brought reward. Briars couldn't hurt me. Beggarweed might try, but it didn't stand a chance sticking to my new outfit, while my professional appearance was proof that I was accepted and forever removed from the demeaning fetch-it role.

Slowly, we moved from the wooded fringe into the tall tan brush at the center of the field to wait until the late-day fly-in, a pause that gave me a chance to admire my feet and to wiggle my warm, dry toes against the protective leather.

"Shhhhhh," my father cautioned.

They were coming. I could just make out the dark-winged birds swarming toward the trees, silhouetted against a sky that would soon boil into hot sunset. My heart pumped. I could hear them now, wings brushing—murmuring—avian voices calling in the thin air. I had never been this close before and had not considered what it might be like for me. My father had hunted since he was my age when, for his family, it was kill or starve. For him, what we were there to do, was simply a continuation. For me, it was immediate, rushing at me and real, and my heart was pounding.

As the birds flew toward our cover, my father "led" them with his gun, sighting them skillfully until his target was sure. Even after my seasons "in the field," the huge noise from the double-barreled shotgun fired so close to me was shocking. Two birds dropped from the sky a small distance in front of me.

"You're a regular hunter now," he said. "You get them while I reload."

I looked at him uncertainly.

"Go on," he prompted.

It took me a while to maneuver my new boots so I could get upright and struggle through the brush into the open. When I picked up the first dove, I was surprised at how light it was, its still-warm body chilling quickly in the icy afternoon. When I found the second, I was stunned to find it fluttering, its black eyes looking up at me from the ground, its wing shattered and blood seeping from it. Carefully, I picked it up. I could see its beautiful head, its eyes watching me, and feel its heart pumping through the stained feathers, throbbing against my hand.

When I stumbled back to my father, my dove was still alive. He took it gently and then looked hard at me, seeing in my face the reflection of what it had been for him in his own childhood moment when death had come, not swiftly, at a distance, but resting in his own bloody hand.

Then he said, "When an animal is badly injured, you don't leave it to die slowly and in pain." With that, he put the dove's head between his teeth and, with the hand still holding it, gave the bird a sharp twist that broke its neck. The body lay limp as he opened his fist. The head slipped through his fingers and hung low and lifeless.

He put the birds in his game bag before he looked at me again.

"You must never leave anything to suffer," he said. "No matter how hard it is, that will always be your responsibility."

He knew we had done enough, and with his gun tucked under his arm, he led me from the darkening field where dormant unseen twigs and thorns drew christening scratches on my tall, leather, grown-up hunting boots.

MARIBU

Nothing seemed more magical than having a tiny fawn of my very own. Nothing! And in mere minutes, just such an amazing creature would be mine, to care for with all the love my six year old heart could lavish.

Maribu was an orphan, as small and defenseless as I. His mother had been killed in a brutal forest fire from which he had miraculously escaped. Alone and left to wander, he had been discovered by the couple next door, a handsome Baritone, Walter, who claimed experience singing at the Met, and his flamboyant, jewelry-laden, Russian wife, Zahlie. She had come reluctantly to our wooded swamp lured only by the idea that she could mistress of a stately Southern manse, grand enough to earn her serious ragging rights with her friends in New York City. Of course, that would take some doing. The mansion was a seedy, cypress box with an old ship's rail parked above the entrance "for decoration.

With little else to occupy her, Zahlie became an engine of industry. Within six months, she had covered it with white paint, added porticos, floor length windows with flanking dark green shutters, and columns, as my mother noted, "worthy of a Mississippi cotton plantation." Before unveiling the renovated house to visitors, Zahlie embellished its perfection with exquisite flowers. Lots and lots of them. A four-week old fawn was the last thing she wanted grazing down her image. So the transfer was mutually perfect.

For the twenty minutes it took to drive over the rough country road to their house, I sat on the edge of my seat, itchy with anticipation. When we pulled into the drive, there he was, tiny and delicate, standing on the patio guarded by Eric, Zahlie's enormous Great Dane that towered above him. Clearly, the animals had bonded and my father warned me to approach carefully, be gentle and steady, and to talk quietly. Then he went inside to finalize arrangements.

Summers spent around animals had taught me not to rush and I gently stroked the speckled, spindly-legged little fawn as it gazed huge-eyed at me. He didn't seem at all shy. Instead, he responded by placing his small damp nose on my face and nuzzling my cheek. My smile must have been gargantuan. Eric stood close by and as I slowly wound my arm around the fawn's neck, to gently hug him, Eric began to growl. Within seconds, he bared his teeth, huge long fangs that left no doubt of his intention.

I backed away but the growling intensified. Slowly, I tried to move toward the house but he pursued me, muscles flexing, crouched and darkly menacing. I turned and ran toward the brick steps leading up to the screened porch. Just as I reached out for the doorknob, he was on me, ripping and tearing at my scant clothes. As I screamed, he threw me down on the brick and closed his enormous mouth around my arm, sinking his teeth into it, tearing my flesh, and then biting my wrist and leg.

He was going to kill me.

My screams reverberated through my small body and were horrifying even to me. As blood spattered everywhere, I thought Eric, roaring now, would rip me apart. Then suddenly, above the mayhem I could hear my father shouting; then he was there fighting the powerful beast off me, sending it flying as Zahlie shrieked from the porch, "Don't hurt my baby. STOP! Leave Eric alone!!" Instantly, my father scooped me up; then rushed me home, and with my mother, we sped into Savannah where my deeply torn flesh was treated with burning medicines stirred into the wounds with a thin, sterilized probe…and finally, bandaged.

Zahlie, meanwhile, refused to allow her precious Eric to be placed in the pound overnight for rabies observation.

Two days later, without notice, the fawn arrived.

I looked at him differently this time. Even at such an unworldly age, I understood how closely we each had been touched by death. I felt our bond and with it, a responsibility to keep him safe.

My father had built a tall, enclosure covered with chicken wire, even across the top. No predator could gain access. Only I, with my warm bottle of formula, would be allowed inside. Maribu was truly tiny but he was far stronger than I imagined. He grabbed the bottle's nipple with such force, he knocked me off my feet. I just hung on for dear life as he tugged and slurped and consumed every drop while I lay there in the dirt.

Gradually, I lost my fear of him and each dewy summer morning I rushed to fix his bottle so that I might go to him and we could savor our bond. Within a month he was allowed to venture outside with me where he followed me like a shadow, nibbling my father's prize roses as we roamed. Without protest, he let me dress him in costumes and dark glasses. And the afternoons when my parents and guests relaxed on the dock Maribu sampled their gin and tonics and ate their cigarettes on the sly. Even the farm's deer-chasing dogs adopted him and, all together, our theatrical band elicited so much laughter, few complained about the outrageous license Maribu enjoyed.

As autumn color fused with summer greens I knew that soon, we would be returning to town. And Maribu? Oh, please. He would be just fine with us there. But I was told that my fawn would be sent away. Weeping, of, course, changed nothing. At six, I didn't understand that Maribu was becoming a young buck. Not only would instinct force him to roam in search of a mate, but as tame and people-loving as he was, he would become easy prey for any hunter who saw him. Quietly, my parents searched for a proper place until they found a wooded, high-fenced farm that rescued such defenseless creatures. Out of kindness to me, Maribu wasn't sent there until I had started school in town.

Every day I cried for him, afraid for his safety, certain that he couldn't be happy without me even as reports trickled in insisting that he was content. He would be safe and could remain "wild." Even better, he had other deer to play with, woods to roam, plenty to eat, and the way the farm fed them meals made me laugh for the first time since he had gone away. It was almost a game they told me. At dinner, they rang a bell and the herd would come running, sleek, swift Maribu always in the lead. My adorable deer was so smart that I knew it hadn't taken long for him to learn the routine and to win the game he'd made of it. But I missed him. My heart had been torn asunder when they took him from my life. Grief that deep was new and incomprehensible. I was inconsolable and I begged to see him again.

A month before our return to the country for the summer, my dad telephoned the farm to set up an appointment for us to visit Maribu. Excitedly, I stood waiting.

When he said goodbye, he began telling me the story about the dinner bell as if I had never heard it before. It seemed curious but as always, I loved visualizing my gorgeous deer racing gracefully and fast, determined to be first in the dinner line. "Maribu……." my dad began, "…he heard the bell and he came racing down the road, quick as lightening…out in the front of the others… just like always." He placed his hand on my shoulder and looked at me. "He didn't have time to see the car parked around that blind corner.…and he ran into it.…head first.……..I'm so sorry, honey. He broke his neck."

DEPARTMENT OF TAKING

The swamp was a dangerous place in autumn when decaying vegetation made everything look the same. Tan and brown leaves rustled in the mucky dents made by our boots and floated on dark pools between the cypress trees where snakes and gators often hid. We couldn't tell what might be near, but it didn't matter. We were determined to get through.

Gradually, as the swamp edge broke away, light poured into the gloom exposing the once-thick forest, lying ripped open and bare. We stumbled across the dirty wound and climbed one of the mountains of clay that lined the construction site: from up high we could see all of it, the swamp, the woods, and far beyond, where huge machines had brutally reconfigured the wilderness into a symbol of progress, a mile long stretch of I-95 that would whisk millions through our rural area without any of them having to notice it at all.

It was hard to imagine. Just fifty years ago it would have taken ages of wielding shovels and axes to wrest a simple woods road from this wild land—our land, that had been loved and enjoyed by our family for more than 75 years. But now, in mere days, the ancient oaks had fallen and the marsh that edged the creek had been torn away. It was stunning in its ugliness. After an hour and without a word, my husband, Don picked up our loaded 410 shotgun, and we headed back into the swamp's gloom.

Don thought the gun was an affectation, but I had insisted. He was a New Yorker, after all, and couldn't be expected to know.

He was ahead of me, following the footprints we had gouged on the way in when he stopped abruptly.

"What's that pile up there?" he asked. "I don't remember that being there."

"Just dead leaves." I was behind him and not really looking.

"Wait!" He put his hand out to stop me. "I think it just moved." He picked up a stick and hurled it. "Is that a snake?"

"The gun is making you see things," I moved up to get a clearer view.

The leaf pile began to swell alarmingly into a huge, towering coil that I could see as well. A huge triangular head rose up from its bulk.

"My god! That's the biggest snake I've ever seen." The reptile's tail began to rattle ominously, but it didn't move off. "A rattlesnake!" He had never seen one before.

"A diamondback," I whispered, now standing next to him. "Stay still. I don't think it wants us here."

"Fine. But how the hell do we get around it?" He picked up another stick and threw it at the surging patterned pile in mid-trail. The snake's tongue flashed furiously and the rattling increased. It had chosen its ground and wasn't going anywhere. "Should I shoot it?"

It wasn't wise to move. I was trying to gauge its size because, depending on its length, we could be within striking distance. "You never know what these things might do," I said quietly. "Besides, it could creep off into the leaves, and then we wouldn't know where it was. And no one knows where *we* are either."

It was so like the time when I was ten and my father had taken me hunting out here. In those days, just beyond the forest, there were acres of rice fields that dated back to the 1700s. They were sectioned off by earth dams that controlled the water, and in winter, some of the fields were flooded to make duck ponds. That day, my father had his shotgun tucked under his arm, muzzle pointed at the ground, as we emerged from the forest onto one of the dams. He was just ahead of me, looking out over the reeds and water. He never saw it. But I did, coiled and ready to spring just three feet in front of us, black and menacing, its huge fanged mouth open and white in the moment before striking. I knew then precisely why they called them cottonmouth moccasins, one of the most dangerous and aggressive of Georgia's venomous snakes. As I screamed, my father instinctively raised the barrel of the gun and blew its head away. I was a small girl. My father was 6'4". We were five miles into the wilderness, and I didn't even know how to drive the truck. I could calculate the outcome, and in that moment I knew about fear. And the threat of death.

Don raised the 410 and aimed carefully at the enormous head whose beady dark eyes were fixed on us.

One shot and the head ripped away. The rattler fell into a writhing heap on the ground. Blood and shattered flesh suggested it was dead, but when Don approached, it suddenly lashed about, big muscular convulsions rippling from the headless body to the rattling tail, menacing, even in death. Up close we could see just how enormous it was. The belly would have been too big even for Don's long hands together to surround it. A horrible pungent odor rose from the carcass. Without discussion, when the writhing finally slowed, Don retrieved a strong stick, picked up the remains, and hung the snake over a tree limb. It measured a full six feet.

"Oh, my god!" was all he found to say.

"I told you we grew 'em big in Georgia."

But I hadn't told him about hanging the snake in the tree, something country Georgia men seemed to do instinctively.

"Well," I said with relief, looking at the awful, blood-dripping, odiferous remains draped over the limb, "We do things differently out here in the country." And I paused. "I see you've gotten the hang of it."

He was the family punster, but it took him a second before he grinned, "Not bad."

Yes, Don was getting it, and before it was all over, before the freeway issue was finished, our "country way of doing things" would go public to impress even the invading forces that sought to overpower us. And they would never forget either.

"Hicks. Bumpkins." We were just more names on the Department of Transportation's 'taking' list, the roll of those to be dispossessed of their land to make way for I-95. Disdain was written clearly on the DOT representative's face when he came to see us. We were wearing battered boots and dirt-stained shirts and jeans, and his dismissive look telegraphed that he thought it should be easy to offer us a little money and we'd sign over our property without a whimper.

Of course, he was more polished and politic than that. He recited his lines with care. He had come to offer us "a very good deal" and to save us "the expense of being sued, and the inconvenience and painful anxiety of having to go to court."

"But it's not just what you're taking to build the thing," Don protested. "That freeway will cut off access to our land on the other side. Can't you just build us an overpass or an underpass?"

"That's impossible."

"Look," Don reasoned. "It can't be that hard to build us a simple road. Isn't that what you people do? We're less interested in compensation than in having a way to get over there." We were very, very naive. The man had met our kind before.

"Sorry. That's just not possible." He paused and changed his curt tone to one more placating. "Now $19,000 is a very generous offer for that little strip we'll need, and that's really all we can do."

"Little? You're taking 129 acres! And you are cutting off at least 500 acres of waterfront!"

"I suggest you think it over. Think it over very seriously. You live in California, don't you?" He looked convincingly grave. "The alternative is a long drawn-out mess with endless delays, not to mention your time, the enormous legal expense, and constantly coming back here to prepare. And then, there's the trial." He rose and looked at me darkly, "And there is no guarantee you'll win. Especially in court *here*." Then he left, leaving no doubt that he knew all about our chances if we chose to resist.

I knew why all too well.

A country court is a place where the tangle of alliances and old history can make the simple facts irrelevant. I kept thinking of 'the sins of the father.' My own had done nothing wrong, but that made no difference.

His background was the same as just about everyone else's in the county—farm-raised and dirt poor with a rowdy entourage of siblings, all working to support the family by struggling in the fields and rivers. From age five, my father had been stumbling behind a plow, accepting his lot until he was taken to Savannah by train for a sixth birthday outing. To a country child, that smorgasbord of options and plenty became a Lorelei, and from that moment, he vowed not to spend the rest of his life "facing the ass end of a mule." At sixteen, he left for Savannah.

As a farm boy, his world experience consisted of what he learned from books backed by the rural ethos that hard work, intelligence, determination, and honesty would someday translate into opportunity. Even then, in 1909, such sensibilities were becoming less expected and more prized. He had many mentors as he rose from awkward country boy to business executive, but while mules and plows faded with success, he never forgot the land that imprinted him so young, offering sustenance if he worked for it and wild beauty to engorge his spirit when so much materially was missing. As did other country folk, he viewed land as security, certain that if you owned it, you would never starve.

As soon as he was able, he invested in it repeatedly, going into debt each time, struggling to pay his way out, and then submerging his earnings all over again until he numbered his acres in the thousands, all the while believing that such diligence and hard honest work earned respect. Instead, many who shared his beginnings, but not his fortitude, never forgave him for his success.

To help with some of the farm expenses, he had sold timber. The contracts were unimpeachable, and the trees to be cut were professionally marked to preserve the remaining forest. Routinely though, the buyers took trees for which they did not pay, trees that were clearly designated to be saved. For years my father had taken these poachers to court in our rural county, bringing with him Mr. Stafford, his polished city lawyer. Stafford came outfitted with a bowler, an English tweed jacket with a belted back, and a large black umbrella that he tapped for occasional emphasis, an out-of-touch mannerism that played humorously to the open-collar-shirted juries.

My father's cases were always solid winners. Stafford, however, managed the impossible. He lost every single one of them.

Now, it was my turn. I had a choice. If I resisted, I myself would have to go to county court with what result? What did I know about contending with such country justice? Exactly nothing. But I remembered an H.L. Menken quote, "What does the faithful husband know of women?" Actually, not much. But he can learn a lot by observation. I had witnessed my father's frustration, and I transposed those lessons into a quest for the toughest, craftiest, smartest country lawyer in the county.

And I found Charlie.

Then we went back to California to wait.

A few silent months went by. I dismissed the case from my life until the day I answered a heavy knock on the front door and found two grim sheriff's deputies standing there.

"We have a subpoena here for a Laura Devendorf."

"I'm Laura Devendorf."

The one with the papers held them out to me. "This is an order to appear in Georgia court." He looked at me suspiciously while the other deputy shifted his hand meaningfully, to his holster.

"You are being sued by the State of Georgia. The Department of Transportation. And you'll have to go back there on the listed date to answer the charges."

The uniforms, the badges, the guns. It was suddenly serious. Really serious. The talk-about-it paper case had slipped into a legal enforcement issue, and I was dry-mouth scared. Second thoughts were roaring through my head. It wasn't too late. I could still accept their offer and stop all this. That night, my fear was matched by Don's steeled anger.

"We can't let them get away with it," he said. "They're just licensed thieves."

The silence from Georgia undermined my confidence even more. I hadn't heard from Charlie in months. When, finally, I decided to call him, he was bubbling with good cheer. After a youthful career of defending the local citizenry on hog poaching and drunk and disorderly charges, he viewed this as his Big Time debut. He was disconcertingly short on information and long, very long, on enthusiasm. "Don't you worry your little head about a thing, young lady. I've got everything under control."

"What, exactly, is going on?" I asked, trying to contain my anxiety.

"Oh, too much to go into on the long distance," he assured me. "We'll have plenty of time to catch up when you get here before the trial. You're comin' a week ahead, right?"

"Yes. A week from Monday."

"That's just fine." His voice smiled. "Call me when you get in."

Approaching the Savannah airport, the plane circled from the south. Over our land.

The dirt scars of government progress seemed huge where dark green bands of trees had been. It was theirs, one way or the other. They had arrogantly exercised their ownership, and there seemed nothing we could do about it except cause trouble.

When we got to Charlie's office, he had assembled our stable of witnesses, who, he assured me, "would prove our case." They were a land planner, a broker, and me.

The planner cheerfully brought out maps for an extensive upscale subdivision with a golf course, docks, recreation center, et al. All this grandeur was ruined, of course, by plowing a freeway through the middle of it.

"But, Charlie," I protested. "We're growing trees."

Charlie looked at me with compassion. "Now I understand that. But this is different. I've been studyin' this thing and there's something called 'highest and best use.' That's what these plans represent. That means the highest use you could put that land to that would bring you the highest price if you sold it. And now, because of the freeway, you'll never be able to get it."

"But, you don't..."

"Oh, I know you want to hang on to it right now and grow trees or somethin'. But your daddy understood what every country boy with land knows, that land is there to enjoy *and* to fall back on. It's why he left it to you. To protect you. Say, sometime down the road, somebody in your family got real sick needin' expensive doctors and hospitals, and you needed money real bad, you would have that land to save you. Now, with what they're doin' to you, that option is gone. *This* is the only chance you'll ever get. The gov'ment wants that land. They're takin' it away from you, and they're takin' it *now*. And there's nothin' we can do to stop 'em. What's nasty is, that they want it as cheap as they can get away with. That's where I come in."

He told me all this, as they say in the country, "jus right."

Equivocation had vanished. He was right, and I was good and mad.

"So," the broker said, "just to finish our 'highest and best' argument on the bottom line, we're asking for compensation based on comparable sales of coastal property," and he pointed to the development maps, "where it has already been sold for a development like this one." He added casually, "One million, one hundred and ninety two thousand, five hundred dollars."

Considering the DOT offer of nineteen thousand, the leap was intergalactic.

Was Charlie crazy with ambition? It would still rest with the jury to give us anything at all. "In this county?" I asked. "With a jury from here?"

"That's what we're askin'," he replied. "We'll just hafta wait and see. You know, nobody's ever thought to use my 'highest and best use' argument before." He grinned.

Oh my god. We were an experiment!

The angst caused by knowing that was soon compounded when we began to learn just how badly tangling with the DOT could end. The local grocery, the post office, the neighborhood were all abuzz with horrific "taking" stories. A few had been lucky, but most ordinary landowners had settled out of court for pennies on the dollar. They couldn't even fight. Their affected holdings were so small no lawyer would represent them, at least, not for a reasonable sum. There wasn't enough money in it.

At that time there hadn't been even the possibility of a class action suit. There was no such thing in property "taking" because each parcel was unique. But the most disturbing cases centered around the poor, often illiterate, subsistence farmers who owned much of the land in question. Their poverty and their lack of ability even to read the summonses made them vulnerable to abuse, as was our neighbor, Joe Willard.

One of Willard's neighbors, a white man named Fred Cotes, was a long-time friend of the system. According to county records, Cotes had an insignificant half-acre of his larger tract condemned for the freeway. Without a court fight, he received $5,000. Willard was different. He was an elderly, black, and nearly illiterate farmer who owned five acres of productive high ground, three of which would be taken by the freeway. Willard said that one day a car pulled into his dirt yard, a car that for rural blacks had always prompted concern. Sheriff's Deputy Barnes stepped out. He was armed and in uniform, just as the deputies had been who had come to me in California. He held the alarmingly official-looking paper out to Willard.

A bewildered Willard took the subpoena and stared at the jungle of legalese he could not read.

"You're being sued by the government," the deputy said.

"But what did ah do? Ah never had no trouble with the law."

"Well Joe, ya got trouble now. Big trouble. They're telling you to come to court."

"But ah ain't done nothing."

The deputy ignored him. "The government wants your land for the new highway, and they're gonna take it."

"But my land's all ah got. Ah farms it for me and my family. We can't get by without it."

"Well then, you'll be needin' a lawyer. And Joe," he warned, "You'd better get the expensive kind, 'cause they're bringin' down an army of those high-priced Atlanta lawyers to go against you."

Willard looked stunned. "You knows ah can't afford no lawyer."

Age and experience had brought a frightened sadness to Willard's face. The deputy looked at him knowing he had brought him to the proper moment, "You know, Joe," he said kindly, "there is another way out of this." Willard waited anxiously while the officer went back to the police cruiser and withdrew a briefcase. He brought it over and placed it on a tree stump, where he unsnapped the latches and slowly opened it. To Willard's amazement, it was stuffed with money, stacks of rumpled old one-dollar bills with ten-dollar bills, for looks, on top of every pile. The deputy said, "It's all yours Joe. All ya gotta do is sign the paper so the state can have the land for the freeway." Barnes paused. "That road will help a lot of people, Joe. They'll be able to get to the hospital and to Savannah and all those other places. And for you, if you sign, it means there won't be any trouble. No lawyers. No goin' to court, and you know, Joe, things don't always turn out so good in court for a fella like you."

For final emphasis he picked up a stack of bills and shuffled it fast like a deck of cards. It did seem like a lot of money, more than Willard had ever seen in one place. Even so, he wouldn't have tempted the deputy's anger by asking to count it.

"It's your choice, Joe."

That country afternoon Joe Willard signed away his three acres for $500 in one-dollar bills—and the tens on top—leaving him too little land to make it life-supporting, even for his undemanding family.

Over and over, the records told of others who had lost their land this way as the highway moved like a glacier, relentlessly carving out family roots, sense of place, and purpose for the future. Dirt was brought in to cover up the past. The DOT "takings" stretched out and melted into hot asphalt as the freeway took over coastal Georgia. Records of those altered lives left in its wake were ultimately assigned to the courthouse basement where, when it was all over, no one seemed able to locate them anymore.

The day before our court date Charlie called, "Just checkin' to make sure everything's all right."

"I guess," was all I could manage.

"So, whatcha gonna wear?"

"Oh, something plain, I guess. Is that all right?" I hadn't wanted to think about it. It made it too imminent.

"Sounds great. Court starts at 9. See you at the court house at 8:30. You know where it is?"

"Oh, yes." Unfortunately, yes.

When we arrived at the courthouse, I was stunned to see the mobs of people crowding the place, filling the courtroom and spilling into the hall. After our family's local litigial history, I assumed it was my own personal lynch mob which, in my burgeoning fantasy, had probably come supplied with box lunches and sweet tea to tide them over so they could enjoy the entire spectacle of watching me taken down.

They stared at us through a ripple of soft comments I couldn't define. I did hear a woman hiss, "That must be *her*."

We entered the court room and took our seats up front at the defense table, while the state attorneys looked me over. Whispering. Charlie saw my unease. "Oh, don't worry about them," he said. "Those Atlanta folks don't know much about country doin's and juries and all, so they hired our local county judge to fill 'em in."

"Is that good?"

"Oh, yes," he laughed. "Seems he told them that this case would be a walk."

"Why?" I asked, horrified.

"He told 'em how juries around here never sided with your daddy when people stole his trees. How they stayed jealous of him all those years. And he's right. It always works that way around here if you've got something they wish they had or they think you're different or high and mighty."

"What could anyone have against me? They don't even know me. So what could he possibly tell them?"

"Well, the good judge told them how you haven't lived here recently and you wouldn't know anything about the land. He kinda embellished that a bit too."

"What did he say?!"

"I heard tell that he said you were one of those California hippies." I sat back, chilled. "A crazy artist. You know the kind."

"My god, that's terrible! What should I do?"

"Why nothin', little lady. It works out just perfect. They didn't take your testimony before trial, now did they?"

"No." I'd never heard of taking testimony. "What's that?"

"Well, hell, they should have. It's called 'discovery.' They could have sat you down and asked you every little thing you planned to say up there," and he nodded toward the witness stand. "But seems His Honor told them that bein' you were a California hippie and all like that…well, there'd be no need to waste time and money taking *your* testimony before trial. You know, with lawyers, time means money, especially with those big-time Atlanta boys from the Attorney General's office. So they were delighted to make themselves popular with the state by savin' both."

Apparently having labeled me a "non-threat," they had left our inconsequential backwater and returned to their warrens of importance in Atlanta. They had never laid eyes on me until this moment when the trial was poised to begin.

It was clear from their stares that they had expected me to appear as cast, in hemp sandals, a muumuu, waist-length stringy hair, and with the vacant demeanor of someone long-dependent on mind-altering drugs. Instead, I was dressed in pumps, a navy skirt, and a tailored white blouse. My clean, short hair was held with a white hair-band, and I even had on lipstick. No one has ever looked so ordinary. To them, no doubt, I sat there as a horrible apparition.

And so it began, highlighted by moments when our experts presented detailed land use plans with comparable values to go with them while the state attorneys stammered helplessly. Another came when their experts testified. Within minutes, Charlie elicited a stunning fact that was a shock, even to us. The DOT had assessed the value of our land at $28,107, a third more than they had offered, making it clear that the state had always planned to cheat us. A rumble traveled around the court that didn't need translation. Everyone in the room had some friend or relative with condemned land, and it was obvious that those people had been, or soon would be…robbed!

The Atlanta attorneys seemed relieved to change the subject. Having moved beyond the shock of how I looked, they appeared anxious to regain the advantage by using me.

I took the stand. The bailiff swore me in.

The expensively-dressed lawyer looked at me long and disquietingly before beginning, "Clearly, Mrs. Devendorf, you never intended to do any of the things your experts said, that would make your land worth that ridiculous amount of money."

"Why do you say that?"

"Because," and he smiled smugly at the jury, "Because you have a current tree planting contract on it, do you not?"

Whatever corner of the brain harbors high gear, I suddenly found it.

"That's right," I said without hesitation. "It was a contract made by my father when he was alive. It was part of a logging contract. He knew he was dying, and he didn't want my mother or me to be taken advantage of."

"That's not at issue here."

"But you should know about that contract." I paused, my mind whirring. "We are thrilled about it. Right now, land clearing prices are around $200 per acre. The contract is for $35 an acre to site prep for planting *and* plant the trees. So, even if we plow the trees under we'd come out miles ahead." The jurors registered appreciation and grinned.

In every subject and with every question the state proved conclusively that they understood nothing about land or forests or me. But our finest moment came when the state's appraiser, Mr. Avery, was recalled to testify.

Charlie began in his slow pleasant country purr, "Now, Mr. Avery, I see that you're a qualified and certified land appraiser."

"Yes. That's correct."

"So Mr. Avery, sir, don't you think that $19,000 is just a tad low for Ms. Devendorf's property?"

"That's not my appraisal. You heard my appraisal."

"Yes. We did. But considerin' the great amount of evidence as to the highest and best use of that land, don't you now think that even your appraisal of $28,107 is ridiculously insufficient?"

"No. Not at all."

"Please tell me sir, did you actually go out on that property you appraised?"

The man was indignant. "Of course I did."

"Would you describe it for us please?"

Mr. Avery had obviously visited the site from the direction and at the same time of year as Don and I had in our episode with the rattlesnake. You couldn't blame him if he'd made his visit brief. And cursory.

He gave a small shudder. "Full of trees and blackwater ponds and swamp bottomland, with vines and briars and mosquitoes everywhere."

"What about the land up by the river?"

"I told you, I went everywhere!"

"Didn't you see the creek out there that, once the freeway goes in, will block access to five hundred…count 'em…five hundred acres of beautiful, live oak-studded, waterfront property by cuttin' them off from the rest of Ms. Devendorf's land?"

"Absolutely not. There is a very small drain at that location, and I was able to hop across it with no effort."

With that, Charlie turned to the judge, "Excuse me, your honor, but there seems to be some kind of discrepancy over just where this gentleman went and just what the creek…excuse me, 'small drain'…actually looks like. It is a substantial part of our case. So could we ask you to take the jurors on a little field trip out there to see for themselves?"

"That seems to me the only fair and reasonable way to resolve this conflicting testimony," the judge said. So a yellow school bus was brought to the courthouse for the jurors. We took our car because, of course, we weren't allowed to fraternize with them.

When we got to the site, we found that the highway construction had advanced far enough that the foundation for the elevated bridge that would cross the broad North Newport River on the southern edge was already in place. The jury climbed the tall dirt roadway to the pinnacle above the river to survey the property. We were all flatlanders, and hardly anyone had ever seen the magnificent spread of rivered marshes from such a wondrous observation point. The afternoon was gorgeous. Sunny and warm. A brisk breeze floated the skirts of the lady jurors and rippled the backs of the men's shirts as they stood at the top of the man-made mountain looking out over lush green landscape. Ribbons of sparkling blue "deep water" brushed along the miles of shore that edged the five hundred cut-off acres. The scene was stunning, prompting one juror to comment, "If there was any way to get over there, I'd surely be honored to buy a piece. It's the most beautiful spot I've seen."

"No comments, please," Sam, the bailiff, warned.

The judge brought them back to duty, "Let's go down and look at this drain Mr. Avery says he jumped over."

Reluctantly, the crowd, with us following, left the breathtaking view and walked down to the contended spot, a place growling with huge earth-moving equipment and dump trucks. Fifty feet of marsh led up to the sides of Mr. Avery's "little drain," now spanned by two enormous two-hundred-foot-long concrete bridges. The wind was at our backs now, and sound floated a goodly distance.

"Damn, Sam," Charlie said in a loud wonderstruck drawl, supposedly to the bailiff. "Good gracious. If he could just hop over that thing, ah wanna enter him in the Olympics!"

There was a float of smothered laughter coming from the jurors before they were herded abruptly into the bus and taken back to the courthouse for summations, jury deliberations, and the ultimate creek-sized amount of reparations they awarded us.

Up 'til then, most of the I-95 condemnation cases in our area had been settled out of court. Many of those cases involved the people now shaking our hands and patting us on the backs and beaming as we struggled to exit the crowded building. The crowd included the very souls who, before our trial, had signed away their land for a pittance because they had had no choice. They weren't bitter or resentful that we had triumphed. Instead, it seemed we had won on their behalf, and it vindicated and rewarded them. Some even applauded and cheered.

When we won, it also became a day of hope for those who had yet to settle with the state. The DOT would have to reappraise all the pending Georgia settlements upward—way upward. But even for those such as Joe Willard who would never recover their land or its worth, intrinsic or otherwise, we had won importantly. And it changed forever our understanding of power, as well as our cramped ideas about community and our original feeling of isolation from it.

The appeal by the state for a new trial took another year while the award money sat in escrow earning interest, and the state Attorney General's office spent thousands and thousands of dollars coming up with "new evidence" to warrant a new trial, all of it in an elaborate and expensive attempt to cover themselves for the mess they had made of the original one. Their mood was poisonous. Their petition even made the petulant argument that although I owned the land, I had inherited it and, therefore I didn't deserve anything.

Points of law, objections, and the presiding judge's rulings on them comprise the substance of such appeals, but our judge had been obsessed with not being overturned. He left none of those ambiguities to argue. The state simply had been lazy. The lawyers didn't do their homework.

Regarding us as the backwater that they did, with me as the mindless hippie, our 'highest and best use' argument had simply been unexpected, a fact not lost on the appeals court when it heard the state's petition. In spite of the state's "new evidence," massive expenditures, and personal jabs at me, they lost the case in the appeals court as well. Unanimously. And to paraphrase the court's decision, "You don't get to conduct a new trial just because you didn't anticipate the defense argument."

For such high-priced Atlanta attorneys, their conduct of the case had been arrogantly sloppy. To neglect such a basic legal opportunity as taking my testimony to learn what I would say in court was elementally unforgivable. Yet these lawyers seemed suicidally compelled to pursue the case over a cliff. Most likely, it meant their reputations. Or even their jobs. So having lost twice, they petitioned the Georgia Supreme Court for final redress. It was no surprise when that court refused to hear the case, thereby upholding both lower courts' decisions in our favor.

To get to that closure took more than two uncertain, angst-ridden years that also cost the state an additional $27,000 in interest on the award money being held in escrow.

But it wasn't really over. Not yet.

The "country Georgia" trump card had not yet been played.

During highway construction, the engineers found that most of the existing roadbed contained earth that was unsuitable for the freeway foundation. It had to be removed. So a farmer friend, Jesse by name, had allowed the DOT, for a price of course, to store the dirt in his cow pasture—piles and piles and piles of dirt that by the end of our trial had become a mesa of imperious proportions. The state still had road work to do, dirt to exchange, and the need, the desperate need after their expensive legal debacle, to cut costs by parking the refuse close by.

One autumn afternoon Jesse pulled his shiny pickup truck into our yard. "Hey. How you?" he grinned as he got slowly out of the cab. Jesse was never in a rush about anything. We had learned to wait out the preamble. His news was almost always worth it. After shaking hands, Jesse leaned laconically on the truck hood and lit a cigarette, took a long drag and exhaled a tall tower of smoke before he said, "You know those DOT boys fixin' up the freeway…" Our eyes narrowed and our lips pinched.

"You know that road work they do is real interesting. I go out there a lot to watch, and yesterday I was standin' on the bridge that goes over the creek over by your land." We grimaced. "Well, they said they wanted to bring another 50 tons of dirt that didn't suit 'em over to my field. I had to tell 'em," he said, sadly shaking his head, "I had to tell 'em I was real sorry but my pasture was full up. My cows were gettin' nervous and I just couldn't take on any more." He looked at us and his lips spread into a big tobacco-stained grin.

"That upset 'em a lot. They'd gotten real used to havin' such a convenient place to put it. I told 'em that I understood they needed to save money since all those lawsuits ran the costs up so high and they were way in the red now." He tilted his head at our stony faces and smirked. "I must say they looked real uncomfortable bein' reminded."

So the DOT was getting back a bit of what they'd handed out to all of us. Our interest in what Jesse had to say was now thoroughly engaged.

"I let it sink in real good," Jesse reported, "and then I said that…the closest place to put that dirt would be right here, you know, right next to the freeway. I didn't have to mention that it was your land. I just let 'em get the whole picture," he said, describing the torture. "Then I said, 'Of course, you've been real mean to those people. They won't be too happy about doin' you any favors.' By then they were lookin' real anxious. So I said, 'But maybe….well, maybe if you were real nice to them, maybe they'd let you dump all that troublesome dirt right there. Of course, they might like the idea better if you offered to shape it into a nice little road and put a couple of those six-foot-high culverts in to let the creek through, and filled around 'em with rock so it wouldn't wash…then maybe, if they had that road promised …they just might let you get rid of all that dirt, right here.'"

He looked at us innocently, "So, I offered to come see if you'd consider it." He grinned wickedly.

A matching wickedness of our own was oozing up from a trove of stored ill will and spreading into unrepentant smiles on both our faces. The money was already ours. They couldn't take it back. And after nearly three years, we still felt happily avenged. That would have been enough. But in the best tradition of country justice, the DOT was being forced to revisit and to satisfy the only thing we ever asked for in the first place, the thing they said was absolutely impossible—a simple little road across that small drain/creek that would connect us to the five hundred cut-off acres.

And maybe—even as soon as tomorrow, they'd be coming, hat in hand, to ask if we'd allow them to build it for us.

TRANSITIONS

1960: In Savannah, things were changing. Even the big park in the middle of the historic district was different. The dark, shady little corners of it that had offered privacy from the streets were gone now because they hid the city's drug deals. Even the trellis that we sat under as children, leisurely feeding pigeons while wisteria blossoms dusted us with spring lavender—even that had been torn away.

Soon, the goldfish pond with its amazingly huge orange and platinum fish was filled in, and the densely foliated hill that secreted it was flattened into oblivion. The larger green spaces were carefully dismembered of shrubs—then grassed and manicured. Everything green was short and open and neat. And new. And bland.

By contrast, out in the country where we lived, many dumpy little Southern towns looked the way they always had. Giant oaks still hulked out of bare dirt and sand leaked through the wild grass where barefoot ten year-olds in faded jeans played mumbly-peg in the sun.

But even there, the city was coming. Just down the road where subdivisions had already replaced the shambling farms, there was a different expectation of beauty. The huge old oaks that survived the cutting down of everything, were surrounded now by emerald grasses that were orderly and smooth like napped velvet, their ragged fringes tidied by borders of liriope and short, dense flowers that offered a luxurious invitation to wander over them barefoot, to sit or spread a picnic. But no one ever did. Lawns were for show. Even children lived mostly inside, their worlds washed with cool blue electronic light. God forbid that anyone should encounter a bug. Or sweat. Or get dirt stains on their clothes.

By 1970, our own bit of "country" was still exempt and we protected it fiercely. The cows and hogs were gone now and pine trees grew in the untended fields giving the term "farm" a new look and intention. But it was still quiet except when the winter leaf fall left openings for the cold wind to blow in from the West bringing with it the demanding roar of the freeway.

I never used to mind that winter West exposure. In the evening I could hear cows mooing far away and animals snapping twigs as they walked the distant woods. When the air chilled and grew thin I could hear the train whistles echoing from the fiery sunsets. Distant, clear and urgent. The winter evening land was cold and empty then and the whistles lured me, calling through the unmuffled space to come and see and go and be. As a child, it excited me. It promised dark adventure waiting in the huge unknown and I could feel each whistle like a personal wound when the trains came hurrying—calling. To me. For me. Before they were gone. Without me.

JAMARKIS

They're laying her down today. Down six feet in the dark earth. The funeral is huge. Hattie, after all, was president of the choir, a mother of the church. Respected. People are crowding around the grave, the ladies at the fringes in their fancy hats and Sunday dresses, laughing and chatting while the coffin sinks and chunks of dirt hit it with big thumps.

The young man standing graveside is big, powerful, black, his face unreadable. She's gone—his grandmother with no legs and three fingers missing, all cut away during those last hopeless diabetic years. Not that that ever stopped her from being the first to gather up a bundle of clothes to send to a burned-out family, or from cooking chicken for the church sale—even at the end, doing whatever she still could manage from her chair with the fingers she had left. Now it's finished. She's down there, this old woman he'd looked after since he was eight—the kind-cruel-caring old woman, hot-tongued blunt and never satisfied, who never gave him peace.

Why Jamarkis? This big strapping teen with his name no one knows how to pronounce much less spell. "Mammy-made," that's what the older black ladies call names like that. Why him? His grandparents had nine children. Surely somebody?

Country funerals are like family reunions where people who never trouble to see each other get all open and friendly the way they do at Christmas. Here, all the grown children stand close to their elderly father, Joseph, and promise to come back and stay with him a while since Hattie's gone. When Elizabeth had asked Joe how he'd manage by himself, he'd said, "Efron says he's comin' back in a few weeks to live with me. He wants us to go in the carpentry business together." Then he gave a half-disbelieving Joe-grin, "Least I sure hope so."

Joe has always been a splendid carpenter, but he's been getting a little feeble lately. So full of grief and tiredness. He hung on to take care of Hattie, to cook for her, to give her insulin shots, and to help her put on her plastic legs so she could move to and from her chair in the morning. After that, he'd still need to do the outside chores, even work a little if he could, until Jamarkis came in the afternoon to help.

The children know Joe needs someone with him now, and they're relieved to hear about Efron. But Efron won't be coming in spite of his promise and Joe's cautious prayer that he will. He won't. They won't. Even with nine of them, not one wants to help pay the two hundred dollars for Hattie's tombstone. Joe's going to have to make it himself out of concrete and draw her name in while it's wet the way they did in the old days before anybody had anything. No, they won't come. All the children act close and caring and guilty right now, but they'll keep being too busy to get away to help him do anything until they won't bother saying it anymore. And it will be silent again.

Hattie and Joe were hard on them. Whipped them, too, some say. Back then everybody got a lickin' sooner or later, and with nine head and both Joe and Hattie havin' to work away from home so much—well. All those children still managed to grow up fine with good jobs. When Hattie and Joe got old and needy, seems none of them wanted to bother. Whether it was about any of what's rumored or just the times we live in—who knows. So they sent Jamarkis to do the chores when school was over and on weekends, and he never complained even when Hattie fussed at him.

All that time Hattie looked to Elizabeth. Hattie wasn't one to complain, even when her foot got a big hole in it. The doctor told her it was just fine. The next week it got so bad Hattie finally had to say something. Elizabeth came over, took one look at the wound and took her to another doctor, but by then, her foot didn't have a pulse. He had Elizabeth take her straight to the hospital, where he hoped he could save her leg, but Hattie came home without it. In a way, she blamed Elizabeth, even though everyone told her that the amputation saved her life.

Hattie had worked for Elizabeth for twenty years before the diabetes made that impossible. She as much as raised Elizabeth's daughter, Caroline, but Caroline got grown and married and moved to England. Hattie hadn't seen her in nine years and had never laid eyes on her son, called Seton. Hattie asked after them all the time. Caroline was special to her. That bright, sensitive little girl used to crawl up on Hattie's lap to show her the latest picture she had drawn or just to cuddle while Hattie sang the old spiritual songs and warmed her with her love. When Caroline married and moved to London, she sent Hattie drawings every Christmas of horses and hounds and castles and fancy balls that were her life now, a life that Hattie would never know.

Hattie shared them all with Elizabeth, who smiled with inner pride that her daughter was so caring. Together, they hoped for the day to come soon when they could all be together and the two boys, so dear to each of them, would meet.

Hattie was old school. Elizabeth and Caroline were her family, and when one of your family came home, you went to visit and to catch up. If they brought their own child, then it was the custom to bring a young relative along to keep the new child company.

When Caroline brought her own four year-old son, Seton, home with her for the first time, Jamarkis was four. Hattie called to say she'd be coming down and bringing Jamarkis to play. What a special day. Now, Caroline's son and Hattie's own grandchild could be friends. All of life was a full circle if you waited long enough.

Long before the two boys met, Hattie and Elizabeth had dreamt scenarios of how that day would be. "Caroline's all grown up now, very different and sophisticated," Elizabeth had warned Hattie. And so she seemed that afternoon—elegant and reserved—meticulously clad in linen, silk and a lot of expensive jewelry in spite of the casual gathering.

Looking at her, Hattie just shook her head and said, "My, oh my. You sho's not my little country girl no more."

For Elizabeth and for Hattie, the feeling was firm. It was full circle, loved ones growing under their watchful eyes, moving on, and coming back together in a new cycle of life and caring. And here they were, *Seton*: The slender, beautiful, quick-thinking little boy from the cultured landscape of London, and *Jamarkis*: The large, silent child as unpolished as his country surroundings—*Seton:* in white shorts, sailor shirt and tie, his soft white feet clad in too-expensive sandals that would far outlast their brief season of need, and *Jamarkis:* dressed up, even in the summer heat, in his best jeans, plaid shirt, and heavy brown oxfords that would carry him sturdily through the coming year. Underneath all that, the way Hattie and Elizabeth saw it, they were just four year-old boys who, by every measure, should know each other.

As the children started to play, Hattie was quick to correct Jamarkis, if he grabbed for a toy. "You be polite, Jamarkis. You knows better!" she admonished, just as she had corrected Caroline when she was small and new.

Soon Seton shoved Jamarkis out of the play area. Hattie said, quietly, "Now Seton, you wants to share things with your new friend." Caroline stiffened, her face oddly alien.

Moments later, when Jamarkis reached out to offer a toy to Seton, Caroline pulled her son away, with an angry, "NO! You get back! Don't you touch him."

Elizabeth was stunned. How could her daughter be so rude and unkind? She did the only thing she knew. She poured forced charm and cheer, her Southern emergency training, on the moment—talking purposefully—airily—almost giddily. Insisting on Hattie's attention. Running on about anything. Leaving no awkward space to spawn another dreadful moment.

"My goodness, Hattie, Jamarkis is certainly grown up for his age. I can't believe he is only four."

"Yes ma'am," Hattie said. "He just turned fo' las' month."

"Is he in preschool?"

"No, ma'am. They charges money for that. He has ta wait for first grade ta go."

"Well, he's a bright boy and he has you to help him. That should be enough."

Hattie didn't answer.

"So, do you help care for him?"

"Yes'm. Ah keeps him days while my daughter, Lily, works."

Hattie's cane rested against the chair and her shiny brown plastic legs shone noticeably in the afternoon light. "Then, you must be feeling stronger these days."

How would she know? Guiltily, she realized that it had it been more than six months since she had taken time to call.

"Mostly, ah do all right. Ah'm still able ta git goin' when ah needs to."

While Elizabeth kept up the conversational barrage, Caroline had no chance to say more. Her body language spoke for her. Repeatedly, she snatched things away from the large, bumbling child, her upper lip pursing in stern disapproval as she pulled Seton away from the little boy, thrusting out her hand to keep Jamarkis at bay. The afternoon stretched painfully until, at last, the sun's long rays began to find the porch.

Both Elizabeth and Hattie understood.

They could stop now.

With some awkwardness, Hattie struggled from her chair. “You come on, Jamarkis. Tell Ms. Elizabeth and Ms. Caroline goodbye.”

He came to her and stood there, mumbling his farewell. Seton never stopped pushing his truck across the floor and Caroline, not looking up, kept her focus on her son.

Elizabeth rose to walk their visitors to the door, still chattering, but smiling with relief that the end was in sight. At the door, she hugged Hattie, maybe too warmly and said good-bye to Jamarkis several times, waving to him lingeringly, as they went away. As she closed the door, she prayed that Hattie was not remembering Caroline’s face and its rejection written there of the woman who had loved her, helped her grow and, this afternoon, had offered her the only gifts she had to give, her time, her love, and the sharing of her flesh and blood.

“Thank god they’re gone!” Caroline muttered. “That child is uncivilized.”

“That’s Hattie’s grandchild!”

Caroline ignored her, “Did you see the way he kept taking Seton’s toys?”

“…and Seton grabbed far more than his share!”

“I don’t care. He has no manners, nor does he know his place.”

“He’s only four! And they’re poor, Caroline. He can’t have much to play with. But I can’t understand how coldly you treated them. Hattie loves you Caroline. That’s why she brought her grandson here so that Seton would have a friend and not be lonely.”

“I would never allow my son to associate with a child like that. Never! And while we’re here, don’t ever let him set foot on this place.”

Two days later, as soon as it didn’t seem too insulting to her mother, Caroline and Seton cut short their visit and flew back to London. Caroline had “scheduling commitments” among other, breezy excuses that could be acceptable to anyone who needed to believe them.

At Christmas, Elizabeth sent Hattie a vase of white roses, knowing they were her favorites. Just as always, Caroline sent Hattie a card, this time a stiff, professional photo of herself, her husband and Seton. Before tacking it up on her wall with the drawings from years past, Hattie called Elizabeth to thank her for the flowers and to tell her that the card had come. “The family is sho lookin’ beautiful,” she said. “I’m so proud that Caroline always remembers me. It’s the best Christmas I could get.”

The call reminded Elizabeth of how sad she, herself, felt these days, but she was deeply glad for Hattie’s sake. If truly, she could believe her words.

Beginning the following year, Caroline and Seton began coming home to visit every summer. Everyone in the neighborhood knew about it.

Hattie never came again to bring Jamarkis. Or even just herself. Nor was she asked to come.

Seton is sixteen now. As is Jamarkis. In all that time, no one has mentioned it.

So many years gone, but it still haunts Elizabeth. She regrets such things, especially today, even though Hattie can no longer be hurt by anything. Even though Hattie is crossing over toward a glorious, heavenly light too blinding to see cruelty.

As the dirt mounds up tall over Hattie's coffin, Elizabeth and Jamarkis stand watching. Differently. A blanket of fake green grass is spread to cover the dirt. Joe slumps a little when his spray of white roses is placed on top.

On Monday, Elizabeth will take time to write to Caroline to tell her the awful news.

Come Monday, Jamarkis will move in with Joe, never asking why he is the chosen one. Never complaining. Just knowing that things are.

CHEAP HAIRCUT

The money mattered. On his paltry income, even a haircut demanded some shopping around, but Cliff didn't really mind. He knew that one day he'd have money for expensive ones. Dinners out, too. And taxis. Yes, he'd have all of that. Cliff was going to be a big success.

For now, he thumbed through the yellow pages with the thoroughness of a stalker until he found the tiny ad for Anthony's Barber Shop that offered a haircut for much less than he'd found anywhere else. He phoned the number and a man with gruff, formality said, "Yes, we are open." And hung up.

It was a good twenty blocks away. But on his budget, Cliff was used to walking everywhere. He had even made a project of it. As often as he could since coming to business school, he had taken his Chicago street map and headed out in a different direction, both for exercise and to explore the city. Today he had the time. It was Saturday, with no heady classes in higher mathematics and statistics, no "ranking" struggles or practice interviews, no untaught-though-implied methodology for killing off your competition. No stress.

These days, Cliff was always well-dressed. He shopped with meticulous care, spending hours buying a pair of shoes, or suit-searching for classic, expensive tailoring and style occasionally built into things that he actually could afford. Once, someone who cared about him had drawn him aside and explained that Cliff's neat but cheap, trendy clothes labeled him as unpolished. The business world, he was warned, had lofty expectations where first impressions were crucial. From then on, Cliff had kept a standard. He wore pressed khakis instead of jeans, button-downs and polished brown shoes replaced his tee-shirts and sneakers, and a tweed jacket took the place of his old nylon windbreaker. In winter, he now wore a classic, double-breasted wool top coat instead of a rumpled parka.

With the change, he could feel attitudes around him change. Now he was part of the game.

Out here on the street though, his "standards" evoked a different response. As in most cities, neighborhoods can change within blocks, and he wasn't underway ten minutes when the streets grew dingier and the traffic lessened. Soon, people stared at him suspiciously as he passed by their battered stoops, and he felt more and more unsettled as the broken, subtly seething place slowly enveloped and isolated him.

The looks from men hanging out in the decaying neighborhood grew from curious to covetous. To them, his handsome coat translated to scores of crack or heroin. It made him look soft, an easy mark. Cliff thought of turning back, but according to the map he was within three blocks of the barbershop.

The neighborhood had imploded and had been abandoned except for a few skinny cats that darted in and out of the buildings. The former shops and homes leading to the barber's were mostly boarded up except for the few that had missing doors and jagged fringes of glass where windows used to be. Finally, with relief, he saw the barber pole standing red and white like a vibrant beacon, and he hurried to close the distance.

Up close, the barber shop looked disreputable. The windows were yellowed with grime and laced with cobwebs. It was steamy on the other side of the glass, making it hard to define what was inside but he could see someone dressed in white, standing in a brightly lit room. When Cliff tried the door it was locked. He knocked. And knocked again. Then he heard footsteps and the door bolt pulling back. When it opened, he was facing a surly young man who looked much like the others on the street—in his twenties, black, with long sideburns and a tiny goatee above strings of chain, black leather, denim and a pair of immaculately white, expensive, leather running shoes. Each ear was riveted with a half-dozen earrings, and he had a diamond stud in his nose. He couldn't be there for a haircut, Cliff thought. His hair was already styled in a Medusa-like halo of writhing dreadlocks.

He motioned Cliff inside and then locked the door before seating himself in the most comfortable chair where he pulled a slick magazine from inside his jacket and started flipping pages. Even at a distance, the content was hard to misinterpret. The pictures of voluptuous naked women in various stages of compromise were huge and explicit.

The barber, who ignored the young man, was the image of a neatly turned out professional with a dense gray mustache that reflected self-assurance and success. It was hard to conjure why such a dignified man would want this sort of character hanging around. The shop itself was spacious and clean even though the linoleum was missing in places. The huge wall-hung mirror had a chip or two, and on the shelf below it there were bottles of old-fashioned liquids, skin bracers and aftershave lotions along with three ancient shaving mugs, soft brushes, straight razors and an old-time leather strop. Clean combs and scissors were placed on a fresh towel beside them. There was a recognizable stability about it.

In front of it all were five brown leather barber chairs. Since there were no other customers, Cliff was invited to sit in the center chair and the barber placed a white cloth around him.

"I'm Anthony," he said. "And how would you like me to cut your hair today?"

"The same way. Just shorter, please."

"You make it easy," Anthony said and started trimming.

"Have you been here long?" Clifford asked, looking around the empty room.

"All my life. I started this here barber shop in 1962 fresh out of barber school. My wife, God rest her soul, and I raised a family right here on this block." In the mirror Clifford could see Anthony's pleasure at remembering. "It was a good, respectable place and," he added proudly, "my children all turned out just fine."

"That's something these days," Cliff said, involuntarily glancing at the dangerous-looking young man seated opposite him. "Where are they now?"

"Oh, my son's a lawyer in the city and my two daughters…one's a teacher at the university and the other…she's a momma. She and her husband got three kids…nice ones."

"I go to the university," Cliff said. "Maybe I've met your daughter. What department is…?"

Suddenly, there was a horrific crash outside. The front door started to rattle and shake. Someone on the other side seemed determined to get in. The barber looked up at the young man who remained sprawled, still engrossed in his magazine. More crashes. "Shank," he said to the young man who glanced up but didn't move. Cliff stiffened. Anthony put his hand on his shoulder to reassure him. Another crash and scuffling, and this time it sounded as if the door might break

Anthony crossed to the door and screamed at the confusion outside. "Get away from here you punks. You get away from here and leave me alone!"

The young hood looked up at the door until the rattling stopped and went back to his magazine. Suddenly, four faces appeared pressed against the dingy window, their features blurred by the coating of steam inside. Their heads started banging hard on the glass. Harder, and harder.

"My god," Cliff said, sitting upright and staring at the window.

"Don't worry," Anthony said. "They won't hurt themselves."

"What do they want?" Cliff asked, alarmed.

"Who knows," Anthony replied as he continued cutting.

Cliff tried to match his calm, but it was difficult as the room filled with more angry noise. Hands began scraping at the glass to see in better but the steam film on the inside prevented it.

Some of them moved back to the door and started assaulting it again. It began to creak—and splinter.

In the mirror the barber could see the shock on Cliff's face and shouted to the young punk still lounging on the other side of the room, "Hey, you, Shank," he ordered. "Get busy!"

With that, the young man got up, magazine in hand, went over to the door and opened it. Once the people outside all got a look at him the assault stopped. There was still some muttering.

Shank said to one of the intruders who, by then, had planted himself in the door frame, "Come on, man. You don't want to come in here." Suddenly, all of them began pushing into the entry—pressing into the room. Shank placed his arm casually across the open doorway, "Look," he said, "There ain't nothin' in here worth anything. So why don't you move along?"

Cliff saw them staring around the shop and looking intently at him, assessing him trapped there in the chair under the white sheet.

More muttering and shifting around, but they hadn't tried to gain any floor space. Shank checked out their jackets—bandanas—colors and said, "Look man, I'm Shank. Just ask Silvo. He's a friend of mine, you know, that crazy bastard, Silvo," he laughed as they relaxed a little. "He knows I hang here on this turf. He wouldn't want no trouble." They shuffled around out on the sidewalk. "Come on now. Why don't you just move along?" They weren't going so he dropped the smile, looked hard at the one almost inside the shop and said, "What's *your* name? I'll let Silvo know I ran into you next time we're chillin'."

Cliff guessed that whoever Silvo was, his name carried enough "mojo" to make the point. The leader, "Yo, manned" and the men did some head bobbing and reassembling, but finally they all got back in gear and swaggered on down the pavement. Shank casually relocked the door and resumed his seat.

The haircut, by now, was finished. In the midst of all that, Anthony had managed an excellent trim that Cliff surveyed with amazement. "Do you like it?" Anthony asked.

"It's wonderful," Clifford answered. "And how much?"

"$7.50."

"Are you sure? You're so good. Why so little?"

"I want you to come back," Anthony said smiling as he moved around the chair to face him. He took the money with the big tip Cliff offered and smiled warmly. "You will come back while you're still here, won't you?"

Cliff didn't respond. A few awkward moments elapsed and finally, he said, "I want to. I do. You did a great job. In fact," he assured him, "I don't know when I've had a better haircut."

Anthony relaxed. He beamed with pleasure that someone with expectations appreciated his work. There weren't too many of those anymore. It gave him a sudden flush of pride. "Then you'll come."

Cliff hesitated before speaking, "I want to come back here, really. But...."

"Yes?"

"...But ...those men...this neighborhood...is it safe?"

"Oh, yes," the barber said, "I've been here for forty years. I raised my family here, you know. Right here. And they all turned out just fine. This really *is* a good place...a *nice* neighborhood."

Cliff rose, hand extended, "Thank you." The older man took it gratefully, his eyes asking, hoping.

Shank unlocked the entry door and looked around outside before he let Cliff pass. When Cliff was on the street again, he could hear the bolt sliding into the old wooden frame behind him.

FINAL CHAPTER

Goodwill had inherited the last of her East Coast wardrobe except for one "proper going-out" dress that was dated and ten years old. Callie's clothes, such as they were, were jeans or shapeless dresses that she had stitched from cheap East Indian bedspreads bought at Cost Plus Imports in San Francisco. But then, where did she need to go? She had become what she wanted to be. A working artist, closeted in her studio, immersed in ideas and dreams with no one to prevent their expression.

In all that time, Callie hadn't been home. She was afraid to go back. She had vanished from Georgia five years ago with nothing, leaving her mother to defend her from the avalanche of disapproval and cruel gossip. Only her mother knew why she had gone—and understood. Her father didn't know and wouldn't listen.

Angry and embarrassed, her father hadn't spoken to her for years. During that time, something terrible had happened to his business forcing him to retire, an emasculated giant, confined to tending his flowers, reading *Standard and Poors,* and pretending she didn't exist.

Six months ago she heard from him. Her mother had suffered a stroke but he insisted that there was nothing Callie could do. Beyond that there were no specifics. He called weekly after that to report on her mother's condition, always speaking crisply and uncomfortably as strong men did when discussing personal matters. "Oh, we're fine," he'd say and his manner closed off further questioning.

Then, one day he brought her mother to the phone.

"It's Callie," he said and then Callie heard the fumbling, clacking, murmuring as her father tried to place the receiver, right end up, against her mother's ear.

Finally, "Callie! Callie! Callie?" high pitched and eager. "Is that you, Callie? I love you, Callie. Is that you?"

"Yes, mom, it's me, Callie. I miss you and I love you, too."

"Is that you? Is that Callie?" several times more before her father would take the phone away to tell her that, really, they were fine.

For weeks thereafter, it was always the same. It never got better.

During the last two months, his reassurances seemed hollow as his voice grew flat with a haunting mix of stoicism and fatigue, wavering with an old-people kind of definition that left her choked and struggling to speak. She realized that he would never tell her the truth. Nor could she do nothing and abandon them to diminish into illness and old age alone. She couldn't ignore it. She had to go home. And soon.

The Georgia landscape flowed flat and green beneath the little prop aircraft, a lush and palpable touchstone of home that intensified as the plane descended over the swamp. She could define the swollen roots of cypress bulging from mysterious dark water and see ripples as some slithery thing took refuge beneath its murky depths. It felt threatening as did coming home, and she tensed as the little plane settled awkwardly on the tarmac and taxied to within fifty feet of her parents.

In those days people went out to the landing strip to meet arrivals and she could see her parents clearly, connected figures standing quietly in the blowing grass beyond the edge. They didn't move. They waited. Expectant. Her huge imposing father, his posture as correct as always, looked toward the disembarking passengers; her mother, hunched and puffy, clung heavily to his arm. His smile, no longer teasing, seemed wistful and there out of habit, and, until Callie came close enough to look into his eyes, he didn't recognize her. She, too, had changed. She looked drawn and older, her hair, once bleached ash-blond by the Georgia sun, had darkened into brown from years spent isolated in her studio.

In spite of it, her mother recognized her instantly. Slowly, with effort, her arms and smile reached out to Callie as if her daughter—her own Callie—were the physical affirmation of life itself. It was shocking to see and, worse, to realize that, this was the best her mother would ever be.

Thank god, Callie thought, Thank god she had come.

There were so many soft, personal things to say, but for the next ten days as they sat together at home, her mother often dozed or drifted in a private world, unfocused and unable to understand. Callie said them anyway. Her father had become near-deaf, and her conversations with him had to be shouted. Each day her parents sat there so quietly, just listening to the sound of her as Callie fought to inject warmth into the silence, struggling to rescue the old bonds.

After dinner each night she helped her Mother ready herself for bed but when her father went upstairs she only watched, never demeaning his independence as he struggled to push his large frame from the chair, and then to stagger the first few steps, grabbing on to the furniture, before finally, shuffling painfully away.

Time was leaden—weighted with empty wishes, guilt, unsaids and impotent sorrow for what they had become, magnified by dread of what was coming. She went to bed at night and sobbed.

As Callie's last afternoon at home withered away, her father suddenly asked, "Would you like to go for a boat ride?" He voiced it with the same casual confidence he'd used every innocent, young day when they shared those childhood summers in the country. Back then, when the tide was right, he'd invite her to go and she'd giggle with delight as he swung her up on his strong, broad shoulders so that she could ride high to touch the trees as he strode down to the dock.

In those days, they had a fast little Chris Craft that he careened, top speed, around the river bends, inciting shrieks of excitement from everyone on board. Back then Isaac and the farm hands repaired and polished the cruiser to a boat show gleam. Now there was no one to winch a boat up on the ways and scrap and paint the bottom, to varnish the mahogany deck or troubleshoot the engines before putting the quick, sleek boat afloat again. Isaac was the only one left and he was nearly as old as her father.

The boat, too, was gone. An elderly bateau was all that was left.

They walked slowly to the dock where her father pulled an outboard motor from the shed. It was tiny by past standards but huge for his ability and, of course, he refused Callie's help. He staggered down the ramp and onto the dock where, huffing and grunting, he lowered it into the aluminum bateau Isaac had tied up alongside. Then he got down into the little craft and with enormous difficulty, attached the motor to the stern. She handed him the gas can that he had allowed her to carry and then he said, "So what are you waiting for? Come on young 'un, untie those lines and let's go for a ride!" It seemed so incongruous, making that big statement over their tiny skiff that with the motor and the two of them in it sank to within six inches of the gunwales. But he said it with that voice she knew—a strong, authoritative command that jump started the connection between them—and the river—and home.

The tide was very high, warning of fall's approach but the marsh was electric with young green and the summer sky above them was enormous—cerulean—filled with the huge puffy clouds that defined summer on the river. The boat purred through the creeks, a dot under the astonishing heaven, pushing away grasses that bent and swayed in their gentle wake. Callie had forgotten how vast and free it was out there. How overjoyed she had always felt. Still felt—in the middle of this constant place—she and her father together, explicit in the soft remembered past, the hard-edged present, and the future they would never be. She looked away from the air beating on her face and turned to smile at him, his tired, mottled face embracing it in kind. It is how she remembers him.

The next morning at the airport her parents stood there together by the tarmac exactly as they had when she first came—the first and final chapters about home remembered—watching her as she boarded the plane. She waved to them from the window hoping they could see her as the little aircraft taxied down the runway. And they were still standing there in the dry, blowing grass, staying with her, as the plane roared aloft and took her West again.

UNCLE FLOYD

Uncle Floyd was too mean to die. I'd figured that out long ago when I was eight and powerless to do anything about it. Certainly, he was the last person I needed around, now that my parents were gone and, at thirty-three, I was left to figure out the future of my family's Georgia farm by myself—from three thousand miles away in California where my husband Dave and I had lived since the early sixties. Now, ten years later, the mythic "California dream" that once drew us there seemed more an empty travelogue than a way to live.

When my parents died and left us the Georgia farm, it only took a year of comparisons to decide that country dull was wonderful—crazy or not, we would start over in backwoods Georgia where nothing was chic or "correct" or "connected" or even current.

Especially not Uncle Floyd. How ironic that he should be the first intrusion into that quietude. I'd just have to make quick work of him.

Just the mention of Floyd's name brought back my most recent dealings with him. Two years before, my mother had been hospitalized with terminal cancer. I couldn't imagine allowing that vibrant, intelligent woman to slowly disengage from life amid a chilling network of tubes and needles in a tiny sterile room monitored by colorless people who moved in and out indifferently. I wanted to bring her home, but first, I would have to make a few changes to the ancient farmhouse.

Floyd advertised himself as a "master craftsman." So I arranged with him long distance to replace my mother's old high-sided bathtub with a more accessible shower. It was a simple job, and he had a full month to get it done. I checked his progress through weekly calls to Isaac, the farm's manager. "No," Isaac would say each time, "I go over ta Mista Floyd's every Monday and he always say he has somethin' else needs doin'. He ain't been here all week, and that tub, she sho ain't finished."

"Isaac," I begged. "Please tell him that I'm bringing Mother back on Friday and it *has* to be!"

"Ah'll do my best." But I could tell he didn't have much faith in the result.

On Friday, when I brought my mother home, her little bathroom looked like a junk shop. It was full of tools, broken floor tiles and other debris. The tub was gone and there were holes in the wall behind where the faucets had been. Black tar stuck to the floor in places where the tile should be, and in the corner stood a tiny metal shower stall that wasn't even functional. A month later, when my mother died, the bathroom looked just the same and I had seen nothing of Uncle Floyd.

Isaac returned his tools to him and then finished the job himself. Floyd's bill came a week later. Infuriated, I priced the shower stall to be sure. It had cost less than fifty dollars. Floyd's bill was for six hundred.

Of all my relatives, it figured that he was the one who still lived just down the road. Not long after the funeral, while I was at the farm alone, he called. "I need to talk to you. It's real important. Can I come over tomorrow mornin'?"

At that time we were absentee owners. If anyone annoyed "a local," the usual retaliation was to set fire to your place and burn it to the ground. I couldn't tell him no, nor could I hide. So, the following morning, there he was on my doorstep, hat in hand, the same hat I remembered from twenty years ago when I'd seen him last, an old tan fedora with dark stains leaking out from under the sweat band.

His bony face had become a hatchet, matching his blue eyes that were as cold and cunning as before. I could never forget the meanness that was waiting in them. It suited him that he was thinner now. His bones stuck out, and he was bent over at the shoulders. He wore gray duck country work pants and a faded plaid shirt. They were clean and pressed, of course. He had come calling. But he hadn't bothered to polish his battered brogans.

He smiled and nodded as I opened the door. "Good mornin'," he oozed. "It's real good to see you."

"Hello, Uncle Floyd." It was formal and cool, and my skin prickled as I let him pass and enter the living room.

When we sat down, he took a ladder-back chair. He was on business. I did the same. There was no need to give him the impression that I was comfortable with him there.

He smiled at me broadly, showing his full set of store-bought replacement teeth, and started with Rule One on how to approach a lady, especially if you want to talk her into something.

"My gracious, it's *good* to have you back. You're lookin' *lovely.* How you been doin'? The fishin's been bad lately. Miss Margie"—whoever that might have been—"says to say 'hello'. She can't get out, you know. I plan on bringin' you some scuppanongs soon's they're ripe. Looks like fall's comin' early this year…and"—all the maddening, ingratiating preamble of pleasantries that smoothed him up to the real reason why he'd come. I knew he'd finally arrived when he got to the part, "Honey, I'm *so very sorry* about your momma and daddy passin'."

My parents hadn't been on speaking terms with him for years, not since I was in my teens. Floyd had managed the farm for my father, John, until the last cattle sale, a transaction that, for once, could be legally tracked. It seemed Floyd's counting method of "one cow for John, two for me" had netted Floyd a brand new, red Chevy pickup truck. My father's share was a three thousand-dollar loss which Floyd somehow thought he could explain away. And why not? He'd always been adept at talking his way in and out of anything. But not that time.

"I know what a burden it puts on you," he continued, his voice a sympathetic purr, "and I know you don't have any experience runnin' this place. It's real complicated and you're such a lady, a city gal and all. You know it's sad, but there are people out there you need to watch out for. They're sneaky and connivin', and they'll try to take advantage of you. But…" he shook his head, "You won't ever have to worry. You and me, we're family. I looked out for you when you were just a little bitty thing livin' out here all those summers, and I won't let nothin' happen. I'm here to help you every way I can."

I thanked him politely.

He moved on. "Now everybody knows you inherited a whole lot of money." I winced. At last report, the gossip mill placed my "fortune" at an insane eighty million dollars! My father's business had been sold years ago. There were few assets, just some wild forest land and a small trust that was about enough to pay Isaac a full wage for life and to care, minimally, for this rough, former fishing shack that had grown randomly over the years into a leaky, haphazard structure covered with chipping paint and with no architectural merit to redeem it. The land was beautiful in a natural unkempt way but it was too far from anything important for anyone to want it—

except Dave and me. So even though the figure was preposterous, there was no arguing with the community's appraisal. My father had been one of them, he had succeeded, and, for whatever reason, they wanted it to be true.

So I said nothing.

Uncle Floyd looked at me solemnly. "We're family and family looks after each other. I would never want to see you get taken."

"Thank you, Uncle Floyd. But I really don't think I'll need to trouble you."

"Now listen. I mean it. You can't be too careful. There're scoundrels out there just waitin' to cheat you out of your money."

"Really, I'm fine. I have the bank looking after all the financial things."

"Oh, you won't need them either. I know all about bankin' and handlin' things like that. I've gotten successful. *Real* successful."

I looked at him fingering the battered fedora in his lap.

"And I'd like to offer you this opportunity to share it with me. It's a blue chip investment. A sure winner."

"Really."

"I have this wonderful place I opened up over in Carolina." He shifted in his chair and straightened up for the pitch.

His tone turned sly, "I've got the sheriff in tow. You know what I mean. And his deputies, too. We don't get any trouble."

I stiffened a little. "What *kind* of trouble?"

"Oh, you know. Raids. We don't get any of that stuff." He lowered his voice a bit. "I was smart enough to see to that. It takes money to make money," he chuckled, "so you pass a little of it around. It's worth it. There's a *lot* of money to be made over there. A *whole* lot."

"Why would you be raided?" A mix of fascination and alarm seeped into the question.

"The girls, I guess."

"The girls!"

"Oh, this is no cat house. Nothin' like that. And like I said, I've got plenty of protection. We just do a little gamblin', and the girls are there to dance with the customers and encourage 'em a little. You know, keep 'em happy. You'd just think it was a dance hall, that's all. It's a *real nice* place. Lots of business, especially Friday nights. Friday's payday." He looked at me with those icy eyes that belied his thin-lipped smile stretched over those perfect alabaster teeth. "You see, I know you've got lots of cash, and I'm worried about somebody tryin' to take it from you. You'd be well off puttin' some of it in my place where it'd be safe. I'm family, you know."

I rose to end the scene. "Thank you, Uncle Floyd, but I really don't think I'm interested."

"You shouldn't say that," he warned. "You'd be bound to regret it. I think you'd best think it over before you say no. I'm sure you'll change your mind."

I thought fast to keep the subject from resurfacing. "I'm sorry, Uncle Floyd. I can't. You see, my father also didn't want me 'to be taken.' He wanted to make sure there would always be a way to take care of this place. So he put the bank in control of everything. I have nothing on my own. I don't have a dime to invest in anything."

Reluctantly, Floyd lifted himself out of the chair. I was already on my way to the front door which I held open for him.

"You think about it, now." I ushered him out. "You think about it real hard," he said as I closed the door.

Uncle Floyd wasn't finished. He came over just about every day. I knew who it was from the roar and clank of his red Chevy pickup the minute it came out of the woods until, at long last, it grudgingly lumbered into the yard. Floyd never believed in undue haste. He'd amble up the steps into the kitchen where he'd drink coffee laced with twelve teaspoons of sugar and turned yellow by a half pitcher of cream. He'd stir it around and around, clink, clink, clink, and then push the spoon standing in it to one side and hold it with his thumb so he could slurp without poking his eye out. He never stayed for less than an hour.

At that point, I couldn't wait for Dave to arrive from California—my creative, charming, highly literate, New Yorker husband, Dave, with his penchant for quick-witted conversation. Surely Dave would find a way to get rid of him.

Instead, Dave found Floyd fascinating.

The first morning he was home again, he and I stood together in the kitchen making breakfast. For both of us there was a magic about morning in this tranquil, private place that cancelled all the false starts and corrupted endings in our lives as if none had ever happened.

As we held each other close, enjoying the quiet serenity, a faint noise became discernible—a rumbling resembling distant thunder—a sinister growl that grew more threatening as it came roaring and clanking down the road.

"What the hell is that?" Dave asked, pulling away.

"Just Uncle Floyd," I grinned. I couldn't wait for the encounter.

The truck hove into the yard and clattered to a halt. The engine went dead, and in a minute Floyd came in. Introductions were made and then we all sat down at the kitchen table. Floyd did most of the talking about the usual inconsequential things while he stirred and stirred his yellow brew. I watched Dave's face as the mug and spoon began its ascent toward Floyd's mouth. Dave's expression was all I had hoped for. I struggled not to laugh as he tensed and sat up straight, ready to stand rescue should the spoon stab Floyd in the eye.

Floyd just rambled on, oblivious. He never missed the chance to cage an audience; it meant he wouldn't have to go back to work, if, indeed, he still had a job. Already he had missed the morning boat to Green Island where, supposedly, he was restoring the old plantation house.

Dave encouraged him to stay. He found Floyd's conversation so arresting that soon he hardly noticed the rise and fall of his dangerous stirring tool.

"You see out there?" Floyd motioned toward the river. "Behind the trees is Green Island. That's where I spend my time, and that's how I know what they're *really* doin' out there." He pursed his lips and nodded knowingly, watching Dave's face, until he could read in it that anticipation had become unendurable. Then, Floyd opened his eyes wide and leaned across the table, looking around furtively before whispering, "They're…runnin'… a white slave operation!"

"A what?"

"You heard it right. I'm not funnin' ya." He sat upright again and the clink, clink, clink resumed.

"How do you know that?" Dave demanded.

"Cause they're bringin' in wimmen. I've seen 'em. They're bringin' em in on planes and landin' 'em out yonder in the cow pasture. That way nobody will know. I've seen 'em do it, lots of times. They're pretty fine wimmen, too…nice lookin'," he mused. Then his voice turned secretive and low. "After they get 'em there, those wimmen disappear. Nobody knows a thing about 'em." He paused. "But *I* do." Dave's attention was guaranteed. "They're bein' *sold!* I tell you, *sold into white slavery*!"

Dave was hooked. Not surprisingly, he'd never met anyone like Floyd, and he couldn't get enough of him. Floyd was the bizarre counterpoint to our reclusive new life of solitude, books, and nature. Floyd—was entertainment.

Even more riveting than Floyd's *white slavery* announcement was his report on drug running. Drugs were one of the reasons we had decided to leave California. We'd seen enough of the wreckage that ensued. The hint that drugs might be surfacing here, even from this crazy old man, was unsettling.

As yet, we hadn't moved to Georgia permanently, and we returned to California for weeks at a stretch while I finished up freelance contracts as a writer and Dave fulfilled his final obligations as executive producer in a start-up cable TV company. We left Isaac as daytime manager to look after the place. We didn't need anyone at night. Out here no one ever locked their doors, even when they went away. Floyd, also, had been keeping an unrequested eye on the place.

After one such trip, we hadn't even unpacked when Floyd appeared and invited himself in for coffee. He took a deep, noisy slurp or so before tilting back in his kitchen chair and beginning his report—slowly—in a voice dripping with smug authority. "You know," he said, "they're usin' your place when you're not here."

"Who is?" Dave asked, his tone brittle. "What are they doing?"

Floyd didn't exactly answer that. "I see the strange cars come in here after Isaac leaves at night."

"What could they possibly do here at night?" I asked.

"Mischief."

"Mischief?"

"Mischief. And I know what it is."

"For heaven's sake, WHAT?"

Crazy old coot or no, he was starting to make us both edgy.

"I'll tell you what, and you need to be careful." He paused. "While you're both away they're runnin' *dope* right across your dock. And you know what's more?"

"WHAT?" we asked in unison.

Floyd paused for dramatic emphasis, "The sheriff is about to arrest the lot of 'em." Then looking straight at Dave, he added, "And he's gonna pin it all on *you!*"

I felt a sudden chill. Ever since childhood I had known about smuggling along the coast. For more than a hundred years, Georgia's marsh hammocks and creeks had provided great opportunities for profiteers outside the law. Crooked little waterways, dense fogs, tricky tides, sandbars, and a myriad of barely accessible marsh islands had made the coast a perfect place to hide almost anything. Allegedly, Blackbeard the Pirate stashed millions in treasure which no one had ever found. Then, during Prohibition, rum runners used the hammocks to conceal their Cuban contraband. Near our house was Bottle Hammock, a place that was once used to store hundreds of gallons of Cuban rum until an all-clear was given to move it to the mainland. Eventually the "revenooers" found out about it, and the hammock's stash was transformed into a carpet of glass that still remained to document the raid.

Even now, the watery, complicated, and largely unpopulated coast remained the perfect place for illicit activities. Instead of rum, ships brought drugs from Latin America, off-loaded them at sea onto shrimp boats which, in turn, transferred them onto smaller vessels that could maneuver the inland creeks. Now, when things went wrong and traffickers had to run for it, instead of rum bottles floating down the river, there were marijuana bales, sometimes by the hundreds. If anyone saw them, and they were impossible to miss, they never said a word. No need to get shot being a hero or, even worse, offend some enterprising neighbor who might hold it against you.

Soon after Floyd's "pin it all on you" report, we returned to California for a week. When we came back East again and heard the news, Floyd had earned for himself a new level of credibility.

He came over the minute he knew we were home. "I told you so." The old man heh-heh-heh'd like the witch in some fairy tale that had scared me witless as a child. "Soon's you left, they raided your place. They captured a bunch of Airstream trailers comin' outa here, 'cept there was no dope in 'em 'cause the fog was too thick that night and the bateaux couldn't find the shrimp boats out there in the sound to make the transfer. So they never got the stuff to shore. The ships probably threw it overboard. There must have been tons of it floatin' around out there in the sound."

Then Floyd made the report personal. "Just like I told you before, the law knew it was planned for your place. Those dopers had your maps with all their landin' sites marked on 'em. Those people they caught, they were all stayin' over there at the fish camp and the law had a wire tap on 'em for months. They got the leader, too." Floyd paused for emphasis, then smiled sinisterly at Dave. "He was a guy about your age. From Ca-li-for-nia. The law was real interested in knowin' where *you* were, and when they found out you'd left, they thought you might have gone so's not to look involved." Snickering, he added, "And when they heard you were in *California*...well...." He held the ends of his thumb and forefinger together to measure an infinitesimal space, "I told ya they were that close to pinnin' it on you." Floyd was hard to dismiss after that.

A month later, we returned to California for the final time before moving our lives entirely to Georgia. In our absence, Floyd also had made big plans, hatching his own concrete inroad into our future. The morning after we arrived, we heard the Chevy roaring out there in the woods and were waiting at the kitchen door when Floyd clattered into the yard. We watched, curious, as he struggled to drag a stack of two-foot-long wooden boards from the truck bed and bring them up the kitchen steps. The wood was beautiful, thick textured, and cut expertly into shingles of varying widths.

"This here's just what you need to put on this old house. You gotta admit, it looks pretty shabby right now." Then he smiled with satisfaction, "I made 'em myself. Hewed 'em by hand just like Dan'l Boone, and I made 'em out of cypress. They'll be here long after you two are gone."

They were beautiful, and I was grudgingly impressed.

"I can do your whole house for you," he said. "Hand cut 'em, just like these."

I wasn't so sure. "I don't know. That's a lot of work. It would take you at least a year."

"Oh, no. Cuttin' 'em should take me two months at most, then another to put 'em up."

Dave was sold immediately, and he looked at them with lust. Just before going West, he had spent three weeks scraping and painting the river house. He hadn't been able to stand the splotches of built-up paint and bare wood that gave the house a leprous look. Not that his intentions equated with results. Most of the build-up defied his efforts to remove it, and in the end he had settled for at least making the house all one color by painting over the top of everything. Within a week, the salt air had caused bubbling and peeling in places. Some thick spots that had repulsed his efforts were now bare, the dead paint resting in messy piles all over the ground waiting for him to clean them up. And start again.

"Think of it," he said. "I would never have to paint again."

For work and materials, Floyd wanted eight thousand dollars which, given the potential savings, didn't seem that much, and Dave was anxious to close the deal.

I had too many cows and bathtubs lurking in my memory. In my opinion, Floyd was a consummate con, and I had vowed never to trust him under any circumstances. I wouldn't even discuss it. If Dave wanted those shingles, *he* could deal with him.

"Don't worry about a thing," he assured me. "This won't be like blindsiding some naïve woman." I shot him a 'could kill' look. "This will be man to man, and I can handle him."

The next day Floyd came by and asked for the eight thousand up front to buy supplies. Dave gave him a check noted, "Paid in Full."

The day after that, Floyd came over driving a brand-new Oldsmobile sedan, eight thousand dollars worth of metal and luxury.

Sumptuous green spring drifted into summer. Sunshine lingered longer on the grass and colored the trees far into evening. The sky turned cerulean above the marsh, and the river lapped in the afternoon breeze in lazy invitation to swim or fish or crab. Both the humidity and temperature began to climb. The lyrics in the song *Summertime* said it all. "Summertime, when the livin' is easy."

Floyd subscribed to every word of it.

After six months, Floyd had cut enough shingles to do two short sides of the eight-sided house, or so he said. He never put any of them up. He still kept coming around for coffee and excuses. By mid-July Dave had to go away on business, and the minute he left, Floyd quit coming around all together, even for morning coffee. Then in early August, the day after Dave came back, there was Floyd with a square of shingles and tools "ready to go to work." The sound of metal hitting nails brought a cautious smile to Dave's face. The hammering continued until noon. Dinner time.

For Floyd, dinner fell into the long siesta category. It lasted until the next morning when he returned, hammered for a while and then came in for coffee. By then, Dave couldn't trust himself and left the room. Floyd was unfazed. His time-out lasted the usual hour. That, as I pointed out to him, left just two hours before dinner.

"Guess I'd best get back to work," he said as he slowly rose from his chair.

"Will you be back after dinner?"

Floyd looked at me as if I had no brains at all.

"Too hot."

Soaring temperatures, however, never dimmed Floyd's inventiveness. His repertoire of reasons he could not work was astonishing. After not showing up for a full week, his Monday morning explanation was, "It's so hot I had to rest my saw. It overheats, you know."

After the next absence, his excuse to Dave was, "My car was actin' up."

"You know you could have called, and Isaac would have picked you up."

"Oh, I never like to trouble nobody."

The look Dave gave him could have disintegrated Floyd and the Olds, and it warned him to stay on the job for a while—"a while" being two whole days. The next excuse was indisputable. It was medical, "My back's been ailin' real bad."

"All right," Dave snarled. "But I'm sick of your lame excuses. Just do the damn work, and it will be over." In answer, Floyd assumed the victimized attitude of someone solid and decent who was being whipped with a cat-o-nine-tails to the point of bleeding. "I don't know how I can make you understand," he murmured. "I just want to do right by you and make this old place look like Dan'l Boone himself had done this job, and all I get is ingratitude in return."

"Don't go there," Dave hissed. "Just put up the damn shingles!" He was spitting uncontrollably with every word.

"But it's you I'm worried about," Floyd said. "You might ought to see a dentist."

At that point, only one wall was finished out of eight. Two courses of shingles had been nailed to the second wall leaving sixteen more rows to get to the top. If Floyd finished the third row and kept going, it would take twenty days to finish the second wall. Of course, Floyd never worked weekends.

Dave's control over the project was now limited to crunching numbers. He decided to do the math. "So, I figure that to cut enough shingles to cover two walls took four months, times six more walls will take him twelve months to finish that part. Then to apply them, let's see, that's twenty-five days per side, times eight sides…that's close to seven months to get them on the walls. Correction. At Floyd's current rate it would come to fourteen more months. Figure rain days and holidays and heat, add a hurricane or two and, oh yes, the inevitable 'unknown', then refigure everything exponentially in 'Floyd time', and we should have a shingled house in just about four years." His face grew alarmingly flushed and he began to stammer. "Four years of watching him drive my eight thousand dollars into this yard. Four years of watching him and that car get more feeble every day. Four years of that old goat hanging around here drinking coffee and goldbricking. Four years of hell, and I'll never even get to enjoy the house if and when he *does* finally finish it."

"Why not?"

"I'll have died of a heart attack from the stress by then."

I laughed. "Maybe I'll just have you put away. That's not quite so final. And when I visit you, I'll share Uncle Floyd's latest reasons for taking so long. And I'll tell you about all the latest projects he's developing for us."

"Very funny."

"Where's your sense of humor? Besides, you're the one who said not to worry, you could handle him. Remember?"

"Thanks for mentioning it."

I laughed again. "You're letting that old dodger get the best of you. I think you're losing it."

"Almost," he said, narrowing his eyes, "But not quite."

That margin grew thinner every day.

Actually, Dave's timeline was overly optimistic. The project started in late winter. Spring and summer had passed and now it was October and time for the emergence of the so-called Georgia state bird, the sand gnat. Floyd made it clear that he didn't work in gnat weather either.

"Why don't you just use bug spray?" Dave asked.

Floyd looked shocked. "That stuff's dangerous."

"Well then, why don't you plug in a fan or something and blow them away."

"Too expensive." Then he just stood there. Waiting.

"Oh. Got it!" Dave said. "OK. OK!!!" He reached in his pocket. "Here." He thrust four twenties at him. He was surly now. "Go get a *big* one!"

"No need to get upset."

The next morning, Floyd didn't show until eleven. He came accompanied by a huge stand fan that, according to Dave, could easily have blown down the Walls of Jericho without the help of either Joshua or a battle.

"The Walls of Jericho!" I roared.

"Right," Dave muttered. "Going biblical must mean the end is nigh. Can't you see how fast I'm declining just having to deal with that jerk? It's frightening!"

I resisted the urge to tease and got serious, "Can't you find some clever, creative way to make him complete the job?"

"What's left?"

"Not much, I guess, short of mayhem."

"And I feel it coming," he said. Without laughing, he gave me a hug.

But at least the fan was working and so was Floyd. He came back after dinner and put on another row. In a few days he was halfway up two sides of the house, and Dave could speak rationally for a change. The next morning, Floyd borrowed our ladder and finished another row. Then work stopped. He came in for coffee. He clinked the spoon around, and around, then pushed it to one side to take a slurpy sip. Dave didn't give a damn if he rammed that spoon all the way through his head, except this would only give him another excuse to stop work. So he sat sullenly. And listened.

"You've seen me havin' to climb down off that ladder every shingle or two to bring up more, haven't you? Now that's real tirin'. Even worse, it's not efficient. Now if I had some scaffolding, I could take up a load first thing and work along the whole side of the house without movin' anything. See what I mean?"

In spite of himself, Dave had to admit he was right. "How much?"

"I figure about three hundred ought to do it. That's what they're gettin' up there at that rental place in Richmond Hill. Three hundred dollars and twenty-three cent to be exact."

After acquiring the company's name, Dave wrote a check made payable to them. Of course Floyd had to get a truck to haul the scaffolding. He'd gotten rid of his Chevy when he bought the Olds. The next day he presented us with a bill for one hundred and twenty-four dollars and eighty-two cents for the rental, plus another twenty-five dollars and sixty-four cents for the extension cords he had to buy so he could haul the fan up and reach the level where he was working.

Four days later, Dave had just ended a discussion with him outside when Floyd put his foot on the scaffolding as if to start his climb. Suddenly he turned around and sagged against the metal rungs. "You know, I'm gettin' old." There was a sad, wistful tone in his voice. "I just can't work the way I used to. This cuttin' the shingles by hand, that's awful hard work and it takes lots of time. Then puttin' 'em up, that's a real strain on an old man like me."

Dave wasn't about to play his game. Floyd would just have to come right out and say it.

Floyd didn't mind. "I figure if I hire a helper, I can go more than three times as fast as I could by myself. We could finish the rest of the shingles and have 'em up in two months. Course, that will take a little money."

"You bid eight thousand dollars on this job and you were paid up front… *all* of it."

"I know, but there were so many expenses."

"Like what? A fancy new Olds?"

"I have to have transportation," he said, hurt. "And here I am, working for you, doin' this special job to make your house look as good as if Dan'l Boone had done it himself. He'd be proud, too."

"Dan'l Boone is dead!" Dave snarled. "He'll never know."

"Still," Floyd went on, "here I am, givin' you my considerable skill and time, and I can't even buy groceries. I'm workin' for nothin'."

"Now wait a minute! You'd be way ahead if you hadn't bought that car or had finished the job on time!"

"Now, that's not exactly accurate. You know that eight thousand dollars I mentioned in the beginning? That was just a loose estimate, and when I said how long it would take me to do it right…*really* right, the way you'd want it, the way Dan'l….Well how could I know that the workin' conditions would be *so bad* and cause me to hold up every now and then?" Annihilation blazed in my husband's eyes as Floyd continued, "Anyway, I don't think I'll be able to keep on goin' if I can't get paid a little more so I can do my job. And not starve."

It was tempting, but Dave kept his hands to himself and held his tongue. He just wanted it finished.

"How much?"

"Another six would do it."

"Okay, six hundred dollars." Dave shook his head. His voice was weary.

"No." Floyd corrected. "Six *thousand*."

"SIX THOUSAND! ARE YOU CRAZY?" Then he answered himself. "No, I think not."

Floyd just slumped there, waiting.

"Tell you what. I'll give you another three. That's to hire someone to help you cut and finish installing *all* the shingles. I expect it done, ALL OF IT, in two months. Not one day more! All right?"

"If you say so," Floyd said sadly.

Things went well for a week. Floyd produced a strong-bodied man in his late forties, with cropped hair and an orderly manner and appearance.

"This here is General," Floyd said by way of introduction. We hesitated. We weren't sure if General was his name or his former rank, although the latter seemed unlikely. We'd just be careful—wait and see.

It was winter now and cold. The following Monday, General showed up alone and Dave went outside to determine what happened to Floyd.

"Oh, Mister Floyd told me to come on by myself," he answered. "He couldn't come today."

"And why not?"

"Oh, he's pretty old, you know, and he says he can't work out in the cold."

It took Dave thirty seconds to get in the car and roar out of the yard. He arrived at Floyd's place with a stream of dust still hanging in the air behind him.

Smoke emanated from a metal flue sticking out of the side of Floyd's dilapidated workshop, a building put together with scraps of lumber, broken plywood, rusted metal roofing, and tar paper. Dave made straight for the workshop door, flung it open—and gasped. Floyd was sitting, tilted back in a wooden chair with his feet up on the edge of an old oil can that served as a makeshift heater. Stench billowed forth from inside, a lung-wrenching, putrid stench Dave couldn't begin to identify.

"What the hell are you burning in that thing?" he asked, his voice choking.

Floyd reared back a little more and drew out the words for emphasis, "C-o-o-n s-h-i-t. Burns real good don't it?"

By now, Dave had recovered. "You thieving old varmint!" he roared. "You lazy, sneaky, good-for-nothing, lying reptile! You piece of worthless crap."

Floyd sat looking at Dave…unmoved.

"YOU BASTARD!" Dave shouted.

Suddenly Floyd was on his feet facing him indignantly.

"You can't prove that," he said.

It took General, working alone, a week to create a machine that could cut shingles that looked nearly as handmade as ones that could have been created by the authentic, he-who-shall–remain-nameless, himself. It took an additional two and a half weeks to make enough for the remaining six sides. Then he brought in a helper and after six more weeks, the house was finished. The final three-fourths of the job cost Dave another four thousand, six hundred dollars. Floyd came away with a brand new Oldsmobile, plus three thousand dollars in his pocket for doing, although even this was debatable, about three weeks' worth of work. And spring had come and gone again, for the second time since Uncle Floyd and his hero Dan'l had hammered themselves into our lives.

But it was over.

That afternoon when we sat serenely sipping wine out on the river bluff, the conversation inevitably turned to Floyd. It was short, of course. Dave raised his glass to me, "At last…to having him finally out of our lives."

We clinked glasses and smiled calmly at each other. Indeed, life would be different now but why did I feel such a sense of loss? Even after all that had happened, the aftertaste was strangely sweet—like the dangerous library paste everyone ate in the first grade. Because it was forbidden, and we liked it.

SEE AND BE SEEN

It was so far back in the woods hardly anybody would have found it. You'd have to have wanted to go there. And seeing the place, who would, unless you were family, or the welfare people, or the sheriff checking up on something.

The spot was recognizably the rural South. The dirt yard was strewn with plastic toys, most of them broken and just left there. Sparse clumps of grass and weeds struggled to grow in defiance of the six small children, half of them in diapers, who relentlessly trampled them. As Ann drove into their clearing among the pines, they stopped doing what they were doing and stared at her, each of them suspicious and guarded as if, for some undefined reason, she had come to harm them.

In their midst stood a battered metal house trailer with a few rows of turnip greens planted alongside and a concrete block in front of the door that served as the stoop. No adult came out of the trailer to greet her, even though a face or two appeared behind a window curtain which fell back in place the minute they caught sight of her watching.

Ann turned off the engine, sat in her car and waited, trying to will away the grinding feeling the place gave her by telling herself to stop obsessing, that she couldn't fix everything. Besides, today her concern was for David.

Gradually, the children lost interest and wandered off. Then the door to the trailer opened, and David, a slight, dark-brown-skinned boy, stepped out.

She was stunned by the look of him set against these shambling surroundings. She had never seen him dressed in anything other than a tee shirt, jeans, and shabby, ancient sneakers. But here he was, wearing a starched white shirt, neatly-new khakis, and shoes so shiny and unmarred they certainly had been purchased especially for today. He looked shyly at her, a little hesitant, almost embarrassed as she smiled and motioned him into the seat beside her.

Carefully, she maneuvered the car through the yard clutter and headed back down the rutted, sandy road to the highway for the hour-long drive into Savannah. David sat erect and silent. It was disquieting. Awkward.

"David," she began, talking to his profile. "Is your family still all right about this?"

"Yes, ma'am."

"If the doctor says he can fix it, are they still willing to let you go ahead with it?"

"Yes, ma'am."

"You remember that today we're just going to see what the doctor has to say?"

"Yes, ma'am. I know."

She had gotten to today with methodical care. She had medical assurance that David's condition was correctable. The money was there in a little fund meant to help neighborhood people who possessed no hope, and in her purse was the signed consent form from his family. Still, she was uneasy. She knew by the way he was dressed that he was prepared for only one kind of news, the words that would sanction his access to a much different world than he had known—the one she had promised, the one that always slipped inexorably out of reach the moment he looked people full in the face. That's when the whole of David, the gentle, intelligent boy she knew, just disappeared, and all that others saw was his right eye, overgrown with blood-red veins, wandering uncontrollably around in its socket while the left eye looked straight at them. At that moment, David became grotesque. People didn't want him around. It was too uncomfortable.

Even Ann had reacted the first day she met him when he'd come to the farm looking for work. For a while, he had skillfully avoided looking at her, but, when finally their eyes met, she had felt a surge of pity and a compulsion to look away. It had felt like falling with nothing to grab, but she had caught herself, grimly determined to concentrate on his face as if there were nothing disturbing about him. Then she had talked to him for some time, curious about him, but also making sure that the unsettling thing she saw didn't reflect something more alarming. Finally, satisfied, she had given him the job.

When David first came to her he was only thirteen. Already, she had tried out most of the neighborhood teenagers. Usually, one of them who needed quick money would come looking for part-time work. There was a predictable sameness to the stream of them. Once presented with the reality of mucking stalls, pitching hay, or splitting firewood, most of them never came back. The sad truth was that it was easier for any of them to peddle a little dope or beg cash from relatives, or simply steal it. The juvenile record book was filled with names from this desperate place.

David was different.

"Yes, ma'am" and "No, ma'am" were about all she got from him in the beginning until gradually, and more often, it was a cheerful, "I could do that for you Ms. Ann, if you'd just show me." Considering his life, his optimism was incongruous. Perhaps the isolation assigned him by his face left him grateful for any kindness. Beyond that, she knew nothing about his dreams nor could she ask. Why bring up something that could never be? She would never want to hurt him.

For months, she had tried to avoid thinking about David's handicap. The more she knew him, the less she noticed. But when strangers visited, it was clear how the eye plundered his life—how even pleasant days were suddenly savaged by others who regarded him as a freak and cruelly, made no effort to conceal it. Increasingly, she felt shame at being normal until it became unthinkable to do nothing.

Fixing the eye wasn't a topic she could broach comfortably. Just bringing it up might make him think she was just one more person who found him repugnant. She could, at least, discover if his condition was correctable.

Ann had been careful in selecting a physician. Dr. Scott was considered one of the best ophthalmologists in the region; and, equally important, when she visited him to discuss David's case, he proved to be warm and understanding. He seemed genuinely engaged when she presented David as a remarkably responsible, bright fifteen year-old whose entire future would be compromised unless something could be done about the damaged eye that floated so disconcertingly.

"Ah, yes," Dr. Scott said, his voice reassuring. "It's called 'wandering eye'—just the way it looks. In most cases, fixing the eye is a simple procedure with virtually no risk of complication."

"So, you really can fix it?"

"Almost certainly. Of course, I'll have to examine him to be sure."

She smiled broadly, awash with excitement and bursting to tell David.

"When should I bring him in?"

The doctor seemed surprised that David's parents wouldn't be coming but he asked, pleasantly, "Is he a relative?"

"No…no, not really," she hedged, surprised by her own vagueness. She looked down at the floor where she noticed the doctor's shoes, his very, very expensive shoes. "David is more… *like* family, I guess." She looked up at him again. "He's…Well, he's…." Suddenly, she didn't want to elaborate. She was aware of other things—Scott's Egyptian cotton shirt, his rich silk tie. His Rolex. And of her own deceit. Her carefully planned appearance in a tailored suit and pumps never hinted at how different life actually was for her, and by extension, for David, and for everyone else she knew back there where expectations fell short of basic. Certainly, everyday experiences there would never fit comfortably into a conversation with Dr. Scott as she now perceived him.

Instead, she said, "The money to take care of this is all arranged."

"Well then, since you have already considered everything, all you'll need is signed authorization from his parents and you can give that to me when you bring him in for his exam. If that checks out, I can do the procedure right away." Then he smiled warmly as he asked, "Could you be ready in say, three weeks?"

"Oh, yes," she grinned. "Oh, yes!"

As she rose to leave, he added, "I hope that boy is suitably grateful to you for this."

She simply smiled, giddy with relief that David's life really was going to change and projecting to the joyous moment when she would tell him.

When she stepped into David's trailer to meet with his parents, she found it clammy and dark inside. The tiny, torn space that barely sheltered the nine family members was crammed with indiscernible objects, and the light was so dim she had trouble defining his parents' faces.

Their reaction was clear enough.

"We don't know nothin' 'bout things like that. An' who's gonna pay for that fancy doctor?"

"Oh that's all taken care of. You won't need to pay for anything."

They were suspicious and tense.

"An' what if somethin' go wrong an' it makes David's eye worse'n it is?"

"Oh, the doctor says that it's a simple procedure," Ann said confidently. "He assured me that it would be no problem at all to fix it."

Since David only worked for Ann, it didn't make sense to them that she was offering help for nothing. White people didn't do that kind of thing.

They didn't trust her or any part of it and summarized their misgivings with, "Maybe it's just best to let it lie."

It must be the money. Perhaps they thought something terrible would happen to them if the expensive treatment wasn't paid.

"Don't worry about the money," she said, digging out the paper that stated clearly that they would not be required to pay for any of it. "See. It has the doctor's signature and mine where I agree to be responsible.

They looked at it quietly, saying nothing.

Their backs were against a tiny window. The glare from the sun outside made them into large still shadows, rooted in denial and too amorphous to read. My god, she thought, how could they resist? Fixing David's eye could make him "normal"—would give him a real chance. He could be different from the other impoverished boys she saw around her, all of them crushed by lack of opportunity, doomed by a rotten school system, and surrounded by children from like circumstances who gradually, irreversibly, became hostile, indifferent, and sometimes even criminal. So far, David had kept himself aloof from all that, as if by working hard he could push reality away and dream of good things that would someday come. She didn't know how he did it. She was often frightened for him. There was an ever-waiting vortex of despair that threatened everyone here. But David didn't need to be sucked down into it. From now on, he could have possibilities. She wasn't giving up, and, to win their confidence, Ann found herself offering guarantees, "It's virtually a sure thing …you have my word…he'll be like new."

But they remained stonily unmoved.

"It's easy…all taken care of…I promise you…no risk…totally safe…" she elaborated on and on, never intending to go so far. But walking away was not an option. Finally, they agreed.

She had been so cautious, so protective of him. So why now, here in the car, driving to see the man who had promised to fix everything, did she have misgivings?

"You know nothing's definite yet," she said.

"Yes, ma'am." He wasn't listening

The doctor's building was awash with people. Five eye specialists shared space there, and the vast center lobby reminded Ann of a bus terminal. The staff was equally impersonal.

From this huge, busy room, they were ushered into a small waiting room crowded with ten chairs. Elderly people sat elbow to elbow in most of them, and, as David and Ann entered, the aging patients looked up at them curiously, started to smile and then, looked quickly away. The space was too small not to notice. David tried to look at some magazines but in truth, Ann had no idea what he could see. Finally, a different nurse called David's name. She saw Ann rise as well and looked hesitant. After leading them to a tiny room, she settled David into the examination chair and motioned Ann to take the only other seat.

There, they waited—endlessly, it seemed—facing each other—awkward—and close enough to touch the silence.

"Are you all right?" Ann asked.

"Yes, ma'am." David looked down at his new shoes.

At last, there was a tap on the door, and Dr. Scott entered, files in hand, registering on her with a pleasant smile of recognition and then, with surprise, on David.

She introduced them, reminding Dr. Scott that David's was the case she had discussed with him. David looked like a cornered animal, his expression frozen, except for the drifting eye.

"I see," Dr. Scott said, studying David. Then he began the examination.

"Look over here. Look here." A beam of blinding light blinked on and off as it focused in on the eye. "Do you see that?" Scott's voice was routine. Almost bored. "Look forward. Do you see that?"

"Mmmm," was all David seemed able to manage.

There was a heaviness in the room that stifled her excitement, a leaden void that made the sound of the doctor's shoes shuffling on the linoleum, the rustle of his starched lab coat, and the snapping of his light seem ponderous. The exam took only about three minutes.

The doctor stood up straight again, and without looking at David, asked, "How old is he?"

"Fifteen," she answered, surprised that he didn't remember. Even so, it should be right there on his chart.

"This should have been done before he turned two. It's too late now," he stated as if to end it. He looked at her indifferently.

"But you said…" she stammered.

She couldn't argue with the doctor here and now; that was nothing David ought to hear. Yet David had trusted her and believed in everything she had told him. How could she walk away and leave it this way?

"But you said you could fix it," she insisted.

"Well, of course, I could fix the eye in place but he'll never see any better. His depth perception is nil and will stay that way." He was close enough to David to feel his warmth, yet he was speaking of him as if he didn't exist. He continued clinically, "When you're very young, both eyes begin to work together so that depth perception can take place. It's way too late for that. He has learned to see, actually, with one eye and has no depth sense."

David's expression was unreadable. There was only the squeak of new shoe leather as he shifted his feet.

The cramped little room was too small for private consultation, but Dr. Scott didn't ask Ann to step outside. "Can't…." she began and stopped for a moment, struggling to find benign words before starting again. But there were none. "Can it be fixed so it doesn't…wander?" It was so blunt. She hated saying it that way. It implied that it didn't matter if David's eye functioned or not as long as everyone else, herself included, didn't have to endure him the way he was.

Scott responded in his same clinical tone. "I told you before that I could fix the eye—freeze it so to speak—but he won't see any better."

Suddenly, Ann stopped breathing. Her mind seemed to explode.

Oh, my god, she realized silently, her body icing. Oh, god…oh, god!!! She remembered. In that first interview with Dr. Scott, "fix" was exactly what he had said. She never considered that he didn't mean repair, make right, make new again, with all the endless expectations for David that the word had unleashed. Those assumptions had been hers. Passed along to David. And his parents. They had heard what she had told them, finally believing in the concrete surety that she offered—giving over to her their child and with him, all their private fears and dreams. She had brought them all to this expectant moment that, now, she saw no way to rescue.

All she found to say was a quiet, "That would be all right."

"You do realize," he added, seeing her confusion, "it would be expensive. It would only be cosmetic and with a boy like that….well, why bother?"

"That's all right," she said again, coldly this time, her expression set to stop him from saying more. "Would you please do that for David?"

"It really isn't worth it," Scott insisted, annoyed. "For someone like him, why would it ever matter?"

"I'll have to call you," Ann said stiffly. Rising.

David and Ann drove in silence most of the endless journey home. Even the angry whine of tires moving on asphalt was insufficient to drown out the voiceless pain that filled the car. There wasn't much time to salvage something—to fix it all in some way. She had to say something.

"David, even if he can't make you see better, would you like your eye fixed so it doesn't wander?"

"I 'spose."

"Will your family understand? Will they let you do it?"

"I guess they would. I don't know. You didn't ask 'em that."

He had heard Ann's assurances. And so had they. When you fix something, you make it right. Whole. Like normal people. He never would have thought to conjure other meanings.

"Just think it over, David. Talk to them. See what they want to do, then let me know." She was trying to sound calm while drowning in grief and shame. "If you would like that, I'll still take care of it, okay?"

"All right," he said looking out of the window, seeing she knew not what.

As they drove back into his broken-treasured yard, a waiting face appeared behind the parted trailer curtain. He climbed out without turning her way, said an automatic, "Thank you, Ms. Ann," and walked across the yard through the spent toys and went inside, no longer careful of his shiny new shoes.

His answer never came. He didn't come to work anymore, and she was afraid to make it worse by pressuring him or his family. She sent out word that she wanted to see him and while she waited, reports came that he had gotten into a string of fights at school, the last one so serious it had landed him in jail. "He got mixed up with the wrong crowd," people said. Only she understood why. She queried neighbors about him for several years. The reports about this kind, bright boy who cared about so many things outside himself and who once had hope—were all bad. Finally, everyone lost track of him. Even Ann. David vanished from her life.

One winter evening about six years later she was pumping gas into her Jeep at the truck stop down the road. The temperature was plummeting. Her breath rose from her in smoky trails and she shivered repeatedly. As she waited for the tank to fill, she noticed a huge black man staring. She looked away. Then she glanced his way again and saw him still watching. Suddenly he started running across the tarmac straight for her. She was aware of the muscle and power in him as he sped closer. She started to leave, but he was too quick and he was there, reaching out for her, grabbing her arm and hand. A huge radiant smile twisted his mouth into the face of joy.

"It's me," he almost shouted. "Don't cha remember? It's me…David!"

He was still holding her arm and shaking her hand vigorously and wouldn't let go. Once she realized it was David, she didn't want him to.

My god. Little David. The grip of his hand dragged her back to a time she never wanted to remember, a time, she believed, he could never forgive, nor forget.

"Oh, yes. It is you," she said, smiling back uncertainly. "But…but you look so different."

He laughed a guttural man's laugh, "I know. I got big didn't I?"

"You really did," she agreed. "I would never have recognized you." With all the superficial comments made, it was time to ask, "How are you, David? Is everything all right?"

He hesitated for a long moment, "I was in a lot of trouble for a while there," he said. "Maybe ya heard. I went to jail." She bit her lip and nodded. "I got in with bad company. Drugs and all that. But I'm out and I've got a job back here now." He smiled again. "I'm doin' all right."

"I'm so glad," she smiled. "So thankful."

So very thankful.

He beamed at her again, then said, "I thought it could be you the minute I saw ya drive in, and finally, when I knew it was, I just had to come over and see ya and shake ya hand."

She couldn't imagine why. She must have looked bewildered because he reminded her, "You remember way back when ya tried to help me?" She nodded. Her throat was tight. "I never ever forgot what ya did for me, and I just wanted to come up and say 'thank you'…so ya'd know."

She answered hoarsely, "Thank you, David," her ineptitude, the sadness, the warmth gone cold, the 'if onlys' all tangling and overflowing. It was hard to speak. Then finally, she said, "I appreciate that, David…much more than you will ever know."

He stood full face and looked at her before they parted. For a moment, their misty breaths mingled in the chill air. And, she swore, both his eyes were looking straight into hers.

WHEN THE WIND BLOWS

There was the hurried thumping of feet coming down the stairs and racing across the bare hall floor. The kitchen door flew open.

"A FIRE!" Maggie shouted. "Oh, mom, a fire! I could smell it all the way upstairs." The logs crackling in flames on the kitchen hearth were as exciting as if the house itself were burning to the ground. "Is it really cold enough out there today?"

"Well," Kathryn hedged, "almost."

The outside door stood open letting the wind blow into the kitchen. It made the fire in the old hearth seem more reasonable. Maggie climbed onto the window seat to read the thermometer.

"Only 65?" she reported with surprise. "It seems so cold."

"Because of how awful the heat's been lately," Kathryn answered.

Although already late October, summer had clung like a damp sheet. They had no air-conditioning in their ancient cottage, and, even though the shade trees and the river made it cooler than the city, the past week of humid, sticky, 90-degree temperatures had been enervating.

"Well, here's to fall!" Kathryn announced as she handed Maggie a steaming mug of hot chocolate. The thought of it was intoxicating. They raised their mugs in salute and clinked them.

With a big noisy northeaster coming in from St. Catherine's Sound, blowing flumes of foam across the river in front of the house, it even looked like fall. White shore birds struggled against the force of the storm as they sought shelter in the coves. The sky was the color of cold steel, and the marshes had already turned tan and reedy like fields of wheat.

Kathryn stared at the turbulent scene, drawing in its energy. "How odd, that the dying of beautiful things should be so stirring," Kathryn mused. Then she turned to Maggie. "Don't you feel excited and ready to take on anything?"

Maggie nodded.

"Ever since I was little, when fall weather finally arrived, I got the strangest sense of being brand new…as if I had new wisdom…new clarity." Here she dropped her voice an octave and made it mock-serious. "I understood the *why* of things."

Maggie smiled knowing that she meant it.

"You know, I've never outgrown that feeling." Then she said, teasing again, "By the way, if you have some heady question for which you'd like a brilliant answer, now's your moment," and with this she patted Maggie condescendingly on top of the head.

"Oh I do. I do."

"Then you may approach the queen."

"The queen, is it?" Maggie replied.

"The queen of all knowledge. The Queen of Sheba. The Queen of the May. The Queen of Denial. Whatever."

Maggie laughed. "Well, I'd like to ask the Queen of Whatever why I need school with a mom like you around?"

Kathryn gave her a pretended swat. "Good try. Next question."

They were sparring again—and happy. It wouldn't have seemed a game that a nine year-old would relish, but Kathryn had always engaged Maggie's mind this way, especially when her child was troubled or in pain. Since the divorce, the disturbance of moving back East, and now, the isolation of their lives out here on her family's abandoned farm, these verbal games consistently turned them away from dark thoughts and silences that, at times, could have plunged them into despair.

Having Maggie learn to relish life again was paramount. The move had meant a new beginning, matched in a physical way by this blustery day that was sweeping away the depressing leadenness of summer and making them quick and focused and ready to have fun again.

Kathryn hated the heat. Her whole being felt indifferent in it. This morning she had snuggled into a bright blue turtleneck and a grey Shetland sweater, a need that brought a deep satisfaction reflected in her mood. She felt healthy, even radiant, and the rawness outside made her feel stronger and in charge.

In the kitchen, the wind gusting through the open door neutralized the fire's warmth, and Maggie shivered in her thin summer pajamas.

Kathryn suddenly realized Maggie wasn't dressed for this, and she held out her arms to envelope the thin, straight-haired child and draw her close. "Let's get you warm," she said as she rubbed her exposed arms, put a jacket around her shoulders and helped her tug on a pair of toasty socks she had hung to warm in front of the fire.

Then they sat on the floor, shoulder to shoulder, in front of the flickering logs and shared the magic over their mugs of steaming cocoa.

"I wish I could go out on the river right now, while it's dangerous and wild," Maggie said.

"Me, too. Or hike all the way to the pond and watch the gators. Up close."

"Of course," Maggie added, "they'd be watching us back and probably dreaming of the yummy lunch we'd make."

"You think we could outrun them today?" And they laughed, imagining the chaos and relishing the reckless prospect of tempting the speedy beasts with all those teeth that way. Anything daring—even thinking the unthinkable—seemed a fitting way to revel in the season's change.

Since coming home, Kathryn had taught Maggie to understand, respect and love wild things; the powerful storms, the creatures swimming in the river or scampering close by, the mysterious, misty dawns and burning sunsets and summer skies whitening with lightning, the rattle of rain on the barn's tin roof, the naturalness of untamed things beginning life, growing, and dying—all things that enriched their lives but were out of their control. She had invested her with confidence. It had taken two years, but Maggie wasn't afraid of much anymore. And neither was she.

"I think I could handle anything today. Anything at all," Kathryn laughed and pulled her close. "In fact, I can even deal with you, my precocious child."

"Then you won't make me go to school?" Maggie asked with mock innocence.

"Oh, that again. If I had any guts I'd say, 'Of course not.' But I'm a slave to the system." She looked at Maggie mischievously, "It's my rigid Southern upbringing. My overdeveloped sense of responsibility. My..."

"Okay, mom, I get it."

"Speaking of which, we're going to be late. You need breakfast. And maybe even clothes?"

"Okay, okay." Except Maggie didn't make a move to do anything about it.

Finally, Kathryn stood and lifted her to her feet. Then she quenched the fire, put the screen in front of the ashes, and gave Maggie a playful pat on the behind to get her moving.

This was what their life was about. Forgetting. And closeness. And freedom. That was the reason she had given up a successful West Coast career and was rearing her young earthling in this remote Georgia wilderness. After ten years in San Francisco formatting life to city sensibilities, confronting pressure and angst and, finally, divorce, she was ready to move on—move on to heal them both, by going backward.

"You're leaving San Francisco?" Her best friend, Judith, had seemed stunned. No one ever left "The City" once they had established a place for themselves there.

Kathryn nodded. "Going back East."

"Where? New York? Washington?"

"No. "

"Boston?'

"No, not there."

"...Atlanta...? Miami...?"

"Actually, we're heading for the Georgia swamp."

Judith was incredulous. "But your work, all those years, the respect you've built.... You can't be serious."

"Never more so."

"Please tell me it's not to that dank old farm in the woods."

Kathryn nodded in affirmation.

"My god! You'll rot there."

Kathryn grinned. "It's humid, true. But it's not that bad. Actually, statistics show that only twenty-one percent of the population suffers from jungle rot. That's manageable."

"Oh, all right. But at least, assure me that you have a good position? Somewhere?"

"You know that I can't work full-time and leave Maggie's care to someone she doesn't know, not after what she's been through with her father. No. I'll have to freelance."

"In publishing? In the piney woods of Georgia? You'll starve!"

"I have skills. I'll find something. Remember, it's only Maggie and me. And we own that little house. Besides, it has a garden with a grape arbor, and there's the river to fish in."

"Fish? You, fish?" She looked at Kathryn who was, as always, meticulously put together. "What unbelievable scenario is that?"

Kathryn laughed, “You forget. Growing up, I spent all my summers there.”

Judith couldn’t get past the image of the fish writhing on the end of a line. “Well suppose you did manage to catch one. You’ll still have to kill it and scrape off all those scales. Cut off its head. And gut the thing.” Judith made a horrible face and Kathryn laughed.

Put that way, it did sound grotesque. But then, Judith couldn’t understand the direct connection between death and survival that constituted life on a farm.

“Really, Kathryn, who will look after you? How will you even afford to eat?”

“We’ll be just fine. Really.” Kathryn said. “Besides, if things get tight, there are tons of mice and snakes I can skin for us to nibble on.”

“Stop!” Judith cringed. “How could you even talk about getting near those things?”

“Oh don’t worry,” Kathryn went on. “Catching them’s easy. They come right into the house.”

Judith shuddered. Then, after a pause, she turned grave. “Seriously, what about Maggie? How can she get a decent education in such a God-forsaken place? Or have friends? Or exposure to important things?”

“You know I’ll find a way,” Kathryn said appreciating that Judith really was concerned for them and was only trying to keep them there in San Francisco, to be safe and nourished, as she understood it. She could imagine what Judith would think if she knew that there wasn’t even a telephone. Cell phones didn’t work either, not in the woods, and there was no one to call for help anyway. The nearest neighbor was three miles away. She had seen him once, a creepy, slumping, middle-aged sort who lived alone. She wouldn’t be cultivating him anytime soon. But she’d tell Judith none of that. Instead, she took her hand and said convincingly, “I will find a way. You know that.”

“I do understand this much,” Judith conceded. “It would be good to get that child away from here. . .from that father of hers. What he’s done….” She shook her head. “Maggie has been through too much. I see it in her eyes. She is so sad and silent. I’ve been worried. And I worry about you too, Kathryn. You have to be healed and level if you are ever to bring her back to life.”

“I know. That’s really why we’re going.”

Judith sighed, “So, if this is your way; then God speed.”

At that moment, from 3,000 miles away and with images of the cottage tinted by the glow of innocent childhood, it had seemed easy. Now, after two years of country reality, Kathryn understood how formidable the struggle would always be if she was to make anything substantive of this life she sought for them. Even more difficult was making Maggie secure and full of trust in light of Kathryn's frequent misgivings about her own competence to handle the endless financial crises or the dirt-hard physical work needed—chopping wood, repairing leaks, maintaining the garden—just to keep them and their little place afloat. Yet she never regretted the decision she had made. She could not allow failure because life in the wilderness was working for her child.

Providing for Maggie's education in a school that would be sophisticated yet gentle enough to encourage her had seemed daunting. But the Montessori school she found not only mirrored her own ideas of how best to guide Maggie's emerging humanity, but it also understood her financial dilemma and let her pay in small amounts as she was able and barter services for the rest. This much she could even share with Judith, who still believed Kathryn had fallen off the edge of the earth and taken her sanity with her.

Driving Maggie the forty empty miles to the Montessori school in Savannah was a worthy trade-off, and it had become something Kathryn just did. As if on autopilot, she traversed the four-mile sandy road to the highway, then moved along the paved road edged with vacant woods and marshes all the way to the outskirts of Savannah. Then, after jostling city traffic and waiting in the carpool line, Kathryn gave Maggie a quick goodbye hug and shifted into work mode on the drive to Arby's.

When she wasn't directly on a job, Arby's was her office. Never crowded, it was the one place where she could spread out the papers necessary to whatever editing work or freelance writing job she had found. Of course, the library offered that too, but it couldn't match Arby's perpetual, life-sustaining flow of nearly free coffee. After greeting Kathryn cheerfully each morning, the manager and staff would leave her, undisturbed, to drink endless refills while she shuffled papers and scrawled notes for the six hours before she would pick up Maggie. In the hot months, Arby's was a cool refuge. In winter, it was a steamy, short-order-pungent place that impregnated her clothes with the greasy odor of cooked meat and french-fries. But she didn't care. Under the circumstances, she rated the arrangement as if she had been offered a corporate suite overlooking San Francisco Bay. Arby's was her place. Her child, meanwhile, was being nourished importantly by the Montessori Method.

Today, however, on this stormy life-renewing day, her spirit prowled. She didn't want to go into town any more than Maggie did. In silence, they loaded up the car and climbed in, letting their private thoughts collect themselves. Kathryn's summer-sodden brain needed time to adjust to the eagerness she felt and to organize her attack on all the issues that had languished listlessly for so many months. She was ready and bursting to share her reawakening. Turning to Maggie, she announced, "As you are aware, I always tell you I know everything. But today I really do."

Maggie laughed. She loved it when her mom was on top of it. It made her feel especially safe.

As Kathryn's Jeep wound through the woods toward the highway, the steady sift of leaves reminded them that the Northeaster was stripping the tree tops bare and that, when its breath was spent, their world below would truly look like autumn. The floating leaf fall was soft. It was beautiful. A deep South kind of snowfall—rust and red and gold instead of white. The next walk they would take along this road would be over a carpet of color.

Neither said much as they pulled onto the highway. They were still going slowly, and that's why they noticed it. A little greyish lump up ahead moving slightly in the roadside grass.

"What's that?" Maggie asked.

"I don't know," Kathryn said, squinting to see it better. "It could be...maybe it's a 'possum. It looks like a 'possum."

She slowed to get a better look. It lifted its head and shoulders off the grass in an attempt to rise and run away, and then fell back. Kathryn pulled up close behind it. This time it shifted its little black head to look at them. Something was definitely wrong. They could see the 'possum fully now, the head rising and falling, the hip a rounded mound, immobile. Just visible at the bottom of the connecting curve, its back and stomach, lay crushed flat, defining the exact width of a tire track.

It was too late to shield Maggie from the sight of it—the little animal, beyond help, struggling to survive, doomed to lie there in agony until its courage broke and the pain and lack of water would bring about its end.

"Oh my god," was all Kathryn could utter.

"Oh, mom, it's hurt. Help it, mom, please help it."

There was no one to call on to help.

Immobilized by the choices, none good, none soft, none placating, all horrible to make, Kathryn sat gripping the wheel watching the little 'possum trying instinctively to drag its broken body back to life. And there she was, the mother of answers, of compassion, of healing, looking into the stricken face of the child who believed she could solve all these things. "Please mom, please, please fix it," Maggie pleaded.

Kathryn took in the 'possum, then the child looking up to her, and she knew she had to act. "Don't look," she instructed. After backing the car up ten feet, she drove forward, purposely aiming for the animal's head. She felt the bump, pulled to a stop and looked at the terrified child. "Sometimes, Maggie," she said softly but with steel, "sometimes you have to do a cruel thing to end a more terrible suffering. We had to kill the 'possum so it wouldn't suffer anymore." Stonily calm, she stroked Maggie's hand. The child remained riveted on her mother, her mouth agape, tears flooding her cheeks.

After a few minutes Maggie looked at her lap and said quietly, "I know, mom. It's all right. We wouldn't want it to suffer." She was repeating instruction.

"You're a very wise and brave girl," her mother said. "The 'possum is at rest now. He won't hurt anymore." Again, she gave the child's hand a gentle squeeze and turned to the road to check for traffic so they could pull away and leave this awful scene. As she did, she caught a glimpse of the little animal in the rearview mirror. Disbelieving what she'd glimpsed, she looked again. It moved and tried to rise, so slowly now; it was still trying to maintain life against this double cruelty. Her suck of breath was hard. She hesitated. Then, without looking at Maggie, Kathryn put the Jeep in reverse and backed determinedly over the creature hoping her child could not see. She felt the bump and brought the car to a stop within ten feet. Instinctively, she looked down at Maggie.

"Oh, mom, you hit it again." Maggie thought the 'possum was already dead. Her voice registered more distress than alarm. They both turned their eyes back to the road.

Now they could both see the furry body close up once again. It took a moment but as Kathryn put the car in gear, she could clearly see the little head, still alive, blood streaming from its shattered mouth, simply staring helplessly at her. The 'possum must have been run over on the paved road and had dragged itself as far as the shoulder. The matted grass on the side of the road only cushioned the 'possum's head, saving it from the death-dealing crush of her heavy car. It would take much more to put it out of its misery.

Forward, she drove. Then backward. Each time the tiny face begged her to stop. Or was it to hurry? Maggie's bewildered face was an accusation. Blood streamed now from its nose and eyes and still it clung to life.

"Don't look, Maggie. We have to do this." She kept her voice as restrained as she could while trying to contain the horror of what she found herself doing.

The Jeep moved again and repeated the process until she could be sure it was over. Dead, thank God in heaven. Dead. Maggie sat in stunned silence.

Carefully, her mother turned the wheel hard in the direction of the highway to avoid the spent creature now thoroughly crushed and motionless in the stained grass. Without glancing at her daughter, she drove into the gray, blowing morning that earlier had brought such renewal, such wisdom, and clarity, and above all, an understanding of the why of things.

SIXES AND SEVENS

It wasn't Scotty's manner or his size that seemed so disorienting to me. Our house painter was a cheerful, well-built, six-foot, fiftyish man with only a budding paunch to suggest that those bottles that rolled and clanked around in his truck when he came to work were the empty six-pack from the drive home night before. It was Scotty's face that stopped me—punched-in like a potato doll, his lips stretched thin in a perpetual grin that revealed two rows of shiny pink gums, permanently clenched on a dead, wet cigar—welded in, I began to believe—and through which he carried on his conversations.

"Ee un ot o or aint en ah eed ih o-ay."** Or something. It always had an urgency to it that set up panic. I couldn't ask him to remove the cigar. I was afraid it would cause his entire face to collapse, and I couldn't even be sure it would make him any more intelligible.

"Ou oin uh ow?" After weeks, I deciphered that to mean, "You goin' to town?"

Apparently, Scotty was sending me on an urgent mission, the substance

** "We done out of your paint and I need it today."

of which I squeezed every brain cell in my head to make clear as his frustration rose. Finally, I learned to resort to displays of paint chips, buckets, brushes, thinner, stirrer, and even drop cloths, in a quasi-Braille method that seemed to make it easier for both of us to avoid panic.

But how could I not love him? Scotty was performance art. Every morning, he would climb the stairs of our two-story house and swing monkey-like up onto the banister surrounding the open stairwell before climbing the eight-foot ladder perched precariously on two narrow planks stretching twenty feet across the void that had all the stability of a trampoline. From the top rung, he could lean wa-a-a-a-y back and attack the ceiling. It was too sickening to watch.

To entertain himself, he listened to the local country radio station and whenever his favorite played, "illin' e oftly ith is ong," (translation: *Killing Me Softly With His Song*) Scotty sang. At times, his voice rose to high-pitched passion, a passion enhanced by Scotty's vivid conducting with his brush baton, swaying and bending alarmingly as the planks bowed and bounced and inched crazily along the banisters. I couldn't bear to watch that for long either, but at least, as long as he was singing, I knew that he was still up there and not twenty feet below, lying broken and in a coma.

Scotty liked us, that was clear. He took joy in teasing me or in having a lengthy conversation with my husband, Don, both end-of-the-day rituals during which Don and I smiled a lot and mumbled many uhhhhs that could be interpreted by Scotty in some appropriate way. We hoped. At least, he seemed satisfied when finally, he put on his cap, went out to his truck, and popped the first bottle of Bud to fortify himself for the journey home.

One afternoon, when he had finished for the day and he and I were alone, Scotty engaged me in animated conversation that obviously had nothing to do with paint.

"Ut ize ah yah?"

"Utt?" I answered. "I mean, what?"

"Ut ize ah yah…ou oh. Ut ize is ya unner ants?"

What? …what was he saying?! To Scotty, it was important enough that with a sigh, he removed the cigar.

"What size are ya under pants?

I just stood there. The silence was crimson and deafening.

"Well, wha are ya?" he said impatiently. "Ya look like a six or seven to me."

"I don't know. Six I guess."

I don't know why I told him. But sometimes shock trumps good sense.

He nodded, got in his truck and drove away, bottles clanking, the cigar temporarily replaced by a beer bottle planted in his toothless grin.

Two days later, Scotty sought me out. He thrust a small box at me. "Oen i'. Go awn oen i'."

"Open it?"

He grinned expectantly, cigar at attention.

Carefully I picked off the top cover and pulled back the tissue paper inside. There were two pairs of nylon panties trimmed in lace, one white with blue ribbons, one pink. I was horrified. What was he thinking? What could I possibly say to get out of this…to make it all go away? Far, far away.

"Oh, Scotty," I said, pushing the box back at him. "I can't accept these."

He looked wounded. And the cigar came out at once.

"Why?"

"I…I just can't."

"But mah wife...she made 'em special for ya." He waited, then said, "We couldn't afford ta buy ya nothing' an' she wanted t' do somepen nice for ya 'cause ya been so nice t' me. She makes 'em to sell ya know. She'll be mitey hurt if ya don' 'cept 'em."

"Oh…..Oh, yes…of course," I stammered. "Then can't I pay for them?" I regretted the stupid, thoughtless words the moment they tumbled from my mouth.

"NO. Oh, NO!" He reacted as if I had taken scissors and cut their gift to shreds.

We both stood there—awkwardly, on my part, and silently on his—the little gift lurking in the void.

"Please…please thank her then," I said. "They really are beautiful….and I appreciate them very much…. and I'll enjoy them and…and…" I looked away, but not before I saw him put the cigar back in his mouth and clamp down on it with lips from which the smile had gone.

MANY MANSIONS

When I drive through this part of town, I wonder who lives here now in those little houses, so many of them broken and flaking paint, with the roofs all rusted and the yards less grass than dirt. There's a kind of life going on there that I don't know about anymore, a life most people shun. Maybe I would have, too. If it hadn't been for Loretta.

Loretta was my friend. She "raised me," as she liked to say, mostly in the kitchen where Savannah's children and black cooks of the 1930s were assigned. It was a time when the streetcar rumbled down Habersham Street at the end of the block. Our own street was still a dirt road, and Loretta would go out there to get vegetables when the farmers came by with carts of fresh produce or she'd swap chatter with the dusty men who balanced huge baskets of seafood on their heads while they called out in their ancient Geechee dialect, "crab, fresh swimps…mullet!"

On days when she wasn't too busy in the kitchen, she let me help her roll butterballs between wooden paddles. She even let me put mine aside for that night's dinner table if I made one nice enough. And there were nights when she stayed with me while my parents went out partying.

They were inordinately glamorous, my parents. On cotillion evenings, my Clark Gable look-alike father would appear at the top of the stairs in high silk hat and tails while I waited below. It was a ritual. First, he would pretend that his hat was too tall to clear the stair ceiling, and in order to miss it, he'd take it off, put his hand on the crown, and suddenly, shockingly, crush that elegant silken tower flat as a plate. I was convinced that he'd destroyed it. But the minute he reached the downstairs hall and came very close to me, he'd explode it into a tall, gleaming pillar again. Lastly, he would place it jauntily atop his head and then tip it to me because, he said, "A gentleman should always tip his hat to a lady." My face would flush, and I'd still be giggling as my mother descended, wearing one of her ball gowns encrusted with beads and crystals or, my favorite, the cerulean blue crepe, its skirt studded with gold stars that burst into a dazzling firmament when she twirled around for me like Rita Hayworth.

"Your mama sure looked pretty tonight, and your daddy does cut a picture," Loretta would comment when they had gone. "He is the handsomest man I've ever seen."

I'd troop after her into the kitchen. "May I have a cookie?"

"No. You had one already." She was always blunt. "But I'll play you a game of Cassina before you go to bed."

I'd wait while she put the rest of the china away in the pantry and stretched the damp towels over the porcelain drain board. Then, after she had hung her dinner apron behind the door, we'd pull chairs up to the enamel-top table and play the card game she had taught me earlier that year when I turned five. I would struggle and concentrate but rarely win.

"That's pretty good," she'd say, if ever I came close. "You just keep tryin'." Her chair would scrape back on the linoleum.

"Please, 'Retta, play another?"

"No. I said 'one.' To bed now." And she would herd me upstairs, watch over my bath, and finally tuck me under the covers. Then she'd turn off the lights and I'd hear her walking down the carpeted hall, down the stairs—one, two, three, four, the landing, and then five, six and down to the hall and into the kitchen where she would stay, reading a book under the glare of the overhead light until one or two in the morning when my parents would return and she could cross the dewy yard and climb the steps to her apartment above the garage.

I knew exactly when I'd see her the next day. I'd already be up listening for the jangle of harness as the horse-drawn milk wagon bumped down the unpaved lane. With a clink of bottles, the milkman filled our box. Then, as the horse started slowly down the lane again, Loretta would emerge from her apartment. She would pause for a long puzzling moment to look into her room. Then she'd straighten up, pull the door shut, lock it, and descend the stairs. She'd stop to pick up the milk before coming into the house and soon after that, the smell of bacon and coffee would call me from my solitary world into the community of day.

To me, Loretta was remote—even mysterious. She was a childless widow. That, I knew. She was *Mrs*. Loretta Lambert, and beyond that, her past, as she put it, was "her business" and no one was allowed to pry. Loretta lived so close to us yet she had never invited any of us into her sanctum. Slowly, I became obsessed with what sinister thing must lie behind that locked door until, finally, I mustered courage to go up there and try to see inside.

I knocked on the door and in a minute, it opened. Just a slit.

"Lolly, why are you bothering me? You know this is my home and you aren't invited up here." She shut it quickly. I'd seen nothing.

I shrank with shame and avoided the kitchen for a week. Then, one afternoon when I came in for a glass of water she asked, "Do you know what day I have off?"

"Thursday."

"Well, that's tomorrow. When you get home from school, I'd like to invite you up to my place for some cookies."

"Thank you," I stammered. "Thank you, Loretta."

After school I ran to the garage, climbed the stair and timidly tapped on the door. I could hear her coming—then hear the twist of the knob. I didn't breathe as she opened the door wide and waited for me to enter. I expected it to be dark and frightening in there. Instead, in front of me was a large, cream-colored room containing two very big, worn chintz chairs with crocheted doilies placed neatly on the arms and backs. An old, highly polished table separated them. On it were her personal things, a bible, framed photographs, a wind-up clock, a painted china crucifix. At the center, were napkins, a glass of milk, and some cookies. A folding screen separated the sleeping area but I could see a steamer trunk in the corner with faded prints of foreign places hanging above it. You could have eaten off the floor. She invited me to sit down.

She didn't seem at all like the Loretta I knew. She was wearing a floaty, pale blue dress and her wavy hair was loose around her face. I'd never seen her out of uniform and so human, so soft. I didn't know what to say, and Loretta was little help.

To be honest, I'd never thought about her as an individual with dreams or a life apart from being a member of our household with the permanent role of taking care of us. From my five-year-old perspective she was a commanding presence in a starched gray uniform and white apron with her hair pulled tightly back under a stiff, tiara-like crown of pleated organdy. Her voice had that same crisp edge and she stood with an authority that stemmed from the most relentlessly upright posture I have ever seen. I didn't think much about her face. It was her eyes, dark and all-knowing, that could stop me mid-sentence if she disapproved. This new demeanor, so different, so personal, was nothing I'd ever imagined. I ate my cookies in awkward silence after which she said, "You can run along now."

"Thank you, 'Retta," I mumbled as I stumbled to the door and fled.

But I had been there. I had seen it. And something more. She had made this exception to invite me into her privacy. No one else. Just me.

For that era, Loretta was very unusual. Aloof and independent, she wasn't the least afraid to stand her ground with anyone, even my imposing father. It was routine. Each year, the night before we moved to our farm for the summer, Loretta served our favorite dinner, a meal begun with tiny biscuits and a delicate shrimp bisque adorned with paper-thin lemon slices and a sprig of parsley. That was succeeded by minted lamb chops, crisp potato croquettes, spinach soufflé, and finalized with a baked chocolate custard drizzled with cream—and fingerbowls—all of it perfection in both preparation and presentation. After we finished my father would ring for Loretta, congratulate her on the meal and ask the annual question, "Are you sure you won't go with us tomorrow?"

"You know I don't cook country," was always her tart reply, and I knew I wouldn't see her again until we returned to town in the fall.

To a five year-old, Loretta's attitude about the farm was impossible to understand. Since I could remember, summers and holidays in the country had provided everything anyone could want—adventure, wonder, fun, and dirt. Lots of it. Holidays were a time of bare feet, swimming in the river, and feeding the farm animals, not to mention riding in the wagon with the farm hands and the special winter magic of hunting down a Christmas tree in the woods with my father. For me it was a carefree paradise.

As I grew older I noticed other things, the broken houses where our neighbors lived and that many of them wore clothes, so old and thin, they sometimes tore into rags. True, I had few clothes myself. For summer, that meant a pair of sandals, a few sun suits, underwear, and nightgowns—enough to last a dirt-prone five year-old until the next batch of laundry was boiled in the big iron pot, dried on the clothes line, and pressed with flat irons heated in the coals. By comparison, my wardrobe seemed luxurious, and in some vague childish way the disparity hurt and made me uncomfortable.

The next summer when I turned six, I was given a weekly allowance of fifty cents, twenty-five cents for milk at school and the rest was mine to save. That remaining quarter, and any other change I managed to acquire, went straight into a little box on the table by my bed where, each night, I counted the accumulating coins, over and over. By the time school started my savings had grown to $3.62 and I showed it proudly to Loretta.

"Oh my," she said. "That's a lot of money. Where do you plan to spend all that?"

"That's a secret, 'Retta. Just wait 'til Christmas and you'll see."

My birthday yielded five dollars and there was also my growing stash of pennies—the kind adults always give to children to win them over. As Christmas neared I thrilled to the idea that, at last, I would have real money to spend.

By December fifteenth the final count was $12.37. My mother helped me with my list and gave me one of her old handbags to transport my loot. Once filled with all that change, its weight suggested a haul from a minor bank robbery. I smiled smugly. I was ready.

Grant's 5 and 10 Cent Store was crammed that day with holiday shoppers, poring through the bins of things that smelled strangely of cold metal, yardage, and the lingering drift of grease emanating from the lunch counter. Distressed, I looked at my mother. The gifts I dreamed of should be sweet with newness—soft and warm—flannel shirts striped like mattress ticking and nightgowns with tiny flowers that had fuzzy surfaces before years of boiling in laundry pots would make them coarse. And where were the warm gloves for the farm hands whose fingers were rough with calluses or the colorful caps or scarves—cheerful things that also would keep the cold at bay?

Smiling, my mother took my hand and led me down the big marble staircase to the basement. The space down there bedazzled with shimmering glass ornaments, colored lights, and tinsel. Treasure overflowed the displays. My Christmas dreams seemed piled to the ceiling, rising from long tables and bulging from shelves and bins. It was all there and I quickly found a perfect night gown. But it cost $3.25. With my budget, I might manage one but there were still ten names on my list. I just stood there fingering the soft pink rosebuds—wanting—wishing—my expectations washing away with the warm tears that rolled down my cheeks. My mother wiped them gently; then guided me to a pile of lady's undershirts, the ordinary kind that everyone wore. There was nothing pretty about any of them. They were plain, utilitarian, bereft of the miraculous. She picked up an undershirt, caressed her face with it, and drew in a long breath of its essence. Smiling, she held it out for me to see how deliciously new it smelled, how soft it felt on my cheek—and how affordable. With Mother's help, I bought the lovely, lace-edged gown for the old farm cook who needed it most and thick socks for the men. For the women, I settled on undershirts, each with a tiny pink satin bow at the neck. Even after buying a little gold pin for Loretta, I still had twenty-nine cents, enough to buy a package of crude holiday paper. At home, I wrapped each gift with care and gave Loretta hers before we left for the country.

Christmas Eve, everyone gathered by the big log fire in the farm's kitchen. Before I offered my gifts, my mother gave a little introduction so that everyone knew the presents came from me alone. Warm surprise shown from every face, followed by big hugs and thank-yous. The moment glowed—personal and connected. And, at six, I learned that it didn't matter what gifts I gave. They would be perfect if they spoke of thought and caring.

From that moment, Christmas became the happiest time of my life.

For the next nine years, whenever we went to the farm, Loretta maintained her resistance. I didn't know it then but, in Savannah, Loretta had status. In those days no one dined at restaurants or entertained other than at home. Social ranking was intimately linked to being an elegant hostess with the ability to serve exceptional food, beautifully presented—arts in which Loretta excelled. So while my childhood summers were spent happily "going country," Loretta had her choice of more sophisticated jobs with Savannah families that spent those sweltering months "up Nawth." It made her independent and my parents respectful.

For girls like me, the ritual catechism for growing up was well-defined, with summers off and a return to the regimen of Savannah society during the school year. As a rule, our program included boarding schools, those high-end brain factories that took young minds and, through rigorous training, shaped them into skilled, well-read, and well-written scholars at the top of the high school academic ladder. At fifteen, I, too, would go away to such a place, and my parents would move to the farm permanently. When told about it, Loretta, repeated her distaste for cooking over a wood burning stove, and preparing food for a dozen farm hands who appreciated nothing more exotic than rice, cornbread, and deep-fried everything accompanied by soggy, overcooked vegetables dripping with bacon grease. For the final time, she declined to go, and on the day my family left for the summer, Loretta, who had been with us for twelve years, quietly said goodbye with a restrained embrace for my mother, a handshake for my father, and a "behave yourself" for me.

When that summer ended, I began the prescribed three-year ritual of intellectual and social polishing—of intensely serious, formal education in the world-proof isolation of boarding school, where we followed a rigid day-into-night schedule of academics, fine arts, and sports. This was followed by equally intense vacations, a spree of dating, parties, and ever-expanding wardrobes filled with summer-crisp linens and tweeds for fall, of lustrous satins, white kid gloves, and all the other accoutrements deemed necessary for the rounds of luncheons, teas and dances at which we were the center of attention. After Spartan boarding school life, the social whirlwind brought high glamour and excitement to our lives, and it camouflaged what was, in reality, more subliminal job training than entertainment. Strangely, none of it seemed imbalanced. In all the years leading up to that pre-college summer we had been carefully taught to accept anything our milieu deemed suitable for us.

Just before my eighteenth birthday, I advanced to the next rung in the academic ladder. Rather than selecting a women's "Ivy," the preferred boarding school outcome, I stunned my family by opting for the largest, most liberal college in the country, the University of Wisconsin, where I became one of one-hundred incoming freshmen in the honors program. Confident in my Savannah-correct sweater, tweed skirt, and saddle shoes, all set off by a meticulously burnished, brain, I joined my Madison honors cohort, brainiacs and mavericks all. Few of them were impressed with 1950s dignities. Most came dressed in scruffy clothes, no makeup, and they lounged impertinently around the classroom, even parking themselves atop the professor's desk while they attacked each premise from an astonishing wellspring of knowledge. Shockingly, to me, almost all of them lived off campus in independent boarding houses away from rigid dorm rules and curfews. I thought of them all as intimidating, brilliant and brave. Unfortunately, they regarded me, not as an equal, but as a sad Southern troglodyte.

It was no place for lazy minds. Or cowards.

Evenings, I worked as a rim worker for the *Wisconsin Daily Cardinal*, considered to be the most radical student newspaper in the country. It was the McCarthy Era and, my editor, aware of my conservative Southern background, delighted in sending me out to cover meetings of people bent on overthrowing the United States government.

The Communist Party meeting was a scene straight out of *Ninotchka*, the people, the place and the conversation all so pervasively gray and ponderous they threatened to put everyone to sleep. After five stupefying hours I decided that they would never overthrow anything. They would bore each other to death first. And it taught me something—not to fear a situation until I had faced and understood it.

In my Southern paradigm, a place like Wisconsin presented a cornucopia of fresh experiences and ideas that dangled like a Lorelei to my uncertain future. I felt like a chrysalis developing my final form. But Savannah had already decided the outcome of my story. Unbeknownst to me, college was just supposed to be "background."

That June, with freshman year and our "finishing" years finished, my hometown cohort emerged as poised debutants, perfected and ready to progress to our penultimate destination—marriage, and our ordination as certified young Savannah matrons—expensive and desirable but with a return expected for the capital of money, education and time invested in us since birth. We were supposed to remain this way, to live out the promise of our training and enhance the men who successfully bid for us. If we entertained divergent plans or loftier dreams, they were dismissed. But most of us never questioned any of it. In all our cloistered lives, few of us wondered if our value as human beings might lie outside the system. At eighteen, as I whirled through that debutante summer, it was easy to put questioning aside. I conformed to expectations. I became engaged.

My husband-to-be, as most of the men we knew, had expectations. Through his marriage proposal, he had contracted a situation—a wife with established standing, disciplined in the art of Southern propriety, ready to slip into such committee work and hostessing as would elevate and sanctify his growing status. He, as did many bright young men, arrived unvetted by the standard, internal family-breeding review, entering instead via its one unguarded back door. Society parties needed extra bachelors, lots of them—well-mannered young men who were educated and charming enough to fit in, and moneyed enough to support the requirements of proper clothing, cars, flowers, dinners, and other escort expenses. In the happy, thoughtless frenzy, he rode in aboard the marriage bus, no questions asked, without ever revealing who he really was. And there I was. Primed and ready. Swept into place by the maelstrom. Just waiting.

Loretta came to my wedding. With an unexpected stab, I looked up and saw her sitting in what was known as the "Negro section" of the church balcony. She didn't smile. Her face was a mixture of knowing and concern as she watched me plunge recklessly into my life, an eighteen year-old child in a beautiful dress attended by innocent, laughing friends, all of us going through the ritual acceptance of womanhood without having the vaguest idea what that meant. All of us had been spewed out in a giddy rush by an orchestrated whirlwind designed to propel us blindly into a formulated future.

Only the settling years to come would reveal what we had really done.

Not long after our wedding, my father folded him into his successful business. We built a house. We lived the life.

We had everything anyone thought we should want.

As with all good Southern wives, my life revolved around things that pleased or interested my husband and smoothed his climb to prominence. I entertained the people he wished to impress and joined groups that would augment his new social standing. As young Savannah matrons, we filled our hours with family, bridge, community volunteer work, and parties where we engaged in shallow, circumscribed conversation that seldom ventured into anything provocative. As well-programmed as I was, I went along, content to fulfill the destiny I was taught to expect with its secure, well-structured future.

Perhaps I had been exposed to too many options. After two years, the limitations and triviality became suffocating. I had been trained to use my brain and I felt it shriveling from disuse in the same stultifying way that, year after year, we could expect the same guest list to fill every gathering.

Getting a job was out of the question. As my husband put it, "having" to work put a woman on a lower social rung, and he wouldn't hear of it.

"No wife of mine is going to work. People might think I couldn't support you properly."

His words stunned but didn't surprise. Disillusionment had already settled into my marriage as I witnessed my husband's slow transformation from a publicly kind, considerate person into a manipulative stranger, quietly tightening his control over me behind closed doors. From his perspective, he was right. We "belonged," didn't we? Why did anything else outside that matter? Didn't we have everything most others would die for? But what was "everything"? Why was its taste so sour?

If I made new friends they became a threat. "Those faggot artists you know…they're ruining your reputation. Those pushy kikes you call friends…the only thing any one of them cares about is your social position." And soon enough, the Lorettas in my life became, "…those worthless niggers. Jesus Christ, they're servants, not your buddies!"

And all the while our friends, men and women alike, made a point of telling me what an outstanding person he was, "…such a gentleman who would never say a harsh word about anyone. How lucky you are, my dear. I hope you appreciate it."

During that time I saw Loretta only occasionally, in someone else's home, where the hostess would take me back to the kitchen to share a few moments with her. The big hugs and "I'm so happy to see you" exchanges were warmly mature, but my new adult position held no pleasure. My daily life seemed empty, even pointless, and the touch of starched cloth and the scent of familiar soap about her made me ache for more innocent yesterdays when she had limited the risks and confusion in my life.

Meanwhile a steady creep of fear seeped through the house as I finally admitted that I didn't know who this man I'd married really was. I also noticed that people I knew well had begun distancing themselves from me. By degrees, they were too busy to linger or to talk. No one telephoned. My husband told me coldly that I had no friends, that everyone thought I was unstable. I wanted to talk to them, to protest, but he convinced me that no one would believe me. He knew this because he had already discussed me with most of them.

After three years, he had isolated me completely and I accepted his appraisal that, except for him, I was totally alone, that I had no skills, that I was unemployable, and that I would possibly starve without him.

Ironically, in the process, he stripped my life of clutter, obligations, and confusion, leaving me only the one thing he couldn't control—my mind. In the void, I began to piece together the fragments of what was happening. Why, I asked myself, wasn't I willing to conform—to be silent—to be caged—or to be owned, in order to protect myself and my comfortable place in society as had so many women before me—a place I now recognized as a waiting tomb? Simply put, to be safe from my ever-more threatening future, I needed to be *free*.

Without money, or friends, or training, the outlook was grim. Secretly, I dragged out the old, unused, manual typewriter I'd had since I was ten, and taught myself to type. When I achieved business speed, I felt confident enough to abandon my expensive prison for a little walk-up in a dangerous part of town, euphemistically called "transitional"—to me, the safest, most beautiful place on earth. Once on my own, I knew I'd never give up that freedom. And even though it took months of living on the edge, finally, I found a job.

I had made it.

The saga finally ended when I met my new husband and I vanished into the West, leaving Savannah and its "expectations" to rot in the sultry dust.

Loretta, meanwhile, maintained her status within the system, moving easily and at will from one prominent matron to another—becoming as important to their social careers as a good address, a proper marriage, and a fine old name. As the years passed, she was there as the downward drift of their lives began, as their energy and interest in Savannah's social life slipped slowly into inertia, and as new young matrons rose to take their places. She was there as their friends became infirm and died, and as interest in them by families or society began to fade. Loretta, graying but still resolute, watched silently as these once-privileged women became widowed, unwanted and alone. They needed her now in a much different way. In the end, it would be she who would shepherd them through to their deaths, imbuing their wasting days with a matter of fact acceptance of their helplessness that protected their dignity.

For those lingering days, Loretta became both caregiver and friend. She was there to spare their family members the daily realities of adult diapers, dribbled food, and the low, eternal moans of the dying. She even spared them time—time taken to make awkward talk about the ever-shrinking list of things that connected them to the ill and elderly—time to stroke the thinning hair—to hold a hand—to read or simply smile. How often she heard "the children" say after brief moments in the sick room, "Well, we have to rush now. We hate to but everything just stays so terribly busy. We really wanted to spend more time. You know we're all so concerned about you and…we do have to go…but please…let us know if there is anything you need." And as if they regarded Loretta as their guilt-absolving gift they added, "Of course, you have Loretta."

With Loretta there they never had to deal with the numbing exhaustion of gradual loss. Loretta made it possible for "the children" to hurry away so they wouldn't have to experience the relentless, gut-wrenching journey toward death, or connect it to their own eventuality.

So she moved from bedside to bedside until the night Agnes Barrington, the latest of her needy women, died. The following day the Barringtons summoned Loretta. She was weary from months of erratic days and long dutiful nights but she stood there, as always, her gaze direct, her back straight.

She wasn't asked to sit.

"We just wanted you to know how much we appreciate your lookin' after Mother," the eldest son began. "Nobody could have done a better job and we hope this token will help say 'thank you'. It's from all of us." He proffered a check for five hundred dollars. "You've been so good to all of us." There was a murmur of agreement among the relatives filling the room, none of whom looked at her.

"But you do understand, Loretta, that with Mother gone…well…we just don't need you anymore."

Loretta was getting old. That hadn't mattered as long as she was there to carry their burden for them. Now, she herself, was a pending one.

He looked around the room to see if anyone had anything to add. They didn't. "Good luck to you, now," he said. The tone was dismissive and final.

None of the Barringtons ever asked what she would do, how she would live, where she planned to go. If Loretta was hurt or afraid, she would never have shown it.

Loretta never heard from the Barringtons again nor from virtually any of the lovely families who boasted about having her in their kitchens. Few of them gave her a dime, a birthday card, a call at Christmas. And the lovely children she reared for those families, took their hand-me-down money and enriched their lives without a thought of her. It was as if she had never existed.

Ten years after my husband and I bid goodbye to Savannah, my parents died, leaving us the farm. By then, we had a child to consider. It was the 1960s, and after commuting from San Francisco to Georgia for two years, we decided to return to the peace and reality of rural life.

While in California, I knew little of Loretta's life other than from scribblings on Christmas cards that let me know she had retired, was in good health, and was still adamantly independent. Once back East, Loretta was the only person I truly cared to see and I arranged to visit her.

It was a glorious spring day. Loretta's house was a tiny, gray clapboard building in what people would have called, "the old, poor section" of town. It had a tin roof, a porch just big enough to sit on to catch the breeze, and a front yard filled with ancient Southern shrubbery. The dirt street in front of it cut traffic and fumes to zero, and the smell of new vegetation and fresh flowers clung in the air in a way that people living in cities hardly know anymore.

Loretta met me at the front porch wearing a breezy cotton dress that matched the morning. She held tall glasses of iced tea that she placed on the tiny table between two rocking chairs. A plate of my once-favorite cookies already was in place. After a lingering hug she held me away. "Let me look at you." She shook her head back and forth as if disbelieving what she saw. "You're so pretty and so young."

"I was going to say the same thing about you, 'Retta." And indeed, the passing years had washed the sternness from her face. "You look beautiful!"

"Now sit right down and tell me everything," she said. We took our places in the rockers, and she offered me a cookie. It was like being five years old again and I felt as awkward. How could we begin to bridge the years of silence with all that had happened in them? Loretta never hesitated.

"You wrote me that you'd married again and had a daughter, but I wasn't expecting such a change."

"Have I changed that much?"

"You look so content," she smiled. "He must be a good person."

"Oh, yes," I beamed. "And you'll love our daughter."

"I'm so relieved," she said, looking at me intently, "You know, working in Savannah the way I did…all those parties…all those people drifting into the kitchen. None of them ever thought not to talk in front of me. I heard all those things they said about you…such terrible things." Being reminded of it must have made me look as ill as I felt. Concern settled into her face. "I just want you to know that I never believed them."

"Thank you."

Loretta pressed on. "I couldn't say anything, you know. I couldn't do anything either except hurt for you. What they were saying wasn't you. I know you."

Loretta's forthrightness was a surprise. In the past, her worried eyes should have told me that she knew, but, then, I had thought no one believed me. It also dawned on me that she understood my rejection by society in a way few could. It mirrored her own.

"I wanted to call you back then," Loretta said. "But I didn't want to seem to be minding your business. Now, I wish I had." She patted my hand and smiled, "But look at the surprise you brought me. Now you're so happy."

"My husband is a wonderful man, 'Retta—a writer—the kind of man I never thought could exist. He isn't interested in all those Southern things that you and I know way too much about." Then I grinned at her. "Probably 'cause he's from *up Nawth*. New York, actually."

"Really?" she chuckled. "A Yankee! I'll have to meet him."

"Oh, you will."

She hesitated. "I really missed you," she said quietly, "but I always knew you wouldn't forget about me."

The closeness between us was old and new and suddenly painful.

So I tried lightening the mood. "How could I forget you when you beat me so terribly?"

She looked startled.

"At Cassina," I teased. "But I bet I could beat you now. That is, if I could just remember how to play."

She grinned, "Or if I could remember how to play either. These days it gets harder and harder to remember much of anything." She paused, "I guess we've both gotten older."

We weren't complaining. She was at ease, while simple survival felt good to me, an achievement of sorts.

"Nowadays," she added with that familiar edge to her voice. "I can do what *I* want when *I* want to do it."

I laughed, "So, what are you doing?"

"I have a job taking care of an elderly lady."

"A job? I thought you were retired."

"Oh, they don't pay me. I volunteer through my church. I cook and clean for her and get her dressed and when she's not too tired, I even take her places on the handicap bus. She doesn't have anyone else to help her, and my being there keeps her from having to go to one of those terrible nursing homes." She shuddered. "I would just hate being sent to one of those places, wouldn't you?"

"Yes…absolutely!"

"With me there, she won't be forced to go. I can see what a comfort that is to her and that's how I'm rewarded. I just hope I'll have the strength to help her 'til she dies."

She looked away, thoughtful, before adding quietly. "Just believing she's independent, that's what's keeping her alive, you know. Without that…well…."

"We have to believe that, don't we…even when believing doesn't make sense."

"That's what my pastor, Reverend Taylor, says." She nodded. "Now, you'd like him. He's an independent one, all right. He'll talk about anything. You never know what he might ask you next and you can't refuse him. You know he graduated from Tuskegee and has a Master's from Yale's Divinity School."

"Sounds like the perfect match for you." And we both laughed.

"I told him who you are and that I was a servant in your home for years." Her directness made my blood pump alarmingly. Back then, we would not have dared speak so bluntly.

"He thought," she continued, "you might just be making a courtesy call …or else, felt sorry for me."

"You know that isn't true!" I protested.

"I know, but he said that only one or two things would cause a white person to make such an effort after all those years, and he didn't want to see me hurt."

Oh, god. Did he think politeness or "white guilt" had prompted this? I despised the thought of it. This visit was no shallow, Southern-manners ritual. And "white guilt" presumed pity and shame, and there was a chasm of difference between that and how I felt about Loretta. No, Loretta and I were deeply connected. I was sure of it. I loved and respected her and wanted to believe that she felt the same. Of course, I had noticed that both she and I were cautious. It's hard to change the form of a relationship you've had for a lifetime into something else. It's easier for strangers to plunge in. They have no past history to limit them, no caution lights, no rules. These days they enjoy a freedom that allows discussion to be far less circumscribed. Loretta and I were both from another time and outside of time altogether.

"He says," she continued, "It's nearly impossible for any of us to change who or what we are, or how it colors what and how we think."

"I hope that's not true."

"We get used to it, whether we're poor and living on the wrong side of town... or rich enough not to worry about it. It's just easier to behave the way we always have."

How could I answer? There were so many complexities to being Southern, such as the genuine love and connection between individuals from different races that evaporate when the relationship tries to move into the broader conduct of adult life. I couldn't believe that we were talking about these things now, but I ventured, "It must have been frustrating to be shut out...to be censored and not allowed to participate."

"We had to be very careful back then." She spoke softly as if she might be overheard. "People liked to think they owned me or that I didn't count. Well, you know how it was." She was quiet for a moment, considering. "I'll tell you. Even when I was working for all those fine Savannah people, I never felt inferior to a one of them. I might not have had their money or their chances, and I couldn't go where they went or do what they did...but it didn't make *me* any less. I knew who I was and I just held on to that and kept it to myself 'til I got home to my place. Once I was inside...then I could let go a little." She paused as if remembering the times, places, and people, and the personal sanctuaries from them she had known. "Yes, indeed. You had to close yourself away. You had to be careful back then."

Suddenly, I could see her standing outside her apartment door each morning, looking in for that long and puzzling moment before straightening up, drawing the door shut, and locking it.

"Loretta, as long as I've known you, you have never put yourself in a position to be looked down on by anybody. And you know what?" I grinned, remembering my terror when I tried to breech her private fortress, "No one should have dared."

Loretta smiled as if we shared a secret.

"And here we are," she said. "After all these years...sitting here together."

"You know, 'Retta, when I was little, you seemed so private. I always thought of you as…distant. Sort of separate."

"And you were such a lonely child. So confused and so different from the other children. You hadn't learned how to protect yourself. And I worried." She appraised me with a smile. "We had a lot more in common than you knew."

The shadows had been quietly falling across the yard in lengthening grays. It was time to go.

But for Loretta and for me, that afternoon began to free us. Living where and when we did, personal feelings were most often expressed in knowing looks, an occasional hug, or a touch of a hand rather than in words. Now we were free to talk from the heart and hardness of life that had taught each of us to become who and what we truly were. Now a real relationship could begin—intimate and private—just as if all the people we didn't trust had left the room.

Later that spring, as we sat again, out on the porch of Loretta's little house, she said abruptly, "I heard about what your first husband did to your daddy. What a shame." She didn't wait for my comment. "I don't know if you knew how much I admired your daddy. We used to talk a lot about how we were brought up. We both came from the country, you know."

"I didn't know that."

"Oh, yes," she said. "We came from the same kind of place…where we had to go to work young. I was out working in the fields when I was five…same age as when he started plowing.

"Well," she went on, "He told me how when he first came to Savannah at sixteen to work, he didn't have money for an overcoat and he caught pneumonia. Almost died, too, and had to go back home. But he didn't give up. He came back to town and got another job. At the new place, the man he worked for had him delivering messages around town and he'd give him a dime to catch the streetcar." She took a sip of tea. "So he'd race the streetcar and get there first so he could keep the dime. And you know, soon enough, he got that coat he needed." She looked at me very seriously. "I like that story," she said. "It shows you can do anything if you're determined to do it."

Details aside, I knew why my father and Loretta respected each other. They shared that earth-born reality that disallows weakness and self-pity.

"Yes," I agreed. "He was determined to make something of himself, and he did. He built that company by himself, 'Retta, from the ground up."

"And your first husband took it away from him."

I just nodded.

"I just can't get over what happened. I really admired your daddy. He had such courage. How could that husband of yours do such a thing?"

For ten years I had kept it buried, and I had no interest in resurrecting the pain. I only wanted to forget and move on. But with Loretta—I felt I owed her an explanation. She had been loyal to us all, never believing the twisted, damaging rumors, and unable to ask about it until now. I struggled to find the words.

"After the divorce, after I left town, I think he believed that my father would find out what he'd done and he'd lose his job. He had to protect his interests. So he sabotaged my dad."

"But he gave him that job…that chance. Besides, everybody respected your daddy," Loretta protested. "How could he get away with it?"

"Just the same way he did it with me…behind his back. It's how he almost destroyed me."

"What on earth did he do to you?"

"I was nothing like him, 'Retta, and I was stupidly naive. For years I didn't realize that he was spreading damning little lies about me until it was too late. Long after the damage was done, I learned that he had even stopped strangers on the street…people he didn't even know…just to tell them awful things about me that I never did."

"They must have thought he was crazy."

"They did. With people we *did* know, he made the rounds, telling them how worried he was and planting doubt about my mental state. Can you believe it…he even cried?" I shook my head. "They swallowed all of it."

Loretta put her hand quietly on my arm and looked at me with concern.

"You know, the worst of it was, no one ever came to me to ask if any of it were true. They never said a word, nor even asked if I was all right…if I needed help. Nothing."

"You can't fight things people *want* to believe. Sometimes, it's best to just walk on by," Loretta said, sadly. "You can't let things that aren't true control your life."

"You're so very right but it hurts and it's a horrible lesson made worse if you didn't see it coming. That's what was so hard on my father. He never suspected that every time my ex took a trip on company business, he took Dad's clients into 'his confidence,' telling them how concerned he was that my father was getting old and even senile. Of course, he asked them not to say anything, especially, to my father because he 'didn't want to hurt him,' and put that way, the clients weren't about to mention it. Gradually, they distanced themselves from Dad and relied more on him."

Loretta looked dismayed. "How ever did your daddy find out?"

"He was ill with flu and was sent to the hospital. That's when my ex made a quick trip to New York where he convinced all the major clients that my father and his company were dying, that he, himself, was leaving to start his own business, and that he would be so pleased and honored if they would come with him. After what he'd led them to believe, they were primed to go. So, he took the business and most of Dad's clients, and he left, telling anyone who would listen that the business was failing, that my father was senile, and that he was lucky to get out in time."

"That's terrible!"

"So, my proud father who had worked all his life to build that company, was left no choice. Dad's friends at other Savannah businesses begged him to sue. They were convinced that Dad would win. But he said that suing would kill him and he was too old to start again. So the business that had been his life…just ended…like a sudden death." I was choking on the words. "He sold it to a firm in Los Angeles for thirty cents on the dollar, and it was gone."

Loretta sat, shaking her head, "You work all your life for your dream and then someone you helped and trusted…just steals it." She sat shaking her head. "It would have killed me."

"The worst of it is that I could have warned him. But I had this crazy notion that my ex's relationship with my father was independent from my own relationships with either of them. My parents had taught me never to blame others for my decisions. So, I kept quiet."

Loretta added, "You know, we were all taught to keep things to ourselves. Never air our dirty laundry. But this explains all the strange talk I was hearing about you and your family. It all came straight from him."

"He poisoned a whole town against me, Retta." Slowly, I shook my head. "You know, I think people enjoy gossip so much they grab onto any innocent little thing and twist it into something vicious, just to have something to add to the conversation…just to keep it going."

We both were quiet for a long while before she asked, "How did you ever manage to survive?"

"I didn't have a choice." Then I added, "When it was at its worst, a wise older woman whose advice I sought, said to me, 'What ever horrible, unjust thing happens to you, it is there to teach you something. You can learn from it, or not. It's up to you.' Of course, I didn't want to hear that. It's terrifying to be without friends, or resources—to be totally alone. I was scared, and I wanted sympathy. But she was right. When I thought about it, I realized for the very first time what I guess you have always known—that no one could give me my life—that my life was mine—my responsibility, and that it was in my control. That's when I first understood. If I believed in myself and worked hard enough for it, I really could be *free*.

"So, I set out to survive. I had little money and..." I grinned, "I even lost ten pounds before, finally, I got work. My ex always said that I'd starve on my own but having almost nothing to eat does have advantages as a highly effective way to diet." We shared a much-needed laugh. After all that time, joking about it felt good. It put it in the past. It had no immediacy, and once again, I felt a glorious surge of freedom.

"I heard about your job," she said warmly. "I was so proud."

"'Retta, getting that job was the dawn of my life. After all those years of being told over and over that I was worthless...that no one wanted me...so many years of being shunned, and desperate...well, it just seemed incredible that anyone would hire me. That first morning as I stood on the corner waiting for the bus that would take *me* to *work*, I felt filled with magic. When people came by I couldn't stop grinning at them. I just wanted to tell the world, 'I *have a job*! They want *me*!'" Loretta smiled and nodded knowingly.

I hadn't been able to pour all this out to anyone, and it had drained me. But Loretta and I were safe in each other's hearts; that was understood. Loretta took my hands in hers. "You have a good life now," she said.

We sat for a moment. Both quiet. Finally, I had to go. "Do you need anything?" I asked as I released her hands slowly and got up from my chair.

"No, thank you, sweet thing. I can care for myself. I have everything I need...just as you do."

When I came to see her the next time, summer had taken over her yard. The shrubs had sprouted alarmingly thanks to consistent afternoon heat showers, and the ground smelled dank and earthy. Blue and pink hydrangeas fought to out-bloom each other in the shaded parts beneath the tree, in all, creating a pleasant place to spend an afternoon.

Loretta and I sat on the porch fanning ourselves with those cardboard advertising fans they give out free in summer-steamy churches where there's a captive audience. It was the preacher's challenge not to bore the congregation into reading what was on them. From what I knew of Reverend Taylor, I doubted he ever had that problem, but the fans reminded me to ask about him.

"He's fine, and he asked after you just the other day. I think he understands you now, and that's important to me. You know, he's helped me through a lot of hard times." And that's when she told me about her "ladies," including Mrs. Barrington. I deeply resented the Barringtons for so callously using Loretta and then setting her adrift to deal with uncertainties of old age. The truth of it was shocking. They, like so many of the town's elite, had long put money and lip service into programs that sought to protect the defenseless and the elderly. Their treatment of Loretta was a form of betrayal I understood only too well. But both of us also knew that, if it had not been the Barringtons, it would have been another fine Savannah family. For Loretta, they just happened to be the last of the run.

"If you knew how it would turn out, why did you stay?"

"Because I'd known all of those ladies for so long. They'd gotten so old," she said sadly, "and I promised them I'd stay and look after them. They begged me, you know. They didn't ever say it, but I knew they were afraid that without me to help them they'd be sent to some institution. They needed someone they could count on. They trusted me, and I never failed them."

Loretta also had known better than to depend on any of the families to whom she had given so much of her life and to whom she had remained so faithful. She had prepared for her own independence long ago.

"I had my house," she told me, leaning back in her rocking chair and proudly surveying her tiny yard. "All those years, the people I worked for gave me bus money to come to work…well…just like your daddy, I'd go on foot and put that change in my pocket to help pay for my house. Sometimes I'd have to walk five miles each way…in the dark, too, to get there on time…and at night in the freezing cold. I never told anyone about my house because I was afraid something might happen. You never knew, back then. But I had my dream and nobody was about to give that to me, but *me*. It took me forty years to pay for this house. And now it's *mine*."

By most standards, Loretta's little home would be considered shabby. Inside, the single window in each room shed light on everything she had collected over the years, cast offs, mostly, much of which I recognized from years long past, furnishings, in enormous scale suitable to the large fine homes which originally housed them. There were no closets. In the two small bedrooms and adjoining bath, clothes hung neatly from hooks on the walls and all the rooms were separated by curtains. Doors were expensive.

Furniture overwhelmed the tiny living room. Two huge faded overstuffed chairs, a large table covered with photographs, heavy mismatched curtains, and an enormous gas heater crowded the ten-by-ten foot space. A thick curtain separated it from the kitchen, Loretta's symbol of accomplishment, which housed an ancient gas stove, a small refrigerator and a chipped, enamel-top table with wooden legs. Torn linoleum showed older layers beneath and a jumble of dented pots and pans hung above a scarred, enamel sink and its corrugated drain board. It was all very clean.

A back door led into what had been a chicken yard.

As the weather cooled, we settled into the big stuffed chairs inside, and Loretta told me about her summers in Vermont or in New York with families such as the Barringtons. "They took me with them to mind the children and keep up things," she explained. "I just loved going to those places. Everywhere we went was beautiful…*and cool*," she chuckled. "Not like around here in the summer."

"Did you get to see much outside of taking care of the family?"

"Oh, I had a day off every week, and I made sure that every one of those days would teach me something. I went to the museums and learned about the history and things they did way back then. And I went to the library and read. You know, up North, they didn't think anything of a Negro woman coming into any of those places."

"Why didn't you just try to stay?"

"Oh, this is home. Home, family, friends…people you trust and who do for one another. That's what counts. I didn't know anybody up there. And besides," she laughed, "Do you know anyone who would want to live in all that ice and snow?"

During the early years of Loretta's retirement, I helped her with little things she couldn't do herself such as repairing the tin roof and manicuring the needy shrubbery. Mostly, she remained joyfully independent. She did have one unfulfilled wish. She wanted some chickens for fresh eggs, and I gladly volunteered to bring her some from the country.

On chicken delivery day, my daughter and I collected three fat panic stricken hens from a neighbor and placed their cages in the back of our station wagon. Even that little bit of activity had worked up a sweat. It was July, and the day promised to be one of those that Southerners euphemistically refer to as "a scorcher." We cranked the air-conditioning up to maximum cool so that all of us, the chickens included, would survive the hour-long drive into Savannah. The cacophony coming from the cargo space made the radio useless. So we just shouted to each other about how thrilled Loretta would be to have chickens in her life again.

After five minutes on the road, we knew how thrilled *we'd* be to have them out of ours. The stench was indescribable. After fifteen minutes we pulled off onto the shoulder, turned off the AC and opened every available orifice that still would allow us, and the chickens, not to fall out on the highway. We arrived at Loretta's, drenched with sweat and permeated to the bone with the aroma of chicken droppings. Loretta never noticed. Once the chickens were launched into the yard, she was far too busy calling, "Here chick, chick…Here now," as she tossed them handfuls of grain and in the ensuing, feathered brawl, we became irrelevant.

We joined her for a while letting the hot breeze cleanse some of the odor *du poulet* from our clothes and hair but it didn't help much. The day was a shambles. We couldn't do errands smelling like that, and it wouldn't get better. We were still ferrying those cages filled with chicken droppings. We climbed into the car and started down the street toward home with Loretta calling loudly after us, "Your tailgate is open!!!"

We pretended not to hear.

We never failed to pay our respects to those chickens whenever we visited Loretta. We had a proprietary interest in them that lingered in the car for months, a car that now had the aroma and desirability of a neglected dumpster. But it was worth it to see her in charge of her brood. In spite of our bringing them plenty of feed, the chickens scratched the lawn back down to dirt. It had the swept-yard look of Loretta's youth, and she glowed when she surveyed the barren ruin that used to be grass. Those chickens were not just a source of food, or even companionship. They were touchstones with her past.

In October, Loretta turned eighty. During the following year, I noticed that she became slow to answer the door. Once inside, I could see the piles of newspapers standing tall in the corners, and, in time, cans of food she had bought still bulged in bags on the floor because she hadn't the energy to take them to the kitchen. Soon, food take-out cartons appeared everywhere. She found it too hard to cook for herself much less take out the trash.

Living so far away made it difficult to help.

She hired a neighborhood child to bring in the eggs and to feed the chickens.

Gradually, the rooms that had been brimming with happy memorabilia looked cluttered and dingy. That winter, they were dark as well, always curtained tightly against the cold, the drapery edges locked together with big safety pins while the gas heater blazed at Miami Beach temperatures. Winter was hard on her. She often had a bad cold. She moved with care and ever more slowly. By spring she stayed only in the living room, huddled in blankets that were unwashed now, nodding off in her fading chair and dressed in rumpled, mismatched clothes. She seemed unaware. To stir her interest, I gave her some new things to wear, but Loretta, ever meticulously dressed, never put them on. For company, she had her radio and the thin crumpled stack of letters on the table that she read over and over.

The yard had gone to sticks and weeds. Paint fell in flakes from the porch ceiling and the posts were rotting. There were rips in the screens. When I mentioned it, she refused help, saying, "It doesn't matter. I can't go out there much anymore."

One day, the chickens were gone.

"What happened, Loretta? Do you want me to bring you some more?"

"Oh, no thanks," she answered sadly. "I had to give them away. I couldn't get anyone to help me care for them."

One day I received a call from Loretta's sister, Annalee, who lived across the street. Loretta scarcely ever mentioned her. They didn't get along, but Annalee was clearly afraid for Loretta's safety.

"I'm old now," she said. "I don't want to struggle to keep up a house and yard anymore and I'm moving to that retirement place, Stubbs Towers, where I can get settled and enjoy life before I get too feeble to take care of myself. You've seen Loretta, and you know how weak she's getting. So, I've been trying to talk her into selling her house and moving there with me."

"Sounds interesting," I said, knowing Loretta would never agree to it.

"She needs to go *now*." Annalee stated with frustration.

"Why now?"

"Because Stubbs won't take you if you can't care for yourself.'

My stomach pitched.

"But..." she added, "they'll let you stay there if you need nursing care once you're in."

Nursing care? For independent Loretta? I had blinded myself to it. I wouldn't think of it. She was telling the terrible truth and, God forbid, it sounded reasonable. But I said, "You know she doesn't want to leave."

"I know she can't stay where she is! But I can't get anywhere with her. You know how stubborn she is. She gets so upset whenever I mention it, she won't even speak to me anymore. So I'm asking if you'd help convince her. She really trusts you." And she added, "Stubbs really is a good place. They drive you places and teach you crafts—nice things like that, and if you need it, they even fix your meals."

"But her house..." I protested.

"Oh that house!" she snapped. "That house literally is going to be the death of her. She can't take care of it now. In a year...well...She needs to get out of there and you're the only one who can get her to do anything. She believes what you tell her."

I promised to talk to Loretta about it.

Just as expected, Loretta was furious. "I know what it is." She regarded me icily. "They just want my house. This is *my* house, and I'm perfectly capable of taking care of it myself." The house had become the unshakable symbol of her accomplishment and her independence. She clung to it and she acted as if I had betrayed her.

Once Annalee moved to Stubbs, a young cousin, Martha, who was a registered nurse, began to look in on Loretta. A few weeks later, Martha called to tell me that Loretta had fallen. She had found her lying on the kitchen floor where she had lain for eighteen hours without water and with no way to call for help. Once rescued, Loretta was unfazed and just as determined to live alone.

Six weeks later, Loretta herself called. Martha hadn't been able to reach me to tell me that she had fallen again only this time she had lain there for over two days. Disoriented and seriously dehydrated, Loretta had been taken to the hospital; then placed in a private, full-care nursing home.

I called at once. "My god, Loretta, are you all right?"

"Oh, I'm just fine now," she insisted. "So you can come and get me and take me back home."

Even Stubbs Tower was now out of the question and, while the words *full-care nursing home* were chilling, how could she live alone?

The address she gave me was on a shady, quiet street and the entire block was lined with large, well-kept homes. The one I sought was surprisingly attractive and once inside it seemed especially neat and clean. I didn't appreciate it then, but later, I would understand the place was paradise.

Not to Loretta.

The owner greeted me and I was impressed at how sincere and intelligent she was. She was not, however, enamored of Loretta.

"I can't do anything with her," she said gravely. "She is so smart. And she does terrible things with it."

"What do you mean?"

"She insults me. And believe me, I am trying to do everything I can to make her comfortable and happy."

"What does she say?"

"It's what she *does*." She was starting to sound very testy.

"What?" I asked, now genuinely alarmed.

"She refuses to eat."

"Doesn't she like the food?

"Oh it's not that."

"What is it then?"

Her voice turned angry. "You may not believe this but she's actually starving herself, and I think she is doing it just to get at me."

I stared at her. "But why?"

"Because she thinks I'm keeping her from going home. She says I'm keeping her a prisoner here so I can make money off her. Well, she can't go back there. Not now." Seeing my expression, she toned it down a bit. "She talks about you a lot. She believes what you tell her," she said. "Please, won't you see what you can do?"

A set-jawed, bed-ridden Loretta regarded me with obvious relief, sure that I had come to rescue her. "I'm so glad you're here. I think you're the only one who understands how much my house means to me. I just knew you'd come to take me home!"

I couldn't answer.

She looked at me suspiciously, "I can manage perfectly well for myself."

When she realized that I hadn't come to take her there she stormed at my deceit. She reasoned. She suggested. She pled. While, in response, I humored, and explained, and most of all, felt like a traitor.

On each of my next three visits I brought her delicacies that I knew she loved, but she just let them stay by her bed, untasted. I tried to divert her with cheerful stories about our family which in the past had delighted her. Instead, the air remained heavy with unsaids as, with deepening concern, I watched the skin pull ever more tightly over the bony frame of her face and body. Yes, she was wasting away, but eating remained the only thing in her life she still controlled. Had I not been afraid to risk it I would have said, "You don't have choices anymore. We're trying to do the best for you and you need to help us." Her answer would have been, "I just lie here alone, in a stranger's house…waiting. The only place that's right for me is home and you, my trusted friend, are depriving me of it." Our conversations became increasingly strained because there was only one subject that held meaning for her.

One day, as I sat by her bed, Loretta was unusually thoughtful.

"How's my house?" she asked.

"Oh, fine. Just fine."

She wasn't listening. She was just staring away somewhere, "I think sometimes I'll never get back there again, and I'd as soon go on and die as stay in this place."

I knew she meant it and I had no answers for her.

"If I can't go there…to my own place…I'd like to just pass on."

There was a time when I would have protested, reminding her that people loved her and wanted her to have the best care. But what did that mean now? Linger on for us in this place you hate, so that we can assuage our consciences by visiting you once in a while?

She turned and looked at me quietly for a long moment and then dug around in her pocket and pulled something from it.

"This was given to me by my mother," she said simply, opening her hand so I could see it better. "It's all I have of her anymore and before anything happens to me, I'd like for your daughter to have it."

It was a worn, heart shaped cameo strung on a simple chain. The setting once had been washed with gold—gold, now nearly rubbed away and showing the plain dark metal underneath. It had never been expensive. It was unremarkable. But it glowed with an undiminished beauty for having been cherished so completely.

She looked into my eyes, a silent plea and urgency combining.

I mustn't cry. Oh god, I just mustn't.

It was painful to answer, to say the words. I choked out, "It's beautiful, Loretta. But are you sure?"

"Yes," she answered.

"Then, thank you. I know she'll treasure it always because she loves you and it's meant so much to you."

She touched me gently as she placed her heart within my hand.

Six weeks went by before I could visit Loretta again. The proprietress seemed surprised to see me but invited me in. "Didn't you know?" she asked. "Loretta is gone."

"GONE!?"

She saw my panic. "Oh, she's all right. Nothing's happened to her. Right after you came to see her last time, her nephew came and got her."

"Her nephew?" I had never heard of such a person. "Where did he take her?"

"Why, he took her to her house."

"Took her home? Who is caring for her?" I asked, alarmed.

"He says he is. He seemed like a very intelligent young man, and he's married. They can care for her, and he *is* Mrs. Lambert's family, you know." She saw my expression and added, "She really seemed to trust him."

I drove straight to the little gray house, knocked on the door and was met by a woman, the "nephew's" wife, carrying a tray of food. I told her who I was.

"Oh, it's you. Loretta's in her room," she said coldly. "Go on back."

I watched as she pulled back the curtain to the front bedroom and delivered her food-laden tray to the half-naked, muscular man sprawled on the bed who, with animal ease, pulled himself up on a pile of pillows to receive it. It was noon.

He looked at me coolly. Alarmed, I moved quickly to Loretta's room, deep foreboding crawling over me at Loretta or me being in that house.

Loretta lay in bed surrounded by clutter. She seemed so frail. So gray. Her eyes were so still. She seemed deeply old. She smiled wanly in greeting and we talked quietly. Then with a slowly pointed finger she said, "Look in that drawer. I wrote you a letter, but I didn't have any way to mail it."

I found it.

"Go on," she coached, "read it."

I opened the pencil-addressed envelope with its familiar handwriting.

It was dated three weeks before.

"Dear Laura,

"I hope you and your family are well. I haven't heard from you in a while. I tried to call you several times but you didn't answer. If you get this can you please come to see me. I need to talk to you.

"My nephew came and took me out of that home. I asked him to come get me and he said he would so I could come back home. They stay here now. They run the house. I have to stay in my room and I can't get out any more. The nurse comes by three times a week to give me a bath and change my bed. She always asks me if everything's all right. But they always hang around and I can't talk to her. I can't phone anybody either. They listen and I can't say anything.

"I want to ask you if you can help me. I can't do anything to stop what he's doing. She may know...but I can't really tell so I can't say anything to her either."

Who did Loretta mean? The nephew's wife? Loretta must mean his wife.

"He comes in here every time she goes out and tells me I'd better do what he says and not tell anybody. And then he pulls up my nightgown and feels me and does a lot of other things I don't like that just aren't right. I tell him no, it's not Christian but he says I can't stop him. I'm his property and he'll do whatever he wants to. I try to push him off but he's very strong. It makes me sick and I'm afraid. So when you can spare some time will you please come by to see me. I need to ask you please to help me.

"Please say hello to your sweet family.

Love,

Loretta'

"Loretta," I said as calmly as I could, "you can't stay here."

"I know," she answered.

"Where do you want to go?" Where would she *allow* herself to go?

"My pastor says there's a nice place two streets over at the traffic light," she answered without hesitation. "You know where that is?"

"Yes. Would you go there?"

"Yes, I'd like to go there."

"All right. I'll go over right away and make arrangements. I'll be back to get you on Monday. But don't say *anything*, OK?"

"Yes."

"Will you be all right until Monday?"

"I'll be all right."

The woman had come back to the kitchen which was just a curtain away. She was being very quiet. I was certain she was listening. We were whispering.

"Now, Loretta, I mean don't say *anything* to *anyone*." I motioned my head toward the kitchen. "I want you to be safe and it's important. Not to *anyone*."

She nodded. She understood far better than I did. My warnings were just to contain my own panic.

There was a problem at the nursing home; no room until Wednesday. Also, the fees were going to take twice the amount of Loretta's social security, about which there was an additional problem. The "nephew" had set himself up to collect it. I arranged to supplement as best I could. But the system seemed incomprehensible. As poor and vulnerable as she was, why couldn't Loretta get help?

Loretta, I learned, had *assets*.

She had her house.

Now, she would have to sell it, become totally dependent, and only then could she get public assistance. The one thing she needed, would not be allowed; just to get a little help so that she could live out her days, peacefully, in her own little place. No matter how downtrodden it seemed to anyone else, that house was her life's accomplishment. She had achieved it dime by dime, never asking anything from anyone. *Assets*? The house and lot together, if lucky, might bring $1,500, enough to sustain her "in the system" for maybe two months.

Instead, the system, set up to help her, was punishing and dehumanizing her by stripping her of the one thing that gave her a reason to live. I couldn't allow it to kill her as well.

One battle, however, had been won, a testimonial to my ability to beg and grovel. The home agreed to take Loretta on Monday. I dared not call Loretta but Monday morning, first thing, I arrived with a pickup truck and crew to move her. The house was locked up tight. To my relief, a neighbor came to see what we were up to.

"Oh, a man took her away Sunday morning," she said.

"*What man*?" I was almost shouting.

"I don't know who he is. But I've seen him go in her house a lot."

"Oh, my god!! Where did he take her?"

"I don't know for sure but somebody said something about some nursing home. I'm not really sure. But maybe the one around the corner."

I jumped into the truck and we sped to the home where I was led to a small, bright, clean, yellow room. Loretta sat in a chair, neatly dressed, relaxed, and smiling. "They had a place come open Sunday and they called my pastor. He came and got me."

⁂

The relentlessly complicated road we travel with our aging loved ones was, in Loretta's case, crater-free for about nine months. That's when they decided to turn the place into an Alzheimer's care facility. Loretta would have to go elsewhere. I spent the next week slogging through the bureaucracy and listening to the same indifferent litany.

"Oh, that will be easy. She just needs to sell her house."

"I'm sorry, but she'll have to sell that house to qualify."

"Yes, she really needs full care now, but, of course, she'll have to sell her house."

"…of course. Of course."

The latest social worker phrased it a bit differently, "If she can't live there, why doesn't she want to sell her house? I know it's a crazy system, but that's all it would take, you know."

I stiffened. "The house is not negotiable. It is the single reason Mrs. Lambert still believes in living and I am getting as stubborn about it as she is."

He looked at me with actual concern. "You've got a problem. You'll have to think creatively." He dug around in the jumble of papers on his desk. "Here…" he said. "Here's a list of places you can look at that we haven't gotten too many complaints about." Then he added, "You know, very few people these days would even bother. I really wish you luck."

For two weeks I reviewed all the disinfectant-scented dumping grounds of life, from the cheap and tawdry to the expensive and spiritless—from the little rooms in family homes where people took in the unwanted to gain a few dollars, to the better ones that suggested "retirement-by-choice," where residents dressed carefully to protect their self-esteem and chatted about their pasts with others, who, like themselves, didn't want to acknowledge that there was no future.

Just when it seemed hopeless, I found a lovely woman, Mrs. Agee, who had three rooms and two very intelligent lady residents. It was much like that first, tree-shaded home where Loretta had begun this hopeless odyssey and in a better time, when Loretta was Loretta, the place would have seemed perfect with its interesting "guests" and familiar homey things. Renewed hope lingered around every china figurine touched with gold, each photograph, and the soft, beckoning chairs, their arms protected with crocheted doilies, so like the things in the little gray house that Loretta had left behind. This was it! But first, I'd have to persuade Mrs. Agee that Loretta was acceptable. As with Stubbs Tower, she only took "independent women" and Loretta now was borderline, occasionally bed ridden and increasingly incontinent. By then, I'd learned to sell Loretta's case, describing her intelligence and her experience, her victimization and abuse, her aloneness, and her need. Reluctantly, Mrs. Agee agreed.

I reported enthusiastically to Loretta, hoping to buoy her, saying silently with all my focus, "Please, 'Retta…please try. There is nowhere left to go."

Once ensconced, Loretta made a small effort, but more and more she took to her bed. I asked her about the place and the ladies.

"They're fine," was all she said.

But Mrs. Agee said in private, "Loretta refuses to get to know them. She won't participate."

The only thing Loretta asked me for was a knit cap to wear. She was balding now, and the thin wisps of white that scattered her smooth brown scalp offered no protection against drafts. I brought her the prettiest one I could find.

"I used to crochet these," she said after thanking me and pulling in on to her head.

"I didn't know that. Did you enjoy it?"

"Oh, yes. I used to give them as gifts and everybody really seemed to appreciate them."

"You know, 'Retta, you could still do that if you wanted. If I got yarn and supplies, would you like to make them again?"

"Oh, I don't know…"

"People would love them. Just think, you could make them for the Senior Citizens…or the church. They would love that."

"I 'spose."

"Would you like to try?"

"I might try."

Two days later I was back with the supplies, a bag full of crocket hooks and colorful yarns, and a book filled with beautiful patterns.

"Look, 'Retta," I said opening the book and holding it so we could share the pictures, "Aren't they beautiful? Have you seen anything like these patterns before?"

"Hmmm," she murmured.

"Some of them are so different. You have such a choice and you could make them, just the way you used to." Loretta looked at them silently and then thanked me, putting the book and the rainbow of yarns on the table by her bed. She never touched them again.

In time, Loretta became more homesick and insouciant than ever. Finally, she refused to get out of bed. On subsequent visits I got out of the car with a mixture of steeliness and dread, always stopping to draw a deep breath and say a silent prayer for the status quo before mounting the wooden steps into Mrs. Agee's little home and confronting what I feared would be final ejection.

"She has to have diapers all the time now," Mrs. Agee said. "She's too heavy for me to move. I'm seventy-two years old myself and I can't help her if she won't cooperate."

I pleaded with Loretta and she assured me that "it will all be all right if you just take me home." I begged Mrs. Agee for more time. But it was inevitable. Loretta would have to move on.

As the deadline neared, Loretta became suddenly ill and was sent to the hospital. Martha called at once to say that it was serious. Indeed, Loretta had been diagnosed with inoperable stomach cancer. Our delusion about her "future" abruptly ended, and we had a week to find a conventional, full care nursing facility that made no pretense of being anything else.

As a nurse, Martha knew the place with the best reputation, one where Loretta would not be neglected, nor left in pain, nor left wet to blister and become bed sore.

How could I tell Loretta that the time had come, that she would have to sell her house to pay for the expensiveness of dying? Thankfully, Martha, whom Loretta had also come to trust, came up with the best possible solution. She would "buy" Loretta's house, restore it, and rent it out until Loretta "returned." Meanwhile, Loretta could afford the full nursing care she needed. The process was deft and final. She quietly acceded.

It was hard for us to look at her as we struggled to believe the lie that Loretta never accepted for a moment. The best we could hope for was that she knew we loved her and had done our best.

The day we took her from the hospital to the nursing home, we made a brief detour. Loretta wanted to see her house once more. It was winter. And desolate. The little structure and its neglected yard, seemed also to be dying. In silence, Loretta gazed at it, making her last connection with what had been; then she turned her face away.

"It's all right." she said. "You can go on now."

The nursing home was a noisy place, echoing with the sanitary coldness of marble floors and the manufactured cheeriness of nurses asking, "And how are we today?" Every footfall, clink of glass vials, and loud voice reminded that this was a place meant to keep life medically under control while letting its substance slip inexorably away. A place like this never pretends to provide more. Just hanging on is expected to be enough.

For some.

In her first weeks there, Loretta sat up in a chair, clean and neatly dressed, and talked with me quietly. She was forced, now, to give up the privacy that had been her refuge, the last silent bastion of her independence—and to share it with another elderly woman.

It made conversation awkward. "How's your lovely family?" she would ask, and I'd try to engage her in some silly story I'd stored up to humanize our meeting.

Before the month had passed, her question was automatic, and she seemed lost and distanced from the answer.

During the following weeks, our conversations dwindled into basics.

"How is the food?"

"Oh, it's all right I guess."

"Do you watch TV?"

"Sometimes."

The other woman in her room was propped up in bed watching a soap with the volume set for the near-deaf.

"Did you see on the news about....?" Loretta always kept up with current events.

"The other lady in my room doesn't watch the news, so I don't get to watch it either."

On my next visit, one of the nurses stopped me to say that, now, Loretta refused to dress in anything other than her robe and slippers. "She'd feel so much happier if she'd put on real clothes. We can't let them give up, you know. You're her friend. Why don't you see what you can do?"

Loretta's greeting was almost inaudible.

I asked, "Do you need anything?"

"No, not really."

"I saw a pretty dress in the mall I thought you'd like. It looked so happy...like a spring day...and floaty, in that pale blue that looks so pretty on you...," I smiled, "... like the one you wore the time you invited me up to your place for milk and cookies...when I was five."

She only smiled, in return.

"Wouldn't you enjoy having something fresh and new to wear?"

"Oh, please don't bother. I don't dress now." Then she drifted away.

In the weeks that followed it became clear that nothing I might try was going to engage her. We both knew that the only thing that mattered was the little gray house, and by tacit agreement, that issue had been dead for weeks. Then one day she looked at me pointedly.

"When I'm gone, will you look after my house?"

"Of course," I whispered, fighting the choke in my throat. Then her face relaxed, and she drifted into quieting sleep.

She spoke less and less.

Within a month, she was confined to bed. Our conversations became more strained. We sat in silence, mostly, and in truth, what can anyone say or do to engage a soul that wants to slip away—and can't. Not yet.

I just held her hand. It was easiest to read to her. It hurt to be there. Knowing.

Then she was moved to a different room with four beds on a quiet hall away from the normal flow of wheelchairs and chatter and visitors. Her neighbors stared silently at the ceiling through a tangle of tubes. Or slept. No one had to ask why.

Loretta was silent too. She spoke once of the pain. One of the nurses said she could not swallow.

Before going out of town for a week, I visited her briefly. "I won't be gone long," I said cheerily. "I'll be in to see you as soon as I get back." It sounded forced and absurd. She just looked through me toward something distant as I kissed her forehead and touched her arm which lay so thin and still outside the covers. I said goodbye and went away.

Two days later she was dead.

At the funeral, I met Martha and we spoke of Loretta's passing. I told her that at the end, I could find no way to comfort her, yet neither could I let her go. The young woman took my hand and held it close within hers. "Loretta knew you loved her," she said quietly. "She truly loved you too." Then she told me of her own last moments with Loretta. On a previous visit she had noticed how dry Loretta's mouth had become, how cracked her lips were. So she had brought a jar of Vaseline that last day and had gently stroked it on her lips.

"Thank you," Loretta had murmured as she drifted off to everlasting sleep.

During the funeral service, Reverend Taylor spoke stirring words forged from his personal admiration for Loretta. He reminded us of her example of wisdom and courage, of determination and faith. Most of all he asked us to be joyous because now Loretta would be free of pain. She had "crossed over to the promised land, a land of perfect happiness where all dreams are fulfilled, a place of rest and love and peace that she will enjoy for eternity."

I prayed that Loretta's special corner in that perfect place held all those things—but above all—I prayed it had a little gray clapboard house on a dirt street, with a tin roof, and a tiny porch, and a yard full of pretty, well-kept shrubbery—and in the back, of course—some chickens.

EPILOGUE

It has been a decade since that long journey toward Loretta's death.

As I drive through this part of town, I wonder who lives here now in these little houses, so many of them broken and flaking paint, with the roofs all rusted and the yards less grass than dirt. There's a kind of life going on here that I don't know about anymore, a life most people shun. I probably would too. If it hadn't been for Loretta. Or for this silent promise it has taken me ten years to keep.

I turn now, onto her street, still unpaved, still fragrant with trees and shrubs and empty with quiet, and I drive to the end where the saga began, searching steadily for the little gray house, fearful that it is finally beaten down or even gone.

The shrubs have grown tall and camouflage the spot. I drive past them before I can really see. Then, suddenly—there! It's really there—shouting to me in a way that makes me break into a joyous smile. The porch is gone but the exposed walls blaze with huge bright paintings of laughing children, topped with the greeting "*Happiness Day Care Center.*" I can hear shrill laughter and the squeak of swings soaring from the fenced backyard where the chickens used to be. And I am soaring, too.

Loretta's house has been reborn and I am five years old again. Starting out again. Old and new and wiser. From the beginning when Loretta was my friend.

www.ingramcontent.com/pod-product-compliance
Lightning Source LLC
Chambersburg PA
CBHW030815310726
48980CB00006B/502/J

* 9 7 8 0 9 7 7 6 6 2 3 3 3 *